HOB'S
DAUGHTER

Also by T. Alan Broughton

NOVELS

The Horsemaster
Winter Journey
A Family Gathering

POETRY

Dreams Before Sleep
Far from Home
The Others We Are
In the Face of Descent
Adam's Dream

Hob's Daughter

by T. Alan Broughton

William Morrow and Company, Inc. / New York

Library of Congress Catologing in Publication Data

Broughton, T. Alan (Thomas Alan), 1936—
   Hob's daughter.

   I. Title.
PS3552.R68138H56   1984   813'.54   84-3840
ISBN 0-688-03911-1

Printed in the United States of America

First Edition

1 2 3 4 5 6 7 8 9 10

BOOK DESIGN BY LINEY LI

The characters and situations
in this novel are imagined by the author
and are only as real as he has
succeeded in making them.

For George Bennett

I have been one acquainted with the night.

ACKNOWLEDGMENTS

The author is grateful to the
John Simon Guggenheim Foundation for a
generous fellowship awarded in 1982–1983 that enabled
him to complete work on this novel.

1

My gentle Michael would rather not kill. His eyes were widely unfocused, the mild expression of a sleepy and tired face. Without glasses he could not see well, and he had thought until I told him otherwise that the field rat on the kitchen floor was the neighbor's cat, a frequent visitor who had claimed our petless house and barn. He put his glasses on, and I could see the world leap into place for him.

"He's dying from the poison," I suggested, "but if you have to finish it, I don't want to watch. What will you do today?"

Some facts would help to place him in my absence. Mike and I hardly ever spent time away from each other. In the five years we had lived together in that house, busy enough with what we had to do to eat and to pay the mortgage, we did not want to waste our free time. Our habit was to rise at six, even in winter when the alarm would send me blundering into darkness to put an end to the rasping somewhere on the dresser. But the fields were lush with green beyond the drooping willow tree, the unweeded gardens—one of those dry, clear July mornings of northern Vermont, as cool as fall. In a land of extreme seasons, contrasts are always present in the mind. I was about to fly to Boston with a box of slides to peddle my latest sculpture at galleries. I had not slept well and wondered if my restlessness had waked him also.

"Take Sheldon to the lake. Perhaps have Melissa to dinner? Go soaring if the weather changes."

Our family net. Melissa was Michael's daughter, and Sheldon, his father, lived upstairs in the extra bedroom, more an apartment since we had added its own bathroom, hot plate, a small refrigerator, and rails placed in the hallway where his hands could easily find them. Sheldon was blind.

"Want to hide while I kill it?" He stood.

I tried not to look but could not keep myself from glancing at the rat, away, then staring again. I have never been able to control my eyes or what they admit or what my mind then forms with the things it sees. My father would lean at me in restaurants to say in a firm undertone, "Don't stare like that, Julie, it's rude." But I would not be concentrating on the surface of the lady with preposterously wide-brimmed hat whose mouth made the nervous snatchings of a guppy when she spoke. I would be on the other side of that pursing face, a tight brim angling over one temple; I would possess her fat hand as it waved embedded rings in air. *An excess of the imagination.* Samuel Johnson regarded it with fear.

Michael flopped in his slippers toward the cellar to find a weapon. The rat was startled, fat brown body convulsing its legs in a dream of running, but poison was the greater enemy now and no scampering could evade it. In the wedge of light its umber fur had the sheen of a rich pelt. A car turning into the drive, Mike's steps mounting slowly. Melissa's arrival let me seem less cowardly. The screen door slapped on my heels, I looked with guilt at the chickweed and crabgrass choking the pinks and vowed a paroxysm of weeding after my trip. Dust surged forward and settled over the field. She waved and stepped out.

"Can I have a cup of coffee before we go?"

She was too dressed up for a mere Wednesday morning, a loose, many-pleated dress swirling out in the breeze, ankles unsteady as the spiked heels of her shoes sank into the newly pebbled drive. Too fancy for her job at a local department store.

"You didn't have to do this."

"But I wanted to." She let my arm hook hers, if only to steady herself until we reached the flagstones.

I liked to touch Melissa. She had her father's big bones, and her flesh had filled that structure fully. Not fat but solid, and something about that body was innately affectionate, ample with ability to give. I had met her mother only a few times but assumed a shift into nervous gestures in some moods came from Frances Feltner, who was sharp-featured, lean, a quick bird in flight.

"You smell good," I said.

"Is it all right? Yesterday when I was buying it, I tried so many at the perfume counter that I reeked and couldn't tell the bottles apart anymore."

She pulled loose from my hand to reach and pluck down a few leaves from the overhanging fringe of willow. A few years ago I would have thought her gesture rose from some tension between the two of us. Only seven years older, I could not be a stepmother to the sixteen-year-old I had first met when I was twenty-three, and even now, seven years later, Michael and I were not married, so what was I? Stepmistress? If in those earlier years I attained at moments the position of older sister, that could not last for long, because who could accept in the roiling dark pits of the mind a sister who slept with Father? We argued often then about menus, about turning the stereo up or down, about whether there was a God or life after death, and above all, how to save mankind.

"Can we sit a moment?" She pulled back one of the metal chairs from its table.

"Aren't you working today? You look like you're going to a garden party."

"Wedding." She brushed the seat with the tips of her fingers and was careful not to lean back against the fanwork. Sitting tentatively in her elegant dress, a silk of pale blue prints through which I could see the patch of sunlight on the stones and solid molding of her legs, she seemed more than I to be the traveler poised for departure. "Where's Dad?"

"Killing a rat."

"That's nice. I don't believe you, of course. He can't kill."

"It's mostly dead."

"Poison? Remember how Dad and I used to argue about that? I said at least traps involved you in what you did to those cute little deer mice with their big eyes and ears."

"Coffee." I cupped my hands on the screen to see through the sun struck mesh. In a pool of light Mike was standing over the rat, spade's point on the floor a few inches from the animal, its handle gripped tightly in one hand. He would often pause like that, frozen before the necessity of doing something he would prefer not to, but I had come to see this was not a pose to make me feel the worse for asking or letting him, only his own tension of deadlock, the knowledge that although he saw both sides, one had to be chosen. *On the other hand* was the expression both Melissa and I had affectionately mocked until he no longer used it, even if the mind continued to act it out.

He raised the spade with both hands and brought it down on the back of the rat. A shriek of puncture. The body, pinioned under the blade, struggled savagely, then was still. Mike leaned, arms still tense. I could not hear what he was saying as he slid the blade under the body and lifted it. He would go out the kitchen door into the field where Ed's corn was already high. The field was ours, but Ed and Tina Bushey were our friends and neighbors, and we let them use it if they would plant us some rows of sweet corn each year.

Mike would probably be annoyed and slightly embarrassed if he knew I had been watching him, so I decided the coffee could wait a little longer.

"Not a pretty sound." Melissa wrinkled her nose.

I pulled a chair near to her. "Whose wedding?"

"Bo Hassler."

She was gazing across the field, eyes half shut against the morning sun. The name was familiar, but during the years that Melissa had been going to the university, living in dorms and eventually her own shared apartment in Burlington, she had come home with so many different boyfriends that they blurred. But the blur had its own form, a composite boyfriend who tended to have a firm, chunky build, athletic but not lithe, and hair that shaded toward blondness even if never attaining it. In that composite was a future I was not certain Melissa could foresee—a tendency to lose that hair, starting with some thinness at the crown, and a penchant for beer rather than wine that would gradually thicken them around the middle until they were no longer able to retrieve balls on the court with much speed. I had wondered one evening as I stood looking down on Melissa and friend from the small balcony that jutted out over the end of the living room whether only Julie Cobb wanted her love to keep his hair forever. Mike would, I was certain.

"Remind me."

"The one Dad liked because Bo liked books, even if he never read them much."

He was coming back, but only through the objects around him. "BMW. Silver?"

"It lasted my whole junior year, off and on. Us, I mean. It's the third wedding in the past month or two."

"Caught any bouquets?"

"None. But I'm a godmother, you know."

"Has to happen."

"So soon? All the ones who swore they would never marry, have. And some of the women who weren't going to have children until they had careers established, have." She paused. "Next thing I know, you and Dad will marry."

"How do you feel about Bo?"

"Oh, that's been over for years." But the wave of her hand was too stiff. She looked at me guiltily. "No?"

I shook my head slowly.

"You're right. Not that I ever expected to have Bo and me take up again. So I don't know exactly what it is, except that he was very special and with people like that I feel possessive. They have no right to become different or go on into their lives." She unclasped the hands she had been holding tightly in her lap and fluffed out her skirt. "I think I'm jealous a lot now. Not because of someone like Bo and another woman. Jealous of my women friends too. They all seem to be going into something, even if I don't like what they've chosen. I'm in a holding pattern. Circling."

She laughed suddenly as she often did, her head tilted back and accentuating the sharp jut of collarbones.

"What?"

"Flying makes you nervous and you're about to travel. I should have put it differently."

I did not want to admit how as usual I had dreamed uneasy scenes, never so blatant as images of wreckage but always drenched in tones of sad endings.

"I think I'm more nervous about the galleries. Are you nervous about the wedding?"

"Reluctant. To drive to Woodstock and drink champagne and dance under the tent and meet the family and hear about stocks and bonds."

"From Bo?"

"From Bo the Broker. Oh, Julie. Do come back soon and come to town and sit in my kitchen with a bottle of wine and let's drink and talk till Dad calls because it's very late and he's worried."

She was smiling widely, and my heart always raced to see her do that, so like Michael too, a way of letting the emotion out in words but posing the face against it. The eyes confessed to seriousness.

"I will."

"You may read my catalogs. I've been looking at programs in counseling. Everywhere. Even California."

I put that away carefully for later thought. California was far away. In spite of all their changes, she and Mike had never really dealt with great distances between them.

"Time for coffee."

We went arm in arm across the patio. Again I was weary when I thought of talking about my work while slides flicked by, a double incoherence since I did not like turning a piece of sculpture into words, and the slides were always grossly insufficient. But beyond that lurked the simpler vacancies of a strange bed and a few days without Michael. Unsharable moments had come to seem a waste of time to me, although we needed our solitude. In the living room Michael was watching the news and waved when she called out to him. I put my hands on his shoulders and kneaded gently. He settled into my grip. I hated to be without his body nearby, especially when I woke at night.

Melissa and I walked back to the table where the coffee pot was still plugged in. I went into the kitchen to get a mug for her, and going both ways I stepped over the freshly scrubbed spot on the floor, so visible because for weeks I had been remiss about mopping.

"When are you and Dad going to take that trip?" She lifted a spoonful of sugar but did not carry it to her cup. Willpower. She caught my glance. "It doesn't taste the same without sugar, but . . ." and she pinched her waist ruefully. Both she and Mike had that propensity to worry about. But I had been given a body that burned off calories as quickly as I stoked.

"The same problem. We can't make up our minds, and even if we did we couldn't afford it now."

"Greece or England?"

"Still. But when I relent and say, 'OK, let's go to England first,' he'll insist on Greece."

"Both?"

"Dream on."

The fact that Michael and I found all the reasons not to go told us something about our urge to travel—weak at best. When our friends came over they would accuse us of inertia, called our house *this middle-aged spread*, a term I resented before I had turned thirty, which

I always thought initiated middle age. But on my recent thirtieth birthday, Mike had said, "Look, at forty-two I'm the only middle-aged one," and when he said it that way I realized again how I would always be living ahead of myself through him.

"After all the suffering you endure here in winter to get to summer, who wants to leave?" I said, but she was thinking of something else, and for a moment we drank in silence—Melissa sipping her coffee, wound into her own thoughts, my mind returning to the rat sniffing his way through some small chink in the basement wall. The dish of bait lies on the mildewed concrete by the furnace. He hesitates, then leans into the light seeds, eats eagerly, scattering chaff. When does the pain begin? That slow cramping, unquenchable thirst, taste of his own blood rising as his gut begins to hemorrhage. He is too bloated to squeeze back through the chink he entered. Gorged with pain, incautious, he drags his clenched body up toward light, air, the hard, clear brightness of sun on linoleum. Surely he knows almost nothing now except the burning inside, lungs filling, his own blood drowning him. Then the edge of metal. Is it as I imagine, flinging out and away everything the body has known, the hook that was life ripped up through the outraged mouth?

I shivered.

"Are you cold?" Her hand was on mine. "You look tired."

"I'm not sure I'll enjoy this trip. Let me show you something I'm making, then I ought to say good-bye to Sheldon.

"Did you drink all the coffee?" Mike was calling.

As I leaned to pour, he put his hand on the small of my back. "I think I'll go to work this afternoon after all."

"Will I tell Sheldon you'll be here all morning?"

He nodded, turned back to the screen. I was caught off guard by the casualness of the moment and could not help slipping through that space somewhere between love and a narcissism that let me see him living on without me, as if I had been flung into a plane wreck or other mayhem on the ground. The sentiment began in my own self-pitying fear of losing all the moments we had left, then dissolved in that dispassionate awareness of his life apart from me that I could never fully enter into at any time.

"I love you."

"Mmmm?" He frowned at the box.

The cellar was my studio. The floor had been earth when we

7

moved in, hard-packed and littered with discarded junk of all the families before us. We had laid the cement floor as a way of making sure the things we stored there would not dampen and rot. Only later did I move my things in from a shed across the road too flimsy to hold the heat in midwinter. Out there once the chisel in my numb hands had slipped and been driven into the floorboard between my feet, and we knew I needed to move. The cellar could be a dark place in winter, but everyplace was dark in winter. In summer I would open the hatchway door to light and fresh air and the songs of birds, and sometimes the Busheys' cat slinked down the steps to sniff joists and rafters for mice.

"It's for Sheldon." I watched as Melissa ran her hand over the polished stone.

I needed Sheldon to take pleasure in touching what I had made as if the smaller pieces were wonderingly found by chance on the shore, shaped as stones or shells smoothed by the sea. I could not say some things to him, mostly because he treated compliments as unfair if spoken in his presence; and anyway, how could I tell a blind man that only after living in his presence had I really begun to see, to touch? Often now, about to work some chunk of stone in the cellar, I would close my eyes and run my fingers over its rough surface and edges, and I would believe whatever I could make of it was a design carried inside, long ago coded under the earth.

"He'll love it."

She put it down and we walked over to the hatchway and bright air. Looking up through the opening at patches of sky, leafy branches of trees that floated unmoored to earth, the droop of weeds and bushes over the edge, I saw that everything was conspiring to turn the world green.

"Why does traveling always make me sad?"

She leaned her head lightly on my shoulder. "That's not really a question, is it?"

"No." I laughed. "A statement. It's not flying, though. Sailplaning doesn't trouble me at all anymore. But I always think of dying when traveling. Do you?"

"Yes. But it's stupid because I always come back. And I don't think you can ever tell when it's coming. Thinking about it is like a silly magic charm that you hope will make it go away."

We went up the back stairs to Sheldon's room. She knocked.

"Come in, I'm decent. In attire."

His radio was playing and his hand moved unerringly to turn it off. He was wearing the usual white shirt, open at the collar. His bureau drawers were full of them, and even after he went blind he did not like shirts with colors. Had he preferred the severity of white or the hint of fallen elegance? He hardly ever wore a tie and the result was a raffish formality.

"Hi, Gramps."

"I thought I heard your car." How can I describe the full measure of that smile? Sheldon's body and voice compensated for the expressive capacity lost when his eyes dulled and their lids drooped uncontrollably. His smile could do extraordinary things to the lines around his eyes as it broke onto that lean, attentive face. But I could understand Sheldon's emotions by watching his hands. They reached into our space, turning, pointing, dancing in air as if blindness had released them into a freedom the rest of us could never comprehend.

"I'm taking Julie to the airport."

"Sit down. I suppose Mike couldn't take you. Lazy fellow."

"I knew if he took me he'd go to work, and I was hoping he'd take the whole day off."

"But he won't?"

I sat in the easy chair, Melissa on the white stool by the table. Sheldon walked three steps and without feeling for it, sat on the end of the bed. He knew the dimensions of the room, the placement of its objects so well that I was certain a stranger would not think him blind at first, and I was so used to spending time with him there that it often startled me when we went elsewhere to see him shuffle his feet insecurely or pause to swing the point of his cane beyond his toes.

"He's changing his mind."

"I'll see what I can do about that at lunch. I can get him arguing. Gardeners hate to walk away from a good argument."

Melissa laughed that relaxed downward swirl she always had in Sheldon's presence, and he smiled again to hear it. He depended on Melissa more than on the rest of us. Mike had told me that ever since she was born and Sheldon first held her, which was only a year after his wife, Liz, had died, they had established a rapport as familiar and thorough as Sheldon's relationship to his room. They knew its dimensions, never groped or stumbled with each other. In social situations sometimes Melissa would laugh as if startled into it, but with Sheldon it was pure song. Often in conversation he would lean toward her as she talked, his voice making small noises of assent because his mind already knew what she would say.

When I had first known the three of them they could be in the room together and not speaking and I would have the eerie feeling that some form of superterrestrial conversation was going on. I suspected they had a space together where they gestured as mutely and eloquently to each other as Sheldon's hands did to his own darkness, but I could not see their motions. When the three of them argued, which they did love to do, I would not be able to keep up. They could anticipate each other by two or three jumps and I would not understand how they got from one position to the next. I yelled out once like a child, *Wait for me!* But slowly they had absorbed me. I no longer needed to translate their language. I spoke it in my sleep.

"Bring me back something," he said shyly.

"Name it."

"I don't have anything in mind."

"What about you, Melissa?" But she only waved her hand.

"Just come back safe."

Sheldon turned to her. "You've got new perfume on. Where are you off to?"

As she explained I stood and looked carefully around the room to be certain everything was in order, whether there was anything I should tell Mike to do before I left. I paused by the window. The grass in the front lawn needed mowing, and the door of the big barn across the road was swinging open in the breeze. Probably some neighborhood kids had been inside again. Melissa was naming friends she would see, reminding Sheldon of any he had met. I closed my eyes. He said something. "Yes, yes, she's the one," Melissa answered, and I did not want to go, wanted only to wander slowly from room to room touching windowsills, watching this blue day flow out into one of those long, clear evenings of crickets, nighthawks plummeting and crying high above, Mike and myself finishing a bottle of wine under the canopy of the willow.

"We'd better go." I kissed Sheldon, and his hand gripped my arm.

Melissa took my suitcase out the side door as she called, " 'Bye, Dad, be back late tonight," and he swiveled on the couch, yelling, "Have fun!" when I hurried in. He padded to the door with me in his bare feet, arm around my waist.

"All my women leaving me."

"I wish I weren't."

I made us pause in the hallway by turning to him. He put his other arm around me and I tucked my face close to his neck, the rasp of his unshaven chin on my forehead.

"Hurry, Julie!" she was yelling from the driveway.

"I'll call." When I glanced back from the doorway he had his hands in the pockets of his bathrobe.

"Not collect, I hope." He grinned, and then I was running to the open car door, she backed out with a jerk onto the road, honked, and we were gone so fast that I did not have time to look up or wave. She rolled her window down, letting the slipstream blow her hair back wildly from her face. We drove in silence for a while and I checked through my purse to be certain I had the tickets.

"Julie, do you think I've changed?"

She was always direct. "Do you feel you have?"

"Something lately seems different to me, but I can't locate it."

"How?"

"For one thing, I'm quitting my job soon." She paused, then blurted, "I think you've changed."

Again, I could only question her.

"Sometimes I think you are becoming more and more hidden. You seem so peaceful, contented most of the time, but I don't believe it. I mistrust it."

"You're not just wishing I was more on the edge? My life less settled?"

"Like mine?"

"Yes. I am happy, you know."

Her hand reached, but the touch was only a flutter before withdrawing to the wheel again. "I wonder if something else is going on inside you that none of us is on to."

"A conspiracy of silence? If so, you'll have to include me among the excluded."

"I hope not. What about you and Dad? Do you think you'll ever get married?"

We had stopped talking about that some years ago, and in those days Mike and I had been firm, even aggressive. Certainly, he had asserted, he had proven marriage was something he did not want. But since he had always tried not to snipe at Fran in Melissa's presence, his own reasoning was constrained, lacking in the concrete proofs

11

Melissa wanted. She listened less to me, I think because I was close enough in age for her to know that my reasons would have been hers too. I wanted no confusion about my independence, if only because I was twelve years younger than Mike, if only because I did not want children or to slip quietly into a slot of institutionalized arrangements. But slowly, gathering years around us, we had made our own private contracts, and we admitted to Melissa one evening that except for some documents, we were as "married" as anyone we knew.

"I guess we still don't need it. Why?"

"What if you became pregnant?"

"Lord, no."

"People do."

"Not me."

"You're saying there are no accidents?"

I did not have to answer. She ran the stop sign in her concentration, we heard an angry horn bleat behind us, and when we glanced at each other, laughing, that conversation was basically over. I think she was as relieved as I was. We were not going to get anywhere.

"You're not pregnant?" I asked.

"No, no. Is that what you thought?"

"I didn't want to be on the plane and replay the conversation and start thinking, 'Maybe she was trying to tell me something, maybe I didn't ask the right questions.' "

"Dear Julie. Do you always replay conversations?"

We slowed for the stoplight at Williston Road, and a small private plane waggled down toward the airport. "I'm always afraid I've missed something important, as if what we're talking about is not really what we're trying to say. Sometimes I sit up in bed in a sweat thinking of how insensitive I've been to what Sheldon or you or Mike have been saying."

We were nearing the terminal when she said, "I'm not pregnant, and I wasn't trying to say anything big. I think my questions were just an extension of what I was saying earlier. About weddings, my friends. And I need to hear you talk. Sometimes I feel you're a small distance ahead of me in every way."

When she started to turn for the parking lot I had to say quickly, "No, please, just drop me."

I pulled my suitcase off the back seat, then bent into the front. "You'll be careful, won't you?" She leaned toward me.

Her question pushed me again into the territory of fears. I was full of my own journey and nodded. I put my hand on the back of her neck, we kissed, and then I closed the door, still bending down to see her through the window.

"Remember . . ." and she said some words I could not understand, but I said "Yes" anyway and she drove off.

And that was it. A morning in July 1969 when I was thirty and Melissa was twenty-three. But again and again in the years afterward, in all that time it took to untangle the consequences of the next few days, if we ever did, I would come back to those hours of that day as if they held an intense and delicate poise that could never be regained. Do accidents never happen? Was it all there in the bright, heavy fall of July sun, the voices I did not listen to, Melissa's footsteps on the gravel? It did not matter. Again and again I wanted it back, to be at Sheldon's window, Melissa and her grandfather talking quietly, Michael on the couch waiting for me to descend. I am talking about safety, about the known fragments bobbing on the surface of a dark sea, but above all about that grace we hope pervades it all: love.

2

My mother, Jane, killed herself when I was thirteen. My father, J. Howard Cobb, known as Hob to his family and friends, died suddenly when I was twenty-two, although by then I knew it could happen anytime. He had a mild heart attack earlier and tried to pay attention to his health, eating more carefully, doing some running, but that lasted only a few months. He was not particularly driven nor one of those persons who knew he would die soon and abandoned himself to plunging at life. But keeping watch on his body bored him so he went back to living as he always had—writing, teaching, traveling but not excessively. He had returned from London in early June and was finishing his seventh novel. He took the last few chapters to New York for a conference with his editor, rode the subway to Union Square, went up to the street, and collapsed. For twenty-four hours the authorities could not find me since I was hiking alone and had spent the night on Camel's Hump—a ritual that I did not repeat until long after that year.

When I think of him on that day, as I often do, I know he is eager to see his editor, have it done. He hates this last niggling. Muggy, hot weather. The subway is stifling. He stands in the morning rush hour, sweating uncomfortably, stooping from time to time to check the names of the stations. He is so infrequently a visitor to New York that he is liable to go in the wrong direction. His present editor is a young woman who has already suggested changes he knows are so misguided that she cannot have truly understood the book. The name of his station slips by, the car stops. He has to hold the briefcase to his chest, pressing hard to part the layers of backs between himself and the door. Dizzied, he blinks, looks for the exit. He recalls those wooden, clattering, forever rising escalators of London tube stops and how he always has wanted to use them in a dream sequence. Two persons, dressed the same, are passing each other. No one else rides the long slant of tunnel. They are the same person turning their faces to each other in mute recognition. He has a pain in his chest, blames the cheap corn oil used too lavishly on his eggs.

I have only my imagination, but for me love is a constant attempt to imagine either the details of the other's life out of the consciousness I have intuited, or the consciousness from the observed details. Even my father. He glides up toward that seedy square, its scattered litter. A gust blows grit against the shove of stale, hot air behind him. A truck shakes to a stop, he sidesteps the unswerving advance of a tight-jawed woman. A man in his path has dropped his umbrella, stoops for it. Hob's breath catches in one harsh clench of pain. The shape of the sky is broken by irregular cornices of buildings, a curious face looking down.

My father. How often I wanted to know what I could never imagine for certain, all the details of his life and what he really cared for. I had given up trying to find those details in his books years ago, and the power of love had carried me through any facts he or I imagined. I tried simply to touch the person who held the words before they became sounds or shapes. His life was not a book. But when he died I wanted the facts his love lifted into that last light of a strange sky before he closed his eyes. Name them, name them. I want to hear him say those words.

Sheldon and my father could not be more different in many ways, and yet sometimes I lapse into a subtle confusion. It goes beyond that usual pattern of the surrogate parent. When I think back over certain scenes in my life with Hob, I almost see Sheldon standing in his place, and the eyes turned to me are blank, the hand that reaches out to touch my arm is asking for something to grasp. I wish I had been able to know Sheldon, then return to my father with that knowledge. Because inside Hob, for all his formidable articulateness, his visionary ability to see far into the puppets on his stage, a blind man groped through new and unfamiliar rooms, passing through doorway after doorway hoping the next space would be known to his hands, his tentative feet. I would give anything to have been able to do for him what I do so unreflectively, so commonly for Sheldon. "Three steps down, and then a turn to the right. That's it. Now we're on the pavement again."

Once when I was a junior in Swarthmore College I came home in late fall for the weekend to see him before he journeyed again. An unusually warm evening in late September. He suggested we take a stroll. We had eaten early, a concession to our confused schedule that had afforded us only one other meal very early that day. The sun was still falling toward the Adirondacks, turning orange and growing larger as it lowered. We had always liked to walk up the hill and into an old estate inhabited now only by a day school. By the time we reached the grove of white pine, tall bare trunks that held back none of the sweep of quivering lake, islands, and sheer lines of mountains, the sun flooded straight into our eyes, and the wind, deceptively mild, was pungent with the scent of fallen leaves and brittle grasses. We did what we often enjoyed most, sitting together so quietly that we almost forgot the other person was there, but that "almost" was essential to the peace and security of those moments.

"Jane never liked it here," he said quietly. "The view was too grand, too open."

The rim of the sun slipped behind the mountains, but the sky was flushing into one of its most brazen displays. The colors of the leaves had been extracted and washed out across the horizon. I waited. He had taken out his pocket knife to whittle the bark off a stick, and now he simply held it, smoothing one thumb along the open blade.

"Why are you thinking of her?" We rarely talked about Mother.

"Been on my mind recently. Often. Perhaps because of my heart attack. Do you think of her much?"

I did not like either subject he had brought up but was willing to listen.

"Not much." Not quite the truth. But had I said "Yes," he might have asked what I thought.

The knife paused, then continued whittling. "Too bad. Maybe you should. Or maybe I should have talked more about her over the years. We've avoided her. Silence for her silence."

If he was referring to the silences I had witnessed, I knew how impenetrable the state could be. She would retreat to her room, smoking and pretending to read a book, or I would look out the window and see her sitting in that canvas chair on the lawn—the chair of my unforgiving dreams—her broad-brimmed hat casting an oval of shade on her shoulders, and even though she might answer or ask something or talk on the phone, there seemed to be no person behind the words. *Premises vacated*, her slow gestures would announce. At dinner he would try to talk to her, leaning forward in his chair as if her silence were a great wind to push against, turning finally to me or my brother Tim. To keep talking was important because the silence was suffocating. Like her death, it was inversely aggressive.

The lights of the ferry boat were slipping in, and faintly the thump and rattle of its docking reached us.

"She had begun retreating into that, you know, even before Tim was born. I never was any good at breaking it up."

I wanted to cry out, "Why do you tell me this?" but even as I was unable to do anything more than stare at the distant lights of cars humping off the ferry onto the dock, instead of the usual memory of resentment I wondered at my mother's silence, at the fact that she could keep reenacting it for so long until she entered it wholly.

"When I look back now, I am sure some things began going wrong for her long before I knew her. But I thought her problems had everything to do with the two of us. I threw it all back on our relationship. My fault. Her fault. What intervened for a while was Tim, then you. But you both grew up."

"Our faults?"

"No, no." His impatience startled me. He stood abruptly, leaving his knife and the stick on the ground, and stood looking down at the lake with hands thrust into his pockets. "Your childhoods brought us some interval of grace, hard as moments in it were. Oh, how I wish I could have held those parts in her together. Not changed her, not changed her, but only to have kept them from pushing off against each other." His hands jerked out as if he might lift them in some wild gesture, but they held tensely still by his sides.

"Tell me." I found it hard to speak, my own throat constricting like a fist.

But he shook his head. "Sorry. It's too much on my mind. And I'm exaggerating. Much of the time everything went well for us."

"Why?" I blurted.

"Because we accepted those times, I guess, learned to . . ."

"No. Why are you telling me this?"

Only enough light was left for me to see the shape of his face, his eyes in shadow, and behind his form the sky was beginning to reveal a few of its brightest stars. He waved one hand, a gesture that was more annoyance with his own inability to explain clearly than impatience with me.

"I shouldn't be talking about Jane and me. I didn't mean to. I wanted to ask you something more important. About Tim. Do you think of him?"

"Yes. Often."

"Good." The light was only a wan glow along the tops of the mountains. One white hand reached to pick up the knife and close it emphatically. "Good. "

The way he spoke and the accompanying motion seemed to close the conversation also, and I assumed he was waiting for me to stand. Did he actually expect me to press him further? I wish I had. But I was puzzled, even a little angry. I had come home to see him, not be reminded of my mother's death, my brother who had long ago run away and not made any contact with us subsequently. But it was only years later, after Hob had died, that we would finish that conversation. He left a letter for me among his papers at the bank. If I had been unfair in not providing an opportunity for him to continue, perhaps he paid me back by making the final conversation so one-sided.

Dear Julie,

Some time ago I discovered that the people I love so much the word seems inadequate are with me all the time, a ground bass under all the varying melodies of the day. From time to time such a person gathers into an image I recognize as you or Jane or Tim, and then I identify it with the word, but there is no surprise because I know all of you have been there all along, present like a heartbeat or necessity of breathing. You more than anyone in my life. I want to tell you some things about your childhood and about Tim's. I am doing so because I hope he will continue to fill your mind, but so much that you will have to seek him out.

Please do not believe I always bring to mind only the painful events. Anyway, I do not remember all the awful things I may have done to you or Tim because I am sure I don't know them. Over the time of a childhood and adolescence there must be many. I can recall my anger when I would vengefully recount some pain my parents had caused me and my father would say, "Oh , you just imagined those things."

But I can never forget the fact that the only time Jane and I resorted to physical violence, Tim was witness to it. A very awkward combination of kicking and flailing. Mostly we both missed, and that has to mean we really wanted to have the physical release without the contact, although I nursed a bluish bulb of swelling on one shin for a few days. In retrospect I wish Jane had been able to let it out that way more often instead of the interior beatings she administered to herself. At any rate, Tim was four and we were standing in the living room where he was playing with some blocks on the floor, and it was the climax of three days of disdain with which we had been treating each other. Whatever I finally said was like a match lit in a room full of gas fumes. We both let loose, not using our voices but flailing earnestly in silence.

It could not have lasted long. We stood apart, exhausted, panting heavily. Tim was crouched over a heap of blocks, his hands open at his sides, his eyes wide, and then a high wail came out of his mouth as if someone behind him were making it, and he ran past us for the hall closet, burrowed into its dark ell, and pulled at the hems of some coats so that they fell on him. I dove for that closet, more than anything to put an end to the sound that kept coming, muffled by overcoats and jackets.

Perhaps Tim was less shocked than your mother and I. At least he responded to our holding and petting him, our quick and thoroughly awkward attempts to be affectionate to each other immediately in his presence as of to say, 'See? See? It was only make-believe.' My own clumsy sermon was to tell him that sometimes people who love each other can get very angry, very angry indeed, and did he remember how only last week he had thrown his fork at Mrs. Jameson when she was trying to get him to finish his dinner? To which he replied with a frown, "Yes, but I hates Mrs. Jameson." That enabled us to laugh and led to the misunderstanding that necessitated letting her go. Tim thought it was very amusing thereafter to tell Mrs. Jameson how he hated her and we did not have the heart to be angry, having encouraged it. So she was replaced.

I know the damage was greater than I am admitting because from then on when Jane and I would begin bickering, before our argument became so pervasive that silence and booze and absence were the remedies, Tim would get nervous, make jokes, pace around the room looking at us warily as if we might explode at any moment. How was he to know that was the only physical violence we ever permitted ourselves? I think he imagined we were at least that mean when alone, or certainly that it remained a possibility. I tell you this incident to remind you that Tim, by being nine years older than you, has seen much more of his parents than you have, and that may make him reluctant to see you no matter how innocent you may be in these family tangles.

But I believe I can tempt you into searching for him because I have never known anyone who needs and wants so much to *know*. If you have as I do an excess of imagination, it is driven, thrust out in the world by an abstract, pure power of the will to know. For what, I have never quite understood, or at least I think most people like myself have tended to channel that need into a pursuit, a discipline. Writing. Teaching. But you gather and gather, absorb and absorb. For what? Your sculpture is part of it, but your interests seem so much wider than mine.

I was present once when you lay on the bottom of the bathtub, your face almost purple, eyes bulging, and I hauled you up, certain you had knocked your head. You were four, and I had been sitting on the stool next to the tub reading *The Pickwick Papers* to you (to myself mostly, since you hardly understood a word) and enjoying it so much I stopped watching you push a toy duck around. You were furious with me, stood there in a dripping, naked rage. "You ruined it," you said. The copy of Dickens was sprawled in a puddle on the floor. "I was going to be a fish." You calmed down finally, explained how a friend's older sister had said that if you held your breath long enough underwater, you could begin to breathe in small amounts through your nose. I spent some time explaining how that was dangerous misinformation, how we were doomed to be without gills forever, although I offered you consolation later that night by showing you pictures of embryos, the fishy shapes of undeveloped human beings lolling in the bathtub of the womb. As I wiped at Dickens and you settled back into tepid water I got around to the basic question and asked, "Why do you want to be a fish, anyway?" You looked at me as if I were a moron. "Because I want to know." Birds, fishes, horses, trees. Henceforth I watched you staring at all of them hungrily. You would have been a rock for a day if you could have pulled it off.

I know where Tim is, know many of the things he has done. Contrary to what you once accused me of when you had one of your more violent teenaged tantrums, I did not banish my son or forget him. I have no doubt that he never forgave me, or if he did, he never tested that against a meeting with my real person. He is my son. He left when I most needed him probably because I had not been there enough when he had needed me, and because, for whatever reasons of survival, unlike yourself he had long ago taken sides in the issues between your mother and myself. Her side. Before he left he told me I had killed her. I was aware enough of my part in her self-destruction to be unable yet to hear that so flatly and from him. I could barely stand to hear it from myself, having not yet worked through to understanding that such an accusation was the last distortion of Jane's and my very contorted dance together. So I slapped him. He did not hide in a closet, nor did he belt me, which he could easily have done given our comparative strengths. Two days later he was gone. No note. The world became his closet. Or so I thought at first until I saw that he had locked *me* in the closet by leaving, taking a whole version of the life Jane and I had lived that could never be revised by some subsequent relationship between him and me. I spent money finding him at various times. Wrote him. Called him once and only got to hear a few words before he knew who I was and hung up.

He must certainly be part of your earliest memories. He would not be hard to find, I think. Most recently in Colorado. For a while he was in the service. Went to Korea. He was in a VA hospital for some time but not from physical wounds. I wanted to go to him then, but he refused to let them give permission. I was hoping his doctors were working with more than war trauma. One of them did go far enough to say I could not visit because I seemed to be part of the problem. Wouldn't Tim have contacted me subsequently if therapy had worked? Or is the real untying of a Gordian knot always the swift, severing stroke? I plead guilty to hoping for some reconciliation of us all through the two of you. But if that is selfish, can't it also come out of a father's love, a sense that you will both be fuller and happier to have touched again briefly, even if in terms far different than I could know?

> Find him, please.
> Your father,
> Hob

Was that a fair legacy? I took my time deciding. What I knew immediately was that it was painful for many reasons, but above all for the stark way it revealed my father's loneliness. I had certainly been aware of that since my mother's death and Tim's departure, but over a period of time I had become used to it. Or his loneliness was diffused by work, wanderings, my own demands from him. The letter's request seemed so futile. What good would my search for Tim do him now? All I wanted was to help him overcome the blankness of such absence. I put the letter aside firmly. He had spoken of my will but overlooked my stubbornness, and although his urgency pained me, it was not mine. My brother had waited in silence. He could wait longer. I avoided the letter much as I had put aside Hob's books when I was young, fearing that those parts of his life were done so excellently they could only limit my own sense of potentiality.

I could hear Hob's voice in that letter just as I had the first time I read one of his books. I was fifteen and at boarding school. Shame drove me to read it. My roommate, a girl from Long Island who possessed everything I thought I lacked—cascades of dark hair, already perfectly molded breasts larger than mine but not so large as to be pendulous, an ability to ride any horse with the consummate air of English royalty—had read my father's latest novel and she had "loved it, really adored it." And didn't I think the way he wrote about horses was "really neat, as if he knows what it's like to be a horse"? I faked agreement although I wanted to say, "My father's never been on the back of a horse and never will, he hates them and I've heard him rant about foxhunting, so what the hell are you talking about?" But I was hurt too. How could my father have left me so vulnerable, never letting me know that in spite of his avowed lack of interest in horses, somewhere in the privacy of his imagination he had lived with them, inhabiting a world he had never shared with me? I borrowed a novel from the library and read it surreptitiously, stowing it under my mattress so that Jessica would not know I had to use that copy.

At first the fragments of his life that I could recognize struck their jagged edges out of this page or that and I could not see the pattern of chapters, the innumerable inventions that transformed anything I thought I knew. But I read that book twice, and what had irritated me the first time through, those seeming inaccuracies, began to disengage themselves from any familiar world. Freed, they sank back into the whole texture, and suddenly I was reading a book, the people in it began to move and speak, the landscape was not one I had ever known. I remember still the simply described scene of a boy who escapes from his parents arguing bitterly over their evening meal, and he crosses a field he and his father had been mowing all day. He pauses to sit by a broken fence and watch a fox angle toward the setting sun, and nothing is overtly stated about the boy's feelings when the chapter ends. But I was weeping.

I closed the book. Jessica had gone to the shower with all her paraphernalia. The water was running, her voice chatted in its tightly fluctuating tones to someone in one of the stalls. I clenched the book hard on my finger and closed my eyes. I could not untangle it all. The hour was late, I marked my place, put the book under my pillow, turned out the lights, and slid into the covers with my back to the door, not even bothering to take off the rest of my clothes. My pain was not only the boy's loneliness, although that was part of it—maybe for the first time in my life I had truly read a passage from a book. But all the people I had thought were part of me, connected by tacky strands when they moved because they were mired in the glue of my emotional life, were separate, complete, and if they were, so was I. My earlier irritation was a way of preventing myself from seeing how my father's private self was rich in imaginings, in things I have never seen or known. The toilet flushed and Jessica's voice ceased its mechanical flutter. She padded into the room, said my name, received no response, and lingered as usual to adore and pamper the surface of her body before she turned out the lights.

But I was not in pain any longer. I would not have known what to call it then. I stood with the boy by the fence. The fox, so clearly described in that lush landscape where a sudden freshet of wind blew the grass upward, paused to stare at the boy. The low sun was breaking over the dark shimmer of leaves, the still fox, the wide-eyed boy, a house behind him he would return to with its web of family. My father's voice was no longer in the words of the last sentences that I could already repeat by heart. What he had made let in something other than himself. For a moment again everyone I knew became as indifferently separate as the thing called language, and then I said their names—James Howard Cobb, Jane Bentley Cobb, Timothy Randolph Cobb, Julie Cobb—and I whispered, "Someday I am going to die." Later I came to think of that moment in my room with

Jessica flicking off her bedside lamp, calling my name quietly, and again receiving no response, as the first time I began to understand the meaning and necessity of love.

How puzzled, finally worried Hob looked when he came to visit me later that fall. I could not talk to him about the books. On the surface some questions formed in me but I silenced them, trying instead to sense that intangible part of him, a consciousness, trying to show him that I knew, I knew. Before he left he had a talk with the dean and the school psychiatrist. He reminded them that my mother had died not long ago and perhaps I had not grieved sufficiently for that, holding too much in. They might want to keep an eye on me. They kept an eye on me. "Love," I said to the shrink who asked me to drop by for a chat ("a little something we do with all our students from time to time") "is . . ." and then I paused, discovering another thing about love, which is that it chooses beyond our will to choose. "Yes?" "None of your business," and I stared out his window until he let me go.

I was right. It was none of his business. His business was reading the text for the incriminating evidence, a spy in the service of Revelations, Incorporated. "Do you think," he asked in the next and final meeting, "that you have really dealt with your mother's death? Are there things about her we should discuss? Recall?" I insisted on coming home to Burlington High School the next year.

I have certain memories I guard carefully, keeping watch over them to prevent myself from using them too much because I do not want them to fade. We often went for drives on Sunday afternoons when I was young. I think that stopped at about the time I was eight. Probably Tim was becoming too old to find them entertaining anymore, certainly we were all floating apart. Perhaps the car was already an illusory container for such different and difficult persons, but for a while it worked—spring jaunts in bright sunshine when we rose from the lake's green shore to the unmelted snows in the mountains, picnics at Crown Point where some vague attempt at teaching history was made by Hob to an audience more intent on catching grasshoppers and butterflies.

One afternooon in fall we take a drive that includes the ferry boat between Charlotte and Essex. My mother's arm stretches along the back of the front seat, her face is turned to Hob as he drives, and she is smiling although nothing in his words gives her reason to. Her hand moves gently on the back of his neck. We are not used to such open affection between our parents, and Tim and I, hypnotized by the slow motions of the hand, the quiet lapping of their words, sit still in a dream of passing landscape. Somewhere near the turnoff for Charlotte a car from the opposing lane pulls out to pass, sees us barely in time to swerve back. Jane's other arm has lifted tensely to keep back the collision, her sternest voice calls, "Watch it"; my father says, "fool" to the empty road. Even as a child I know the danger, and my heart does not slow until we are near the lake. We have left on a clear day in Burlington, but near the water the colors of leaves are subdued by mist, and in the middle of the lake we enter a fog so deep that even the ferry boat loses its way, slows, begins a steady hooting into the blank, then cuts its engine.

We drift. None of us speaks. The hooting stops. We are all deeply asleep, a spell cast over us by a goblin of the lake. But I still hold those moments of suspension carefully. Four of us safe in a world of possible collisions, arguments, unseen objects. My mother's hand perfectly still but relaxed on Hob's neck. Tim's hands on his bony knees, my legs crossed under me on the seat. We drift in utter peace. And then I see the globed shape of a tree, the curve of a parapet. The engine explodes into motion, pulls us back, but we do not leave sight of the shore again, groping toward the arms of the slip and the rest of a journey that I have long ago forgotten.

3

I could not look closely at my mother's death for many years. But perhaps I was able to gaze with fascination at the violent lives of Art and Bessy Sprague because they were so distanced from me in class and temperament. I was middle-class, protected without by the house I lived in and the street it was on, protected within by habits of mind. Because of that I lived in my city for long spaces of time, even traveled through and into the countryside experiencing only as much contact with most of the people in it as those tourists who perched on the edge of the lake in summer, their backs to the land, eyeing the water and testing the wind before stepping off into their sailboats. My life was not unreal but carefully disjunct from another whole state within Vermont that lived on lower North Street, or in a trailer park in Milton, or down near the river and the dead mills in Springfield.

Arthur Sprague lived in a trailer with his wife, Bessy, and his daughter Annette. Or it was a trailer once. The shape still had some basic reference to that rectangle narrow enough to be trucked down a highway. But over the years it had been permanently beached on cinder blocks, its metal obscured by patches of plywood, rotting window boxes, a few slanting excrescences barnacled to the sides. It leaned back into a precipitous hillside of unmown grasses and encroaching saplings, and here and there were the midden heaps of old car parts, bottomless pots and pans, an embedded oil drum. A rut that also served as spring runoff from the woods above zigged once, then zagged into a wooden shed almost as large as the trailer. But unlike the place where Art and his women lived, the shed was pure in line, the two windows reflecting cleanly, the foundation stones patched here and there with fresh mortar. The shed was where he worked, where much of him lived.

I was a sophomore in college, home for the summer, and Hob

had arranged a job for me as helper to Mr. Sprague, furniture maker. It was an odd idea Hob had hatched that if I was going to continue working in sculpture, and my earliest attempts were with wood, I should know more about woodworking in general. "It's sort of like a writer working as a newspaperman," he said, so pleased with the comparison that I did not have the heart to argue or to tell him that by spring of that year I had graduated to stone. He knew Art Sprague because of his own hobby of collecting antique woodworking tools, but I had never met the man until that first morning I went to work.

A glint on the trailer's windows was the last sunlight of that particular day. Dark clouds had been slowly edging in from the south, and even as I walked toward the shaky stoop, the reflections dulled and a mist of fine rain gusted at me. I pushed the doorbell a few times but heard nothing, so I knocked. Bessy eventually came to fill the doorway, her hennaed hair so thin that she was nearly bald in places, thick legs splayed by her weight and ending in slippers of crushed and bedraggled fur. The television prattled behind her.

Her eyes moved nervously over my face, never making contact with my eyes, and as long as she withheld expression, her flesh was a barrier of weight accumulated to stand behind safely and peer out at the world. Later, after I had come often and Bessy trusted me as much as she could anyone, I was amazed at how mobile, expressive, even lovely that face could be. That first time, however, I could not avoid the oppression of bulk, the way her head was joined to a neck and that in turn to her steeply sloping shoulders so that there was no articulation of parts. I could barely tell she was holding back a laugh.

"He's up there." she jabbed a thumb past her ear.

"Who's that?" A very high voice. Another woman, shorter than Bessy but almost as heavy. Unlike her mother's, Annette's face was totally round and her flesh was simply fat, lacking that weight lifter's solidity. I could not really see any more than her face at that time, but I judged Annette to be about forty.

"Someone for Mr. Sprague." She did laugh then.

Annette stared for a moment, then grinned. "Mr. Sprague," she repeated heavily.

Bessy nodded and I could tell she did not want the mockery to go further. "Walk up. If he's got something running, pound on the door. He don't hear too good sometimes."

27

I worked my way around the side of the trailer, avoiding the rusted coil of barbed wire lurking in the high grass. As it does so often in Vermont, the landscape tilted inexplicably out of a flat, marsh-pocked field, a hillock of tough stone that had stood obdurately against the slow grind of glacier. It was crowned with woods that would be cut again and again, always growing back, a few old trees so misshapen that they had never been worth the using, now mostly dead limbs and deeply seamed, rotted trunks. Equally inexplicable, though, was the way someone always chose to perch a habitation on these knobs and scarps, as if agreeing with the landscape in its stubborn adherence to unreason.

At the door I turned to let my gaze sweep down past the backside of the trailer where the worn dirt grew nothing because it rarely had sunshine all year, the battered truck looking more abandoned than parked, past my car incongruously clean in lines and polish, over the fields of planted hay and random patches of swamp or ledge humping up like the gray back of a whale. If I had never seen something like it before I would have thought it bleak beyond enduring. But I had come to sense that areas like this were maybe the most beautiful of all in their inviolability. No strangers in the form of tourists or developers or entrepreneurs of the picturesque would ever seize on it. Even the practical, farmers or lumbermen, would not choose it except to scratch up a little hay or firewood from time to time. But people like Art Sprague would pound in their stakes and cling to its sides, hardly changing any of it in doing so, as native as the birds that nested in the brambles. I knew I could never do that, but somehow I was grateful to him for choosing to. It made me feel that we are meant to be here after all, at home in even the least accommodating patches of an earth our species is said to have defiled.

"You looking for real estate, or you coming to work?"

He stood in the partly open doorway. I had heard the intermittent whine of a sander and now I could smell resinous dust. His eyebrows and creased face were finely powdered.

"I'm Julie Cobb. Howard Cobb's daughter."

"I know all that. I saw you drive up."

I stepped in, he closed the door and turned back to his workbench, where he had been sanding a slab of cherrywood. The shed was lit with a bright tier of fluorescent lights, his tools hung neatly along the walls, and even though the floor was covered with sawdust and wood chips, it was only one morning's litter. Some of the tools still very much in use were like ones my father had collected.

He picked up a piece of steel wool and began rubbing gently. He was much taller than he had seemed, his height diminished by an habitual forward stoop of shoulders. He was lanky and big-boned, and the knuckles of his hands bulged hugely. When he glanced at me he squinted as if trying to peer through a haze.

"Table I'm making for Mrs. Cox. You know her."

I didn't. He talked about the table for a few minutes. Mrs. Cox was from Vergennes. He would lean closer from time to time to blow and he had a piece of fine-grained sandpaper in the other hand. He invited me to look at the tools, so I wandered around the various racks and cabinets.

"What's this?"

His hands stilled. "Hold it up. A sash fillister."

My father had one. I knew it was some kind of plane but could not identify its use.

"You look at it carefully and you'll see it's just a skewrabbet and a molding plane put together. I got no use for that much, now."

I could not tell if his grin was because he assumed he was bewildering me, or pride in the object itself, so I accepted the challenge, if it was. "Could you use it for shaping muntins?"

Do initial gestures define relationships, or are some relationships defined clearly even in their earliest gestures by the rub of characters? Henceforth we tested each other often, and even when we were not doing so, we tended to express ourselves as if we were. What pleased me at the time was how my memory was able to retrieve enough facts from Hob's explanations made while he had pointed to pictures in a woodworking book.

Art put down the sandpaper and steel wool. "You could. Look here."

He was beside me in two long strides, the loose sandals slapping loudly on his heels. Everything about him hung loosely, his shirt and pants shapeless as a jumpsuit, the jowled folds of his stubbled face. For a while we moved around the room slowly as he picked tools up, put them down, showed me an old book he had with illustrations of more kinds of planes than I had ever imagined could exist. But I should not have faked my knowledge. What I knew was limited to a defiant interest in woodworking brought on by reading a sentence in a shop manual at school: "The jigsaw is one of the safest tools. Even girls can use it easily." Art had to discover my ignorance the hard way when I ruined a whole slab of oak later that morning.

"I thought you was smarter than that." He stared fiercely at the gouged wood.

Mine was a cold anger now, determined. "Do you want me to leave?"

He laughed, showing how many of his back teeth were missing. "Lady, you can do what you want. I don't usually work with nobody. Waste of time. But I got orders to fill. Let's see how fast you learn."

I crossed my arms. The job, after all, was Hob's idea, and my pride was a measure of my lack of concern with keeping it. "I'm not staying till you tell me you want me to. I didn't come here to be made fun of."

"I thrown Bessy out of here on her ass once. You want the same?"

The wood was between us and he unbent his back, staring at me flatly.

"Listen, woman, I trust your father. He said you was all right. But I think you're a little crazy, and I got enough crazy women around here. I said you could stay. What more do you want?"

"Fine." I was weary suddenly. I worked the rest of the day in silence, following his orders, letting his hands guide mine when what he asked for was a motion I did not know. At five he turned off the lathe, told me to sweep up, then held the door open for me. It was drizzling and I hesitated, buttoning up my jacket. He looked off toward the foggy green expanse of fields below, then lowered his gaze to the trailer, a narrowing of his eyes that made his expression as harsh as the nearer landscape. I started to turn away but he put his hand on my shoulder to stop me, drew it back, and wiped it along his shirtfront.

"You'll do. Come back tomorrow."

I already knew that was near the upper limits of praise I would get. "Tomorrow." I put out my hand.

He looked at it, tugged it once. When I glanced back up the hill, the door to the shed was shut, and the drab rain made both buildings seem utterly deserted. All the way to town I thought of how I had spoken and I could not believe what I had done. But later when we reminisced, he admitted he had been impressed by that directness. "I hate your sneaky types. I don't like getting greased and then slid off somewhere I don't want to go." Soon he seemed to like having me there, sometimes already in the shed before he stumbled up from the trailer in the morning. He had his bad nights and his hands would show it the next day, trembling, scattering screws as he cursed under his breath. Occasionally he would spend an hour trying and then walk out, slamming the door, not coming back till afternoon. I liked getting there early, watching haze gather over the fields below as the air heated up.

He started taking me with him in his battered truck when he went to the mills and I learned about various woods, met the few men who still knew the art of milling. He taught me haunched mortise-and-tenon, rabbeting, subtleties of simple cross lap joints I had not thought possible, although there was never any question which work was his, which mine. Once driving back from New Hampshire when we had gone rummaging for some quarter-cut ironwood he finished his bottle of beer and threw it in the back, where it rolled around for a while, and then he said, "I always wished Annette could have been like you, but she wasn't good for nothing but screwing around and eating and getting kicked out of school." I waited but that was all he said, as close as he ever came to saying I was part of the family.

Not that I wanted to be. For a long time I could not hold together in my mind the two worlds of trailer and shed any more than I could see as capable of violence those rough but deft hands testing the surface of a carefully planed board. A few times I would come to work and he would not even be at the trailer. "On a bender," Bessy would announce from the doorway in her bathrobe, and then she would ask me in for some coffee, tell me, "You might as well go on home if you're looking for him to work today. Even if he gets back he won't be no good and you won't want to hear him if he's still ripping." I always took her advice after the first time. I was finishing some work we had abandoned the day before. The truck slithered and whined up the muddy road, Art stumbled out leaving the door open like a slack jaw, and then their voices rose toward me—his, Bessy's, Annette's—the crack of something breaking, blows, one of the women yelping like a dog in pain. I feared murder, was halfway down the path when the noise subsided, only whimpers as I stood by the back of the trailer, then Art's voice, heavy and dull, "Get up and quit that noise.'' I closed the door to his truck and drove home. The next day Bessy lifted a curtain to stare at me as I got out of the car, a purple welt closing one of her eyes. Up in the shed Art was sweeping the floor.

''You left this place like a pigsty yesterday,'' he muttered.

Annette treated me with indifference on those mornings when I was ushered in, stepping around piles of old magazines and newspapers, trying to avoid bumping into dilapidated easy chairs and a sofa that exuded wads of stuffing. There were cats everywhere. On the hottest days I could barely endure the odor of grease from the pans, the scats of the animals dropped too close to the trailer, Annette's and Bessy's flesh suffering in the heat that relentlessly pressed down on the metal roof. We would talk about things Bessy had seen on the TV or on her last trip to Burlington in the truck with Art, and I tried to bring her things if she would mention them to me—hair rinses, bottles of minerals for various complaints. Often Annette would not be up yet, her presence expressed in the scrape of springs giving to her weight as she shifted and moaned on the other side of a beaverboard partition they had set up so she could have ''her own room.'' In a whisper Bessy told me how Annette had been ''knocked up twice before she dropped out of school some twenty years ago or so,'' but they'd given the babies away and Art nearly killed the last boy she'd fooled with, ''and that was a long time ago.'' Bessy said she and Art had two other children, both boys, who had left and never come back, and she didn't know what would happen to Annette when she and Art passed on because the girl had never ''took care of herself too good, and she was already pretty feeble in the mind.'' Girl? Her age still evaded me. I would go home, aching in the new small muscles of my forearm or in that taut line of tension up my back from pressing and not letting the tool do the work. Standing in the shower, washing sawdust out of my hair, I would close my eyes and try to imagine their lives. But I could not. They were foreign to me, even if I came to know Bessy well enough so that she could look me in the eyes when she talked, even if I loved that part of Art Sprague that lived in the shed. The best I could do was numb my aversion by flailing at it, blaming it on my ignorance and an insufficient sympathetic understanding. I rarely got beyond merely superimposing the crisp, accurate slither of his plane onto the brute and wordless muttering of anger from the trailer window.

But for a moment my own experience at least showed me the double nature of those hands so that they were never wholly simple in function when I watched him urging a coping saw through some delicate curve. Art was impatient sometimes but usually gentle with me, and I suspected he had begun to enjoy my presence in the shed with him, my constant and unconcealed admiration for what he could do. Was he lonely? His customers or patrons certainly knew his worth and paid him accordingly, but most of them had that offhand kindness of the wealthy. "How very lovely, Arthur," Mrs. Cox had said of her table, and she added an extra thirty dollars to show her pleasure. But that was that. The table was delivered, hers now to be eaten on, to accumulate the scars and patina of her own widowed life, and when she died no one would know who had made that table shipped to heirs or auctioned off to some antiques store. If Bessy did not resent me it was because she did not know or care anything much about that aspect of his life. He made a living by it. But she only looked puzzled when I tried to tell her something about my growing respect for it. I was welcome to it. "You'll ruin the skin on your hands" was all she could say.

But Art and I made each other angry in some final area where he would not give up his predetermined notions about the limitations of a woman. I accused him of protecting his pride, or by believing I could never completely know some things because I was a woman, he was even holding back some part of his knowledge to keep me from sharing it.

We went in late July to a woodlot that he had rights to above Johnson, where he had stacked lumber hewn and sawn the winter before. We walked the half mile to the place, began carrying down loads to the truck. It was heavy labor and I could tell he was testing my endurance, since we had often argued about the relative strengths of men and women. My shoulders ached after two trips, splinters worked their way deeper into my bare hands, but I would not give him the satisfaction of seeing me quit. He had brought some beer with him and whenever we reached the truck he had one or two bottles. I did not want any. The beer ran out and he began nipping on a pint of whiskey. It was midafternoon when we finished and climbed into the cab of the truck. I stretched out my feet, let my head rest against the seatback, relaxing like a cat to the sun pouring in the window on my face. He put the key in the ignition but did not turn it.

When I lolled my head toward him I saw he was hunched toward the wheel but his face was turned to me.

"You know, you're some kind of woman."

So I had passed through that last hesitation with which he had regarded me. But I had not expected a verbal recognition. "What kind is that?"

"Tough." Not much was left in the bottle, and he diminished that further, wincing as he swallowed. He looked at the last measure. "Might as well sit a minute. Want some?"

I shook my head. The wind gusted through our opened windows.

"My sons couldn't do that well, and they was bigger than you. Lazier, too." He hardly ever mentioned them, and never by names. They were always "my sons" or "my boys," and all I could imagine were two sturdy images of himself.

He drained the bottle and flipped it into the woods, where it shattered.

"I tell you what. I wished I'd come across you when I was younger. We'd've had some time, eh?"

That seemed like a simple compliment, and I could not help thinking what that would have been like, his face less worn and seamed by use, less coarsened by the wear of heavy drinking.

He lurched toward me with a look of surprised embarrassment, his motions as awkward as if he were trying to move fast in a dark room. One hand clutched the top of my thigh, the other held fast to the nape of my neck. My own pulse raced. The grip in those two hands proved that no struggling would prevent him if he went further. He was so close I could see only the mouth twitching, tightening as he said, "C'mon, Julie. How about a little pussy?"

"No." I tried to keep my voice steady.

"C'mon."

The hand on my neck tightened, and I had to hunch against it. I kept my legs crossed, but his other hand was burrowing between them.

"Ease up. I won't hurt you."

His mouth was on mine, the barrier of his teeth bearing against me until I thought my lips would break. When he drew back, panting but close, I said again, "No," and this time I placed both hands on his chest and began to push. The hand had wedged its way into my crotch, was clumsily, painfully prodding.

He drew back so suddenly that I almost fell with him toward the other side, but when I knew I was released, I had the door open and was out. Nowhere to go. I turned, breathless, wiping at my aching mouth, then gripped the frame and handle of the open door. He was hunched on his own side, staring forward, hand poised on the key in the ignition.

"You getting in or you walking?" His voice was slurred but toneless.

"Damn you." I held on to the truck. I could see the tools in the back, thought coldly of grasping an ax, bringing it down on those rolled shoulders.

"What do you want me to say? Sorry? I'm sorry. To hell with it. Now get in. I won't touch you, and if I was you I wouldn't want to have to walk out of here alone."

The hand twisted, the engine choked, groaned, and rumbled. He let off the brake. I climbed in, slammed the door, but leaned as close to it as I could, my arm out the opened window. There was not enough room in that cab to put between us. He jerked his foot off the clutch, the engine stalled, but the truck was rolling. He muttered "Fuck it," turned the key again, and then we trounced down that rutted wood road as if a dam had broken behind us. Again and again tree trunks massed ahead, the back slewed as he yanked the wheel, but somehow we made it to the highway.

I was exhausted, watched the road unravel, letting the air buffet me. The drive down out of the woods had distanced me from my anger to a simple concentration on survival, and all I wanted was to be away from him. I would think it through later. When he began to speak, I had to draw my head out of the slipstream to hear him. He had both hands on the wheel, his expression dazed with beer and whiskey, and he was not even glancing at me.

"It's the booze, Julie. It always makes me do things."

But I was in no mood for his self-pity. "Then quit drinking. And that's just an excuse. It doesn't do it. You do it to yourself."

He nodded. "That's a fact. I didn't mean otherwise. But you're a damn beautiful woman and . . ."

"I don't want to hear. I don't like the way you compliment me."

"Lookit." He frowned heavily. "I'd take back what I did there if I could. Or you'd let me."

"Generous of you."

But he did not bother with my response.

"That was dumb. Ugly old critter like me. But not what I said. If I was younger I would've done a lot to know you better."

"Why the hell did you do that? What am I going to do now?"

He looked puzzled. "Do?"

"How can I keep working with you after that?"

The truck swerved in response to his surprised glance at me.

"You figure I'm dumb enough to pull that again? I don't get it."

I did not mention the incident to my father, and later that evening I lay for an hour in the tub letting all the aches of heaving and dragging grow numb. I kept sponging hot water on the nape of my neck without realizing for a long time how I was trying to wash away the touch of his fingers. I was no virgin by then and had no fears of the kind of sex I knew, but this was not just brute violence either. I could not understand what his attitude was showing me, but I kept coming back to it. Only years later did I have time to think it through with the help of some other experiences, and I could see that what happened to us in the cab of the truck was the bewildered interfacing of two cultures. He had tried something simple and it had not worked. What did not work was wrong. Some women do, some don't, and he was too old for my liking. That was over. A blunder as if a hammer had missed the head of the nail and pounded his thumb. Well, you try not to do that again. Mine was that world of shivering consciousness, of gestures made that sent their endless ripples here and there or had consequences to be weighed, measured, seasoned with guilt and retribution, and tightly parceled out into time. I could not accept his way any more than I could change mine. For me what had happened in those woods would not dissolve. I had shown him I could compete even on the level of hard labor, but in the end he had held up the strongest symbol of counterbalance he could find, refusing to deny the body and his immutable view of it. He was a man, I a woman. Only a truce was possible, and I went back to work in the same room with those hands whose skill I loved and whose violence I would not forgive.

I lasted almost one month more.

August. I drove up the rutted drive, thought Bessy was only out early, sitting in a patch of sun on their front stoop. She seemed to be dozing, her massive form slumped awkwardly across the doorway, one shoulder and her head leaning on the frame. I stopped the car quietly, hoping not to wake her, and climbed out before I looked again.

Her face was swollen and bruised, eyes puffed shut, her lower lip torn in a bloody seam. She was breathing irregularly in short heaves, and her hands lay palm up beside her.

"Bessy?"

I was not sure if the eyes in their narrow slits could even see, but she nodded.

"Can you walk?"

I had to get her to the hospital, but how could I carry her? She tried to pull in that lower lip and make her jaw work. Her words were as misshapen as her face, snatches on the wind of her gasping—yes, don't worry, am OK, need to rest. I put my hands firmly on her upper arm, but even both hands could not reach around it.

"I'm taking you to the hospital. You've got to help me. Walk to the car."

She tried to pull back. No, no, mustn't. Everything all right. Just needed to rest. Didn't want to go to the hospital.

"She'll come 'round."

The bloated form of Annette in the tent of her nightgown was standing in the doorway. Her short-cropped hair hung straight over her ears and forehead, and her stare slid lazily between her mother and myself.

"Bessy's hurt, Annette. Help me get her to the car."

"I seen her worse."

"Do as I tell you."

Her face stuck forward at me. "You ain't my mother. I don't do what you say."

"Where's your father?"

Her columnar arm lifted, a small thumb poked back over her shoulder. "Sleeping it off. He won't be no good till tonight."

I tried to step over Bessy and edge past Annette, but she did not move.

"You can't come in here like that. This ain't your house. You wasn't invited."

I leaned close to Bessy's face.

"Can you hear me?"

A nod.

"Please try to come with me. You're very hurt."

The eyes rolled, snagged on me. She nodded again. Her legs flopped down onto the next step, she tried to heave against the frame. I tugged; she sat upright but nearly fell backward. She mouthed some words to her daughter, and Annette stooped, grunted, hauling at Bessy on the other side. The three of us staggered down the uneven scrabble, I flung open the car door, we pushed and lifted her onto the seat, and her head rolled back against the rest. I slammed the door and did not say anything to Annette, but she hulked around to my side. As I started the car, her high, wheezing voice was saying, "My dad's gonna be pissed as hell at you, none of your goddamned business, you high-class cunt."

Bessy was still bleeding thickly from her mouth. She muttered from time to time and I took the curves carefully for fear she would slide and pin me against my door. Two attendants had to help at the emergency room, and they wheeled her off to surgery. After an hour of trying to read through ragged magazines, I went back to the desk.

"They've decided to keep her overnight for observation."

"Could I see her?"

"She's under anesthetic. You might try this evening in visiting hours."

I had no intention of going to the workshop that day and had made up my mind about the whole situation by the time I reached home. That evening when I went to see Bessy she was gone.

"Her husband came. We told him we thought she should have some other tests done, but they both wanted to go."

The next morning Art was stooped over his bench, wood curling up in bright shavings from his plane. "You'd best turn those legs so we can finish the desk today."

I stood beside the bench until he stopped working. His eyes were tired, almost furtive.

"If you want to talk about all that crap yesterday, I don't. I'm sorry you had to get in on it, but you ought to know better. None of your business."

"How is she?"

"Hell, she can take it."

I kept one hand on the flat surface and pressed down. "She didn't look like she could yesterday. Anyway, I can't. I'm leaving."

He waved a hand disgustedly at me. "Lay off. It's between Bessy and me. We been going at each other for years."

"I didn't see you getting sewn up at the hospital."

"She ought to know better than to try to lay into me like that. She always gets the worst of it." He paused. "Look, I said I was sorry you had to see it. I'm off the booze now. Me and Bessy had a long talk and I'm giving up that stuff. It always does that."

"Good. I hope it works. Well, that's it." I held out my hand, but he let it hang there.

"I suppose now that you know all you want, you'll set up on your own. Shit." He slapped his hand down. "Was I played for a sucker."

"I'm not going into business. I'm going back to college."

He barked out a laugh. "I bet."

When I looked back from the door he was still standing there.

"Good-bye, Art."

He did not answer.

The door to the trailer was open, I could dimly hear the energetic, false laughter of a quiz show, applause. I was about to stoop into my car when he strode into the drive and stood in front, one hand on the hood.

"Julie."

I stood, keys swinging against my wrist.

"I wish you wouldn't go." He glared at the hood. "How am I to get on without you?"

"I can't forget that." I pointed as if Bessy were still slumped in the doorway. Instead, Annette's figure had risen like a large bubble out of the murky interior.

His hand slapped the metal. "But you're the best thing that's happened for years."

Part of me wanted to compromise, say, "Well, I'll help finish up those orders." But such an evasion would have been as sentimentally vicious as the self-pity he must have lapsed into every time he woke from one of those bouts. I sat, closed my door, started the engine. He leaned with both hands on the trembling hood, peering intently at me through the windshield. His long, seared face was immobile, eyes as obsessive as in the portrait of some Byzantine saint, and then he jerked up and stood aside.

"Goddamn, goddamn" his voice was muttering as I drove by, those long arms hanging as if their fists were rocks.

I told Hob only that Art did not need me anymore. For me they stand like three hieratic figures within one frame: Art, Bessy, and Annette before a background both desolate and deeply known. But that framework does not always contain them. I am drawn into their lives again and again, touching some terrible core that even love must struggle to penetrate.

4

The first time I met Michael Gardener I kept a screen door between us. I was fifteen. The library wanted my father's papers, and Michael, in his first year working for Special Collections at the university, had been delegated to cajole and wheedle Professor Cobb, even tacitly appealing to his conscience. Hob's response was irritation but not anger. "They're just doing their jobs." The university had been good to Hob but had received more than enough in return if only through the use of his name in the catalog.

My father's strategy with librarians was to be "not at home." In this instance he was on his way out the back door as I stood at the front. "I'm afraid he's not in," I said, having waited for the slap of the back screen door to preserve me from lying. The chug and grind of our jeep starting, the view of it easing around the side of the house, my father's grim and airy wave proved my statement. I rubbed it in: "You just missed him."

"You're Howard Cobb's daughter, aren't you?"

I had heard nothing against Mr. Gardener and disliked him at that moment only for disrupting one of the few afternoons of a fall weekend when both my father and I had been home, not doing anything together, but his presence giving me a comfortable sense of another person in the house. Since my mother's death some of the rooms could seem empty.

"*J*. Howard Cobb," I said slowly.

The gauze of screen obscured his expression.

"Exactly. Sorry to have missed him. Will you tell him Michael Gardener called?"

"Sure." But he was not showing enough reaction to his treatment. "You didn't call, you came. And obviously he knows already."

He laughed, threw up his hands in mock surrender, said, "Obviously," and walked down the steps.

I watched him from my bedroom window as he strolled up the street.

I was twenty-three when I talked to him again, this time in his own office at the library.

He rose from his desk. "J. Howard Cobb's daughter?"

"Yes." That old flinch at being identified through my father was not a good beginning.

"This time you're on my territory." His expression gave away nothing yet.

"You remember that? I wouldn't have expected you to."

"How could I forget? Call me Mike or Michael, I don't care which."

No screen between us, so we shook hands. I was relieved that his was firm, not mushy. I hate puffy handshakes, like squeezing a frog. He offered me a chair, and we sat down.

"I haven't thought of that afternoon for years, but for some time afterward I tended to see you standing at the gate like a guardian angel."

"No angel. But I would have slammed the door on your foot if you'd tried to go farther."

"I'm sorry about your father's death. I didn't know him very well, but certainly much better than I did that afternoon. I read all of his work. I was getting used to asking him for the papers once a year."

"Did you like his books?"

"I wouldn't have kept trying so hard if I didn't. I won't tell you how good I think he is because you'll accuse me of flattery."

"I didn't write them."

"If you did, I'd like to be the first to know."

I did not wait for the next meander, though. "I want to sell my father's papers."

His grin was so infectious that I ended up laughing.

"I was hoping. But I didn't dare ask again."

We moved quickly to details, how he would have to look over the boxes of papers and manuscripts I had stored in the attic and basement following Hob's death, how he had to be honest in admitting that the university would pay less than some other places. But just as we were arranging his visit he blinked and raised his eyebrows. Someone was directly behind me. I assumed the secretary, but he said, "Hello."

I turned to a girl in her midteens, almost a woman but still a filly in the way she tried to assume a relaxed pose while only managing to make it a parody.

"My daughter Melissa. This is Julie Cobb. Miss Cobb and I discovered a mutual memory trace."

"I've seen you around," she said, not doing much with her face. "I'm going to Mom's for dinner and then to the movies."

I had stood when their conversation began, and now I wandered out of earshot to let father and daughter confer. Looking back I could see how mature she was in body, even if she did not yet know how to possess it. They talked with increasing intensity, Michael emphasizing by tapping with his finger on the desktop, her voice lifting into an exasperated, "Oh, Dad." She shrugged and walked away pouting but managed to say something polite to the secretary as she passed.

He was all business when I returned, leading me into Special Collections to show me how carefully they would catalog and preserve the papers. The split glasses he wore when peering at a manuscript made him look older but no less attractive. "I hate bifocals." He replaced them with his regular glasses when we walked on. His long fingers were the right shape to touch and hold something valuable.

"She's sixteen, I'm afraid," he said when I mentioned how young he was to have a teenaged daughter. "And I was nineteen when she was born. Her mother and I married before we knew each other well enough, as we've come to rue. However, sixteen is a very difficult time. It seems everyone is to blame."

"For what?"

"For making one be sixteen." He was holding a book open with his hand cupped carefully under it to prevent the binding from cracking. "Do you remember being sixteen? My sense of history is not very good, but I think of adolescence as . . . what? No single word works, does it? I was going to say painful, but that's not right, because I remember some very happy moments. Whatever the state of mind was it was extreme and liable to reverse itself. A lot of energy and no clear focus. Makes me tired sometimes to watch Melissa."

As he described the jagged intensity I wondered if I had left adolescence yet, except for the recent past that was more a matter of numbness, a paralyzed inability to decide whether to move or stay in our family home, whether to continue working on my sculpture in Burlington or push myself into New York.

He walked with me to the exit and we set up a time for him to come. My telephone number? He had a bedraggled datebook held together by a rubber band. I thanked him, then all the way home I looked forward to showing him the papers. I was grateful to Michael Gardener, if only because his interest and motion toward resolving the problem of Hob's literary remains was removing my numbness.

I am sure that is why I recall the first meeting with Michael and Melissa so well. I was already waking without knowing it—because when I think back certainly nothing in the whole scene was exceptional enough to warrant the clarity with which details come back to me. The secretary wore seashell earrings, the patch on one hip of Melissa's faded Levis in the shape of an apple exaggerated the fullness of flesh beneath, Michael changed his glasses hesitantly as if he knew they would shift his appearance and he was vain enough to recognize that but not vain enough to have concentrated on whether the change would be for better or worse. Michael's pencil was broken at one end, the point a stub, and he carried it in a side pocket of his jacket. New details. My formal period of mourning was over.

That week I was able to pack away or sell Hob's personal belongings also. Any sorting was in discarding things too worn to give to the Salvation Army, or perhaps storing away in a box an item or two that seemed so characteristically his that a presence invested them. By now I did not feel great pain in handling them, only a clear proprietary sense that these were extensions of his body and that I might years later wish to lift them out of their boxes for only a moment as tangible evidence that the complex love imbedded in my memory was no illusion. But other things were harder. In certain closets were boxes representing his own attempt to sort and banish objects belonging to my mother and brother, but the jumbled contents, the stuffed and hastily taped appearance of them showed he had been less successful in that process than I was being. I, in turn, could not yet deal with the evidence of his panic, so those boxes were obdurately unresolved and gathered slowly in a pile in the middle of the basement. I held down my own rising confusion with logic—first things first, I muttered, concentrating on all the immediate objects of his life.

But I did find a manila envelope full of my own childhood draw-
ings and scribblings inscribed as gifts. That was a time when dashing
some crayon strokes on a piece of scrap paper, calling the representa-
tion "Me, Mummy, Hob, and Sun" was sufficient token of love for
any occasion. For a long time I held close to the light blurring in
through the basement window a drawing of a woman with golden
hair falling to the floor, coiling in a heap there. Behind her was a
square window, sky, clouds. The arms were held wide, fingers
splayed out, and the face grinned toward me. The caption read,
"Mummy in her tower" in a childish scrawl, and beneath that in my
mother's tight, minute hand—"Me as Rapunzel, July 10, 1943."
The wide, upturned mouth covered most of the face—no miserable
princess here. And then, unfocused, no clear sense of a particular
day, a brief burst of memory made me aware of a lap I was sitting on,
a breath by my ears, the brush of fingers gently pushing aside the
hair straying into my eyes. I wished I could find more such moments
before her own dark witch climbed up and cut her hair.

On the afternoon before Michael came to dinner I wondered how
knowledgeable he was about cooking and wine, and I began to feel
wary. I can cook, but my father was one of those men who found the
kitchen a natural place to be, and only after his death did I realize
how much I had depended on him when he was around. My years at
college had done little for my culinary talents.

Michael looked through boxes while I cooked, and when we sat
down he announced that the contents were valuable, not just
manuscripts but above all Hob's correspondence with other writers.
I was not willing to believe the sum he mentioned as rough estimate
and felt so peculiar about hearing my father's personal effects
translated into cash that I told him we had to talk about something
else first.

"A toast, then. To my divorce."

"Recent?"

"Last Wednesday."

"Will you stay in Burlington?"

"No place else I want to go. Besides, there's Melissa."

"What will she do?"

"We gave her that choice. I'm staying here, keeping the house.
Fran is moving to Chicago. My statement was as simple as I could
make it. 'I want you to stay, but I will accept your decision.' "

"And what was your unstated position?"

He frowned. "Do I have to have one?"

"Fathers always do."

"All right: 'Stay and show me you think I have enough love for you to help you grow up through these last years of your childhood, go and show me you think I have love enough to continue caring even if you are not with me.' "

I thought for a moment. "Hard test for a daughter to deal with, if you want word from an ex-daughter. One can rebel against clear bias: 'To stay is right, to go is wrong.' But no matter what she does with you, you'll judge yourself harshly, not her."

He took a sip of wine and stared at the glass when he put it down. "You're saying I tried to make it a test without choices? Does that come from an ex-daughter's experiences?"

"I never had a choice. She decided to stay with you?"

"Yes. But it wasn't easy for her. Fran was sometimes a harsh mother, but they were very close to each other. Melissa and I like to argue, but not on personal matters. That prevents me from knowing some aspects of her that I glimpsed only because of Fran. They argued a lot."

"Did she have a deadline?" I was having trouble imagining how a child decided such a thing, beginning to wonder how fair even allowing that could be.

"Fran left last week. That was one deadline. Then Melissa made her own. She marked it on a calendar. She's always been that way, setting her own boundaries. When she played with other kids she would get the rules very straight first. If they were changed at all she would be angry. She never minded losing, but it had to be a fair encounter with limitations."

More and more Melissa was interesting me. I wondered if I would ever meet her again, and then I had made my own decision. I would, whether or not it was through Michael. Burlington was a smaller town than it liked to think. I was bound to see her.

"She wasn't playing games, and if that's the impression my description of her gives, it's wrong. Dramatic, because she has a flair for that, but she wasn't trying to build a Solomon-like position for herself by pushing us into demonstrations of comparative love for the baby. That day she went to school, then came home. When I returned I could not find her. Her books were on the couch, the door to her bedroom open. She wasn't in the attic. I called out a few times, figured she must have gone downtown. I was in the kitchen getting out some steaks when I looked out the window. We have a large Norway spruce in the backyard. The branches start close to the ground and it was always her climbing tree. She was sitting on a little platform of planks she and some friends had put high up. Lately she'd been going up with her recorder and tootling the sun down. You can see the lake from there, wonderful sunsets. She wasn't moving, not playing, just sitting with her hands folded on her crossed legs. I thought I'd make her a pie, since she likes that and I had some cans of cherries. I kept looking up at her and she was still there and then the sun went down. The tree was a large black shape against the sky. I cooked the steaks. Everything was ready when I heard the door close and she came into the kitchen and helped me put things on the table.''

He was not looking at me anymore. He was in a room of a house I had never entered, across the table from his daughter. And I could hardly breathe, acutely discomforted by the idea of making such a choice, finding it impossible to keep myself from becoming Melissa.

"I had tried all day to tell myself it did not matter, that she was my daughter and always would be. That I would rearrange my life to see her if she went away, or alter it to accommodate her if she stayed. But after I saw her up her tree I could not hold back panic, terrible regret. I knew I wanted her to stay more than anything in the world. If she left I would never be able to forgive myself for not fighting harder, tooth and nail with every reason or pressure at a father's disposal. I tried to begin eating, but it was no good. I put down my knife and fork and sat back. She was looking at me very calmly. Oh, she knew it was dramatic, her way of saying, 'OK you guys, you have your show called divorce. I have my own production.' But even if she had set it up that way, I could see that in the last moment she did not want it anymore. She looked very shy. She said, 'I am staying here.' I said, 'Thanks.' '' He looked up at me and then away.

"That was it?"

"And then I wept. Not for long. She asked me please to stop. She said that if she had not and was not going to cry, she didn't think I should. I agreed. She had never seen me weep before, so we were both a little confused but not embarrassed.''

We were silent for a while. Because it was getting dusky, I lit the candles, but I was not willing to fill the evening with casual discussion of the papers and his job. My curiosity about his life with Melissa and Fran made me impatient, and perhaps I already sensed that Michael was the sort of person who would not offer personal information unless asked, although behind that reticence was no lack of willingness to reveal. In fact, I am sure the tension between that surface coolness and the considerable heat of intimacy beneath it was one of the things that made me want to be alone with him. So I asked him in the first available silence "Didn't you ever think of leaving here? Giving it all up to start new elsewhere?"

"I tried. Some time ago, a year or more. Melissa would be able to tell you when because I disappeared for a month or two, took a leave to look for some rare books in Ireland, I said. But I didn't go to Ireland. I went to New York, stayed in a friend's apartment. He had gone to Ireland, actually. I should have. I drank too much, spent as much money as if I had traveled but without the diversion. I walked a great deal all over the city. Couldn't seem to concentrate even on movies, concerts. Finally self-pity ran out and I was just bored. And I missed Melissa, my father, even my office."

"Why did you go?"

A glance at me and an unsteady grin. Embarrassed? "Oh I suppose I had a grand idea, a sort of Malcolm Lowry or a Gauguin. My friend came home. We talked. I confessed to being a very domestic creature. He laughed at me, and that helped. A new panic, though. What if I got home and Melissa didn't want to have anything to do with me, or lawyers had me for desertion and Fran took the house, or someone had replaced me in my job?"

"None of the above."

He laughed easily now. "You see me. I love routine, I worry and fuss about my daughter. I need a good argument with my father from time to time. *Homo domesticus.*"

The candles were smaller when the phone rang. A woman's voice. Was Michael Gardener there? The background noise had all the matted confusion of a barroom. Another woman? I knew nothing of Michael's private life.

When he came back he stood behind his chair. "I'm afraid I'll have to go along."

I stood. Whoever she was had not sounded very pleased and I imagined myself in the middle of a considerable misunderstanding.

"Melissa. She had a ride back from a rehearsal, but it fell through."

"I have a lemon caramel soufflé, if she likes that." I flicked on the porch light.

"Melissa never refuses desserts. Her undoing."

I cleared and cleaned, made the table ready, and pondered some of the new things I had learned that night. But I should have been trying to imagine ahead, to anticipate what it would be like for Melissa to come to my house with her father, entering a setting where two people had already been enjoying themselves, one her father and the other a young woman she had met only once and probably not heard mentioned again. If I had, I might have foreseen how it would be perfectly natural for her to be watchful, even a little remote.

But all too soon the doorbell chimed me out of a boozy reverie. I ushered them into the dining room, feeling a little foolish because my gestures had to include Michael but he was already as much host as guest since he had witnessed the hour that had reduced those candles and covered the sticks with folds of wax. Did she want some wine too, or something else? Her dark hair was gathered in a ponytail, the scent of greasepaint had been absorbed by that worn, blue button-down shirt that must have been her father's once, and a slight smear of some flesh tone was left on one side of her neck. Wine, please. I made the mistake of glancing at Michael for parental approval, and she saw it. I retreated, brought back the bottle of Sauterne and a glass for her, tried to make amends by filling hers first and liberally. Neither was talking when I carried in the soufflé. I glanced at Michael, this time for help, for he was concentrating on running two fingers up and down the stem of a glass. I served, said a few inane things about how I had never quite understood whether such an object should be torn with forks or cut like a cake. She stared at me in silence, only making what I was saying seem more insignificant. Michael suggested a spoon. The adults were in trouble.

"You made it yourself?" she asked.

Oh, yes, I loved to cook. Did she like to cook? Her father did, but she was not sure. Well, she must be careful about that because I had lived with a father who loved to cook, and I had neglected my own skills for too long.

"But you're doing fine now. Besides, who says women always

have to cook? Maybe we shouldn't have to at all.'' The tone slid steadily upward from stubborn to belligerent.

I agreed emphatically. I would be perfectly happy to marry someone willing to do all the cooking.

"Oh?" She was looking at us both archly, and I knew she must be a good actress if so capable of playing that far forward into an older woman's spite.

"How old are you?" she asked when I was bringing on some coffee and liqueur for Michael and myself, tea for her. I barely told her when she asked, "What do you do for a living?"

I suppose I wanted her to be more reticent, and Mike's manner then as often afterward was a bemused mask of the parent who has decided not to interfere. My irritation at such times was often at him for not protecting me. As it was, I had to fight back against my self-protective instincts that would have found an ironic answer more easily.

I explained my circumstances briefly—Hob's death, my own helter-skelter life after college although all in the same location, my art, and the income from my father's books. I found myself talking faster as her interest wavered, wondering what it was she really wanted to know since her questions never seemed idly asked. I was trailing off when she frowned and said, "Do you believe in communication with the dead?"

Michael's hand hitched on its way to the bottle of Cointreau. "Even I can't follow that connection too clearly."

"She doesn't have to answer if she doesn't want to. I asked only because your father died. My friend Lisa's brother died last year in a car accident. She's been in touch with him. Have you ever read about spiritualism much?"

"No."

"I don't know what to believe. Lisa got very angry when I made fun at first. She tells me some things he said and described that I don't see how she would know otherwise. But he's begun to stop appearing. Maybe it can happen only for a little while afterward."

She stared at me, waiting to hear my séances described.

"I'm afraid I haven't been in touch. Not the way you mean."

"What other way?"

"I think of him, and sometimes I recall moments in our lives and then find myself not seeing them from my own eyes, but as if I were looking out from where he stands. At other times it's stories that I've never seen myself, only heard him tell, but I sort of become him in remembering.'' I had begun by feeling foolish again, but for the first time Melissa was leaning toward me and listening intently.

''I know what you mean. I do that sometimes daydreaming. Oh, not about anyone dead, but I've done it with Jemmie, our cat, thinking of crawling out over the hot driveway on my belly to hunt a bird. I keep telling Lisa that's sort of what she's doing. Imagining, like dreaming, and that she doesn't have to make it so spooky as if she's moving objects in a room with her mind.'' She paused to gather words, her eyes widening to see in some inner distance. ''It's what I do when I'm acting, too, like dreaming you're someone else with your eyes open and you can see all the other silly people at the rehearsal and someone pounding sets together but they're not nearly as real as what's going on behind your eyes.''

Michael started to say something, and I could tell by his expression that it was going to be humorous in the wrong way so I found myself staring at him, saying to myself, ''No, Michael, don't, don't interrupt.'' He sipped his Cointreau instead and I wondered if that might be sufficient witness to Lisa's belief in psychic powers.

''Do you think,'' she whirled on, ''that when you do that, when you think of your father and live his life, it's because he's in your cells, that he's really still alive because you're alive? Wouldn't it be amazing if someday they found something in your cells that was just for all your relatives to be and speak to you and go on living when you have children?''

''I think they have.'' Michael went on to discuss cell structure in ways that surprised me in the wealth of facts.

Melissa waved her hand. ''He's hopeless. He has a memory for facts that isn't fair because I can never win in arguments. You know what, though? When I'm dead I'm going to spend my time experimenting. I'm going to try to reach someone hard and get this whole thing settled once and for all.''

Michael sat close enough to put his arm around her shoulders, then keep it draped over the back of her chair. ''Do you want me to try? I'll be the first to go.''

''Would you? I promise I'll be very open. I tell you what.'' Again she leaned eagerly at me. "Let's make a pact. Whoever goes first, tries first."

"I'm not in your cells or your father's. If that's the theory, how can I reach you?"

"I forgot. Oh, well. I guess caring isn't enough."

That she was willing to suggest we cared about each other was encouraging, but I was ready to see the evening end. Their presence together required the concentration of reading a thick book in small print.

"But maybe memory puts you into the cells." She was pleased with her idea. "Let's make a pact anyway. Dad?"

"Why not?"

"No, really. Don't boff it up. Julie and I are serious, aren't we?"

Melissa and I against Dad. I accepted that. He put his hand palm up over the table between the candles, she flattened hers on his, and I put mine on top of the pile, palm down. His hand curled, and we all did our best to hold, and I regretted having to draw back from that touch of father and daughter layered in my grasp.

I would have liked for Michael Gardener and myself to be coming to the end of that evening, conversation lapsing, both of us pausing awkwardly in that moment when we would sense that it was time for him to go, neither of us quite willing to have the opening phrases stated that would lead him inevitably to the door, snuffed candles smoking behind us, good-bye, thank you, compliments, some silly words about the hour, the brightness of the stars that could be seen from the porch. I knew we would both put out a hand, both feel at the same moment how inappropriate that gesture had become, but neither of us would rush beyond the first light kiss on each other's cheeks, like two diplomats about to separate at the border. I would have waved to the pale face turning toward me at the car window below and stood in the cold breeze, staring at the late and empty street, the houses of dark windows. My own house would seem vaguely different when I walked in, deciding to leave the dishes until the morning.

Instead Michael and I sat back into an increasing stupor, until even Melissa's energy waned and he suggested they must go. Emphatic agreement by Melissa since she had another rehearsal tomorrow and a new scene with half-memorized lines that she must at least read through before sleeping. The three of us stood on the porch, and the stars were not visible anyway because harsh clouds had blown in. The intricate web of the Dutchman's Pipe rubbed and rustled in the corner. Mike had his hands in his jacket pockets, a slouched form on the other side of his daughter. So it was Melissa I kissed, meaning to, and grateful that she would accept both my outstretched hands. Perhaps lunch sometime, we agreed. Her cheek still smelled of greasepaint, she pecked at my cheek as well, mumbled something about the dessert, and then they were walking together down the stairs, Michael's arm around her shoulders, talking to each other in quiet tones. By the car door he paused long enough to raise his arm to me and then they were off with no time for a backward glance.

But in my dark bedroom, unable to fall asleep quickly, I could not help returning to the spruce and Melissa on her platform. She can see far to the west across the sweep of lake—Juniper Island, the tongue of Shelburne Point, the broken horizon of the Adirondacks. Perhaps she imagines climbing high into a spruce on the opposite shore to look back at her Vermont, that lake reversed, the long and irregular ridge of Mount Mansfield's profile stretching from forehead to chin, the isolated saddle of Camel's Hump defining the edge of her view. But she is not looking across the broken curve of earth at herself. She is Melissa high in a tree almost as familiar to her as her own body, legs folded in front of her, hands clasped loosely, her back straight but not stiff. She can look directly at the sun now, red disk in an orange sky that washes to purple except for those slim clouds melting into gold on their undersides.

She lowers her eyes to the house in her foreground. Why have they always lived in the Castle of Bickering and Confusion? The roof slopes toward her, juts into the tilted flap of the long dormer on the second floor. The angle on the side is still colored by the sun, but the back of the house is dark except for the window of the kitchen. The sink, refrigerator beyond, and her father cooking. She longs for him to be someone else, for him to put down that rolling pin he bends over, strip off his apron, burst out of the house with flaming brand, an ax in his other hand. He will chop down the tree, and in a leafy rush it will descend like a parachute only partially opened. But her father is crimping the edge of the pie. She tosses the straying hair out of her eyes. Anyway, you bring things down on top of you, and you just get crunched.

She is angry at the unruly nature of her imagination. Can't she be serious? This is serious. She holds out her two hands flatly. She sights along them to the horizon and the last slip of sun that sinks into her palms. In the right hand she holds Mother; in the left, Father. She has come far enough to know that she can have them both, but she cannot have them together anymore than she could inhabit both sides of the round earth at the same time, living night and day simultaneously. Her father stoops to the oven. He stands. He turns to the window. His hands wipe down the sides of his apron and then hang still. He is a babushka, and she can lift him apart, father within father within father. She knows he cannot see her anymore. Does she believe for a moment she will picture him this way when he is no longer to be seen and his eyes are staring forever into the dark? She chooses what she senses she had chosen long ago and refuses to weep.

When I think of those weeks in which I was coming to know Mike, I find it hard now to see around the figure of Melissa. Partly the distortion of events made us want never to see around her, but also much of our courtship was tangled in her life. In those days after his divorce she was constantly on Mike's mind. She had been with us from the beginning, and what else did we have to talk about except Hob or her in those moments when we knew each other so slightly that silence could seem awkward and we needed to fill it with some shared experience? But gradually the more we did things together and made some known history we could call "ours," the more those silences did not need words.

Sometimes the words we did tell about ourselves were contradicted by actions. If Michael had chosen to present himself as a highly domesticated male, happily clinging to home and work and maintenance of an adequate nest for his child, he was presenting a wish as well as a reality. At times another Michael literally flung himself free of earth to glide and soar and reluctantly settle down again only because of the undeniable promptings of gravity. Spontaneity was something I had not had a chance to see in him until one bright, windy day. He telephoned me at home.

"Are you busy?" he asked.

I was not, but I was also happily alone, considering the long-denied ritual of a quick ride out to Huntington and a climb up Camel's Hump. I had waked that morning to a half-remembered dream and began imagining myself at timberline—that passage through stunted trees to shrubs permanently windswept in shape, to the final bare and crumbling rock that always swept me to the verge of rising from the matter of earth and water into air and fire. Standing on the peak I would feel the absolute loneliness of apex, the contact point between one realm and the next where I would close my eyes to imagine that one small step farther beyond gravity, beyond the pressure of one foot trudging after another. So I was not busy but planning to be busy, and what I had in mind I liked to do alone. If he heard irritation in my voice, he ignored it.

"Not really."

"Come with me. I want to show you something. It's a perfect day."

"For what?"

"Trust me. You'll see. I have an instinct you'll love it."

That intrigued me. What did he think I would like? He was offering to reveal some estimate of who I was.

"For how long?"

"Rest of the day. And I promise you dinner afterward."

"I shouldn't." I was letting go of Camel's Hump. It would still be there later. "But I will."

"Dress warmly."

"No other clues?"

He laughed. "Pick you up in an hour."

We sped faster through a late fall countryside than I would have thought Mike liked to drive. He seemed tense, expectant, as if he might make some elated, wordless cry.

"Christ." For a moment he gripped my hand. "It's just one of those perfect, perfect days."

"Look," I said when we finally turned off along a dirt road edging a local airfield, "gliders."

Far over us I picked out two, then a third glinting against the red-splotched hillside. A small airplane had overtaken us, towing a sailplane that had already left the ground, and then it rose also, so much more clumsy and blunt than the sleek, silent bird tethered to it.

"Let's watch for a while. Do we have some time?" After all, his urgency was not mine, and I was beginning to regret giving up for his purposes what could have been a random day.

"No." He glanced at his watch. "We'll be just in time."

He parked in a small lot beside a corrugated shed. From that moment I was swept along as if a wind had lifted us once we stepped outside the sanctuary of our car. He walked in long strides, I ran to catch up. He was talking to a man at the shed who seemed to know him. "Next one," he said, "or you won't get another till after lunchtime, take the two-thirty-three." Michael's grip on my elbow was firm, and as we kept our breathless pace toward the sailplane that looked wounded as it leaned on one wing, he said, "Just do as I tell you. We've only a few minutes left."

Was this Michael? *Do as I tell you*? I had no time even to act on my resentment. I was no child. What were these orders? Now that I was understanding why we had come, I wondered why he thought I would enjoy standing around in a field watching him demonstrate his soaring talents? I remembered Ted Conte, a boyfriend I had finally abandoned because he had insisted I did not love him if I missed a single one of his wrestling matches, and yet I had hated the acrid reek of stale sweat filling the steaming gym, the sight of his body that I knew in gentler guises flexed and wound in the grunting body of an opponent.

The towplane was not alone, banking sharply near the distant ridge of mountains, condensing into a beaded line as it descended directly toward us and the landing strip. Michael was throwing a bag of weights off the grounded wing.

"Lift at the tail and push."

It rose so lightly in my hands that for the first time I worried for Michael going far up in the sky in something so insubstantial.

"Keep the nose into the wind!" he yelled as the airplane taxied toward us, and he began to pull us forward. The man ran out to us from the shed, the plane turned tail, and now Michael was gesturing at me with a waggling arm, soundless mouth open, eyes wide, and for a moment his elation seemed to have driven him as mad as a prophet overcome with vision. That same arm pulled me firmly around the waist toward the open cockpit and two seats in line, and he was lifting, his full voice close to my ear, crying, "There, up front, hurry!" I struggled, he took my motions as attempts to climb, I gripped the edge of the cockpit, his hands heaved on my butt, I went where he propelled me, sat in panic because he had disappeared and the snug seat clutched me down. What was this nightmare being enacted for, a recurrent one I had dreamed since childhood of being suddenly alone in a plane without the vaguest idea of how to fly it? But his hands were firmly buckling me in place, adjusting the strap to tighten against me.

Then he was climbing into the seat behind, the canopy came over us and with it quiet, the sound of my own panicked breathing. The man outside was hooking a towline to our nose, then gesturing impatiently. "Michael!" I yelped, but he said calmly, "He wants me to test the towline's release." Now I was aware of the stick between my legs and how my feet had come to rest on two pedals. A panel of strangely marked gauges was in front of me. I could not turn to see him. The man was making signs, I could hear Michael mouthing something in his breath, I said "Michael, what the hell," and then the man had lifted the wing, the plane was moving, its muffled engines rising in pitch, the man running with us, and with the slightest thump, the scratch and slither of weeds against the belly beneath us like a canoe gliding through reeds, we were moving, bobbing, soon no longer even touching the earth in spite of the fact that the airplane still trundled and bounced on the uneven field.

I closed my eyes and missed that first levitation. What I heard was the steady hum of a propeller too far beyond us to let me feel we could control our fate. What I sensed of motion was in the roll or chop of slight jerks, and I was angry. Was he crazy? What kind of egotistical trick was this? How could he dare to assume I would put up with the risks of his own wild needs? If I survived, I would walk away from that sailplane and into his car, and he would drive me home immediately, my furious silence ending any conversation between us. I had been deceived. I opened my eyes only a slit, concentrating through the dim crevice on a sky and our frail line. When I could no longer take the strain in my eyelids I opened them wide but would not look down.

"You pull the release this time," he said in my ear, a voice incorporeally godlike, stern.

My arms were stiffly folded. I glared at the red knob.

"Quickly." The voice was urgent now.

He had me, of course. I saw too clearly a huge blue sky, a horizon stretched taut to its edges, a field that might have been ours but reduced to a small green patch. I yanked, and as if it were my own body pulling away from my mind, I watched the yellow towline slipping loose and the plane veering away from us. I held my breath.

There was nothing in front of me but a curved surface, then air and a distant landscape too far below. He had even tricked me into releasing us, a gesture of complicity.

For a moment I did not know what to do with my body. My posture must have shown that, perhaps I was even making slow snatchings like an infant on a table when she fears she is falling.

"Sit back into the seat. Please. Relax. I've been doing this for years."

"But I haven't," I said with a wail.

"It's absolutely safe. Safer than if we were in that little plane."

"But we can't do anything. We're just floating around. Please. Take me back, Michael."

"Put your hands on the stick, your feet on the pedals. Don't do anything to them, but you'll see I'm moving them. I'm in control."

The anger was subsiding. Save that for later. Survival now. This recent voice reassured me. He was Michael Gardener after all, and I had already imagined that giving myself into his hands might not be unpleasant. But not quite so extremely. So for the rest of the flight I did as he said and he must have known that holding something moving slowly on its own, a ghostly tilt or pump that I had to dance with to keep myself from impeding the controls, would relax those muscles in arms and legs and across my shoulders. The silence itself began its appeal, a quietly fluctuating whistle and hiss as if it were the air unraveling on the spool of everything I could see, and more and more I opened my eyes to let it all in, finally even leaning to look down so that space began to seem not like a possible fall but like an introduction of irregular patterns of great beauty, the uses of earth revealed. I was learning to trust the air.

We moved slowly back and forth along a ridge.

His own voice again. "Down there. The Hump."

I was looking at the summit I had dreamed of when I took that final step away from granite, and now I breathed deeply, wonder filling the place where fear had risen. We were not alone. Below us hawks were soaring, long wings held wide and barely shifting as they balanced on air.

"Oh, Julie." Now I knew what wordless ecstasy he had been speeding us to. "Isn't it perfect?"

It was. But I was stubborn enough not to forgive him yet for the way he had brought me to it, so for an hour in silence we soared gently downward through hawks until alone again, through air I would never again be able to think of as insubstantial since it was the upward flow that granted us our freedom, and I have not forgotten how my own body followed his motions as he rode out those forces. I would come to be able to fly us as well as he, sitting where he was while he followed the ghostly manifestations of my skill. We have often called it a true parallel for the dance of our own lives.

At the end the ground rose toward us with speed I mistrusted, we turned in a wide arc, shed, fences, cars became their own sizes again and too solid to be met, the fence rose as if Michael were aiming at it and then the nose lifted, we flared out, I waited for a bump that never came and we were skidding to rest in green. Stopped. Our right wing tilted dejectedly onto the ground.

"Out," he said, and the canopy lifted.

I followed him reluctantly onto the ground, helped him push our plane back to the weights, and all things were burdened by gravity, even my feet stumbling on hummocks. When the sack was in place on the wing, he said, "Thank you."

I was standing in front of him, he was looking down into my face, grinning. I thought back to my anger, could even touch some part of it still there, imagined a quick lashing of one hand across his face, and then I began laughing, perhaps a little too hard, but he joined me, hooked my arm, and we walked toward the shed.

I stopped him, though. "Don't do that again. Please. I don't like being told what to do. Or not being told what I'm going to do."

"I was afraid you wouldn't do it if I asked."

"I might have." But I thought that through. "Or might not."

The arm had slipped around my waist, but we were on earth now and not well enough known to each other for such unself-conscious gestures to last long.

"I'll ask first from now on."

"My turn first. Can we do it again?"

He grinned as happily as a child. "I knew you'd like it."

Lunch at a nearby inn. Two more flights that afternoon because the conditions for good wave lifts held. Some long conversations as we lay on our backs in the stubbled hay waiting our turn. I told him my dream of rising beyond the peak and thanked him for fulfilling it. I lay there and listened and stared up into a space far more familiar, and by the end of that day he too had begun to seem familiar, especially after a long, full dinner in the dark corner of a dining room where a fire had been lit in the hearth, and even later in the parking lot after he had put his hands on my waist and pressed close against me, his mouth on mine, my eyes closing again but this time not in fear.

Soon afterward I met Sheldon, who was at first more formidable than he had been described to be. He lived in an apartment near Mike's house. "Come meet my father," Mike said on the evening I came to sample his cooking. Melissa was there ahead of us, keeping Sheldon company at dinner before she went off to the final performance, a cast party, and an overnight stay with a friend in Underhill. She was washing dishes when we entered and pushed back a wisp of hair with her arm.

Her smile to me was genuine. "I thought we were going to have lunch soon."

Sheldon rose, one hand splayed on the edge of the table. Then he lifted the hand and shook mine. "I met your father once. He was reading at a bookstore in Montpelier. I read one of his books before I went blind. Don't know why the later ones weren't recorded. Maybe I could get this wretch," and he gestured carefully toward the running water, "to stop reading Tolkien to me. Please sit down."

Melissa was wiping her hands on a towel, Michael sat by his father on the couch, and suddenly I was set apart from them, father and daughter regarding me from the same plane, Sheldon between them as if they were there to transmit what they saw to his waiting face.

"I wish I had a camera," I said.

They smiled. Melissa's hands kept moving in the towel.

"What would you do with it?" Sheldon put one finger across his lips and waited.

"Only a family portrait. You seemed perfectly composed."

"A group statue?" Melissa's voice was quiet and musing, so I did not take that as a wisecrack.

"You're hardly older than Melissa, are you?" Sheldon asked.

I felt at a disadvantage then. Had he not been blind our expressions would have done more of the talking for us, and I sensed for the first time how much energy it could take to translate all meaning into words alone.

"Gramps. She's much older."

"Seven years," I murmured.

He smiled broadly. "Nothing. That evens out fast."

"And what did you have in mind, Dad?"

"Don't know. You know I never know till I say it, and then I usually don't anyway. Maybe I was trying to figure how old her father would be."

"Sixty-two."

"Hah."

"Hah, what?" Michael was watching his father now, and I was glad he intervened.

"I'm sixty-eight and a grandfather. I could almost be Miss Cobb's grandfather, but I'm not much older than her father. I hear you let Mike sweep you off your feet the other day."

"He means sailplaning, and I'm jealous." Melissa perched on the arm of the couch and accepted his hand in her lap. "Dad never takes me."

"You're too busy."

"If I had it to do all over again," Sheldon said to me as if I had suggested he would not be given that option, "I would have done a lot more things. Gliding. Flying real planes. Traveling. Especially that. Always wanted to go to Africa and see the animals. Have you been there, Miss Cobb?"

"No."

"Anywhere?"

"Not much."

"What's eating you tonight, Gramps?"

He tugged his hand but even I could tell it was a mock withdrawal and she did not let go.

"Michael brought me a friend to meet tonight, and I can tell by her voice she's beautiful."

"She is." Melissa smiled.

"Thank you." Sheldon nodded at the space between us. "I'm happy to know I can still tell the difference. Miss Cobb, don't be miffed at me. You'll get used to it."

"I'll certainly try."

He would have said more, but Michael rose to announce our chicken might burn if we delayed returning, and so my first meeting with Sheldon ended. I felt as if I had gone through an audience with a very special dignitary. But I did not resent that. Clearly, he was special. Father and daughter kissed lightly, he cautioned her, gripped his own father's shoulder, Melissa and I promised to pursue that lunch date, and back in Mike's house it was my turn to sit in the kitchen while he moved from counter to stove. I was hungry, and having someone cook for me for the first time in over a year was going to tempt me into eating too much.

What happened later that evening was simpler than anything I had imagined, certainly simpler than any such experience before. Surely that was because we both knew where we wanted to go and what we needed, and I suppose we also knew that with the matter of the papers settled, we had no minor excuses left to bring us together. But simplicity is something that has stayed with us. Sometimes we tangle on the surface in bickerings or irritations, but we have always been able to retire to separate rooms, maybe leaving behind some broken crockery, tears, or tense silence, and in that space alone breathe deeply, remind ourselves how we never want to be alone as we were before we knew each other. Often later, in the hallway or on the porch, he or I will be standing, waiting, and we will not have to explain or even refer to the squabble that drove us to the other side of closed doors.

We were standing in the living room. He had brought two snifters of Cognac. I put mine down on the table, and he did too. We were facing each other, and as I reached my hands up to his shoulders, he placed his on my hips. The gestures were simultaneous, as was our uttering of each other's names, and then we held tightly and moved against each other. How long, how long since my body had been touched or held. I could not get close enough. Often at other times in my life I and whoever it was had ended up in bed or on a couch or anywhere convenient to what followed. But always in confusion. Who is leading? Who follows? Who will be responsible? The politics of loving. Will the clothes be dropped about piecemeal or in one decisive removal, as if we are changing into our bathing suits? Sex when both are willing and eager but still unfamiliar is usually humorous.

I stepped out of my shoes and walked with him up the stairs into his bedroom. We took off our clothes in the dark without hesitation; he pulled back the covers. We moved like dancers who had rehearsed at a time before we could remember. We did not have much to say. Later that night he asked me if I was surprised and I thought briefly and said no, except I had not had a lover for some time and had not wanted one. Why? I tried to explain that I had pulled back into a solitary state to simplify my life after my father's death, when close relationships had seemed too complicated. Probably it happened to everyone when both parents had died.

"First comes panic. I looked around at the funeral. All those relatives were almost unknown to me. A good friend named Polly had come, but she lives far away and for a few years we had only corresponded. I thought, 'How can anyone actually wear a hat like that?' and she seemed very different from me, farther away than geography can make. I knew some men, but what did they give me? Dinners, entertainment, a weekend in the White Mountains. My parents were left only in my mind. I was an adult. I had no idea how to be one, or what to do.''

He said something about his mother's death, I thought about what I had said, and then we were sleeping. A sound woke me, I assumed I was in my own bed, but all was misshapen. The ceiling was sloped and shadowed by unfamiliar patterns, a flat, dark dresser hunched against the wall, and an abandoned arm was draped across my side, bending upward from the elbow, a hand cupped laxly over my breast. Someone was breathing in my ear. Someone else was moving under us. A door shut quietly. Footsteps rising. I was still too confused to be certain if this was something good or evil. In that hazy moment before I let the room and house be Michael's, the footsteps led me to believe my own home had been maliciously transformed and that my father was about to call out from the stairwell, fling open the door, letting harsh light pour over us. I tossed off Mike's arm, sat up, reached wildly for covers that were strewn around the floor.

A voice said gently, "Dad?" Pause. "Dad? Are you awake?''

Michael rose dazedly on one elbow. I put my hand on his shoulder, shook him lightly.

"Who's that?''

"Me. Melissa. I'm sorry to wake you, but I wanted you to know I'm home.''

He sat up quickly. "What's wrong?'' He swung his legs over the side of the bed, groped into his bathrobe, and was at the door before he stopped to look at me, then back to his hand on the knob.

"Nothing. I couldn't stay. They were all being obnoxious.''

In the dark I could not tell which pile of clothes was mine. I settled for finding a sheet, covering myself to the waist.

"But you're all right?''

"Yes." Her voice, however, had a high and injured tone. "Mr. Daniels drove me home."

He stood with his head down and cocked to one side. I was certain Melissa would not yet want me to hear her talking to her father as if they were alone.

"Jackson was being awful and I'm sure Helen set it all up for him to be there too. She knows I don't like him anymore. I'm never going to speak to her again." Now her voice was really rising and falling, a petulance that could lapse into rage or tears.

"I'm sorry."

"Can I come in?"

Instinctively I raised the sheet to cover my breasts, but it was too tangled to reach.

"Not right now, sweetheart. Can we talk in the morning?"

"Tell her," I whispered, only thinking that if she had to know, I wanted her to make the discovery with a possibility of graceful retreat.

A silence. Then, in a different tone, "Sorry. I'll see you when I get up."

"All right," he said to the sound of her retreating footsteps.

He did not move for a while. I abandoned the sheet and sat cross-legged in the middle of the bed. He walked away from the door, bathrobe high on the white columns of his legs, both hands in pockets except for the brief gesture he made of touching my shoulder as he padded by on the way to the window. He flipped the blinds and stood looking down into the street. I thought the right of first speech belonged to him, and besides I was not certain whether his silence was intended as concealment. Melissa's tone of voice had led me to believe she had either heard me or sensed someone else was there, but I did not know her well enough and she might have been merely miffed at being put off until the next day. Finally he discarded his bathrobe and came back to the bed. He lay on his back beside me, one hand reached out, and I held it in my lap. He did not whisper, and I was grateful for that since I had already begun to feel that to have to be furtive for the rest of the night, to sneak out into the city at early dawn, would have done something unpleasant to us.

"Not exactly the way I would have planned it."

"You're sure she knows?"

"Your car is out there."

"But she did want to talk. She's not that good an actress."

"She is that good, but she did want to talk. We often do. Sometimes when she's vexed she'll wake me, come in and sit on the end of the bed and talk about how she knows she's playing Ophelia just right but Mr. DiAngelis doesn't really understand women."

His hand was as relaxed as when he was asleep. I held it loosely in both of mine and had an inkling of that peace beyond the surface anxieties we were struggling with, as if our calm hands were really where we lived.

"Will she be angry, upset? Will she forgive me?"

"All of the above. She has nagged me recently to go out, meet people, not sit at home reading, watching television, listening to records. She was happy about the evening at your house. But when the real thing happens I imagine it always has to be a shock."

"I felt like a child discovered in mischief."

He laughed. "We were. Please make mischief with me often."

But I was not quite ready to let things go. "You're sure it wasn't too sudden? She'll blame me, you know, not you. It will be easy for you to laugh."

"I'll try to help." He lifted his hand, pulled me down beside him. I stretched along his body, my face on his chest, and we dozed, waking from time to time when the light began to wash between the blinds and the city roused itself toward business.

He would have made breakfast for us, determined to be casual. But I did not think it fair to Melissa or myself, although he assured me she would not be down till noon. My shoes, of course, were in the living room where I had stepped out of them, clear witness to my presence if she had seen them. I looked up at the house from my car. The paper boy was on his way up the driveway, folding the paper he plucked from his orange sack. Mine would be already stuffed behind the storm door at home. A skift of snow had fallen and I drove slowly along the hillside. I was glad to be alone again but too tired to think, and in my own house I found myself wandering slowly from room to room as if to look out of every window. I took a long, slow shower, my face to the steady stream of hot water, then lay down on my bed and slept for hours.

Only three days later he came to my house for the night. The next morning I tried to tell him what it was like to wake at night in a house I had inhabited since childhood, in a bedroom I had dreamed in since

I was four, to the breathing shape of a man beside me, to make love in a place where my own body had spent more time than anywhere else on the planet and yet in which I had never been entered. He listened and described to me how he had felt that morning watching my car drive away, standing in a bedroom where only he and Fran had made love, and not for years. We agreed the effects were very different. We also agreed the similarity was that we had altered those two spaces completely.

No, Melissa had not been angry. A little distant. "That was Julie Cobb, wasn't it?" she had said abruptly. Yes. Did she mind? Of course not, but did he love her? He thought so but would have to see. She had said sagely, "Well, you don't have to get married right away you know." He laughed remembering. "I told her that was good advice."

I looked at him and waited. He seemed to have nothing more to add.

"That's too easy."

"Maybe. But that's all for now."

"I guess the next is up to me."

"What next?"

"How can I keep coming back to your place until I've talked with her?"

"I'm not sure you should try that."

"What?"

"What if she'd rather not talk with you?"

"That's her choice, then."

"Isn't she a little young to be telling us what to do?"

"Old enough to be given the right to, whether or not we agree."

He was annoyed, and we had begun the inevitable process of tracing the tangle we had made. Sometimes, lying alone in a bed that was no longer entirely mine, listening to a night wind off the lake that made me think of the summer to come, I would turn restlessly, almost angry that I had permitted that alteration of my night space. I could say rationally to myself, "Julie, this man is twelve years older than you are, has a grown child, a blind father, burdens, entanglements, things that can only restrict your freedom, confine that space of solitude you love to move through. It is not too late to stop."

I could call. "Michael, we have to talk." In his office would be best, no way our gestures could become intimate. "I shouldn't have let it go this far." Remain friends. Deeply affectionate. Need your friendship. Such a pleasure to have come to know your family.

And then I would see Mike clearly. My arm would stray into the space in a bed that had come to seem much too large.

One morning I called Melissa and suggested we have lunch together.

5

I reached the restaurant early, looked for her, and went back to sit in my car. It was raining, squalls followed by gusting wind that shook the puddles and scudded papers into sodden piles. I almost did not recognize her. She was riding her bicycle and was tented in an olive green poncho with hood. As she took it off I saw her hair was differently arranged into a tight, neat coil on the back of her head. We sat opposite each other in a worn booth. Did she mind if I had a drink? No. Did she ever take a long trip on her bike? Yes. She had a new play coming up? Yes. I twisted the swizzle stick, made myself sip the Bourbon I was tempted to bolt.

"Do you believe in Christ?" She fixed me with a very serious and unwavering gaze.

"How do you mean 'believe'?"

She smiled slightly and nodded. "Then you don't."

"I didn't answer yet."

"Your question was an answer. If you did believe, you wouldn't have to define."

She was right, but I was annoyed. "There are all sorts of belief." I knew that Melissa was attending a Catholic school not because her parents were Catholic but because Michael did not like the local high school. I could not help wondering whether some process of conversion had begun.

"I bet you're going to say you believe in myth, like you believe in the Greek gods, or Hindu gods, or Buddha, or any of the figures that represent the religious in all of us."

Again, irritatingly right.

"Do you believe?"

She bit the corner of her mouth. "I try to, but then I really can't get beyond some things. I can even see miracles, all that, but the business of a God sending his son off to be human, then getting him

68

crucified, and that final thing of judging everyone . . ." She shook her head.

"Does this have anything to do with your school?"

"Oh, no." She tossed her head, forgetting her hair was in a new style, then reached back quickly to be certain the pins were not loosened. "The nuns don't bug us. There are prayers and religion classes and all that, but plenty of us aren't Catholic, and they don't expect us to be. Just sorry we aren't."

"Orders?" The waitress stood with her thighs pressing the edge of the table.

Melissa's request for a salad put me to shame. I could not resist the spaghetti and meatballs.

"Do you always eat a big lunch?"

I tried to believe she was not rubbing it in. "Sometimes I can't restrain myself."

She nodded. "I'm that way about fudge sundaes at the university dairy bar. Do you drink a lot?"

I put my Bourbon down. "Melissa, are you trying to make me very self-conscious?"

Her face flushed. "Sorry. Gramps says I do that too much. But I'm curious, that's all. Do you love my father?"

"Slow down." We were looking at each other, but her eyes might as well have been covered by dark glasses, they were so unexpressive. "I can't get there that fast. Can we go back two tiny steps before we take a giant step? You're good at asking questions but not so hot at answering."

"What did you ask?"

"I was trying to find out why you were asking about my religious beliefs."

"Oh, that. A group of my friends have started getting off on Christ. They don't believe in any of the churches because they're all corrupt, and they want to be in direct contact with it all, you know, right out of the Bible, or better yet, just zapped by the Spirit. They sit around in a room and hold hands and pray together for the Spirit to descend."

"Do you?"

"I've tried. One of my boyfriends believes very much. I joined them once or twice, but then they asked me not to. I guess they could tell I was faking it."

I shook my glass, and when our plates were delivered, I ordered another drink. She waited for me to begin eating.

"You didn't answer my question," she said.

"Michael is . . ."

"No, I mean about drinking."

"I like wine with dinner. I never drink in the middle of the day."

She stared at the waitress's descending hand.

"Hardly ever," I muttered.

"One of the ways you're supposed to be able to tell an alcoholic is he says he doesn't drink much, just a little here and there. Then you find out it's every day, and here and there is a little bit everywhere."

"Melissa, dear, I am not an alcoholic. And I can't answer the third question because it is too soon to know, and if I say it, I want your father to be the first to know."

"Wow." She chewed on a large section of tomato thoughtfully, then rested her fork under some lettuce. "You mean you guys never said you loved each other?"

"It takes time," I pleaded.

"But you make love and everything, don't you?"

Irritation again, and a slightly Puritan fear that I was corrupting my lover's daughter, but I barged ahead into candor. "Yes. You know that."

"I'm not snoopy. Really. Dad and I are very open about sex. I let him know I was making love with Jackson. I sometimes tell the person I'm making out with that I love him. I mean, at that time you do, don't you? It doesn't mean you have to think it's forever. I use the Pill. Do you?"

So far I had managed only a small mouthful of spaghetti, and my stomach was beginning to flip-flop in response to conflicting emotions—a hunger for those savory, spiced meatballs in their sauce, a reticence that made me want to shrink under the table. I've never been good at talking about sex directly until I know the person very well. I put my fork down and folded my hands above the plate as if it were the Sacrament I prayed over.

"I know people have sex without love," she continued. "I didn't mean to sound sappy. If Billy wasn't so sure Christ didn't do it, I wouldn't mind having some fun with him. But he's right. It's best not to get your spirits mixed."

"Please."

She looked over her partly lifted fork, saw my expression, and set her fork down. "Did I shock you or something?"

"How about a small postponement? Right now it's either a further discussion of your father and myself and you, followed by cold spaghetti if I have any appetite left, or it's eating my lovely lunch followed by discussion."

"I'm sorry," She was not acting. Her eyes even began to fill.

I reached quickly across the table, touched her arm, and retreated before she could accept or reject the gesture.

"I said that too harshly. I'm glad you want to talk, because I do, too. But my emotions are too complicated."

"And mine aren't?" She bit that out.

"I know they are."

"Sorry. I promised myself I wouldn't be bitchy. Let's eat."

We did, while nibbling at minor topics. Did I go to any church? Were either of my parents religious? I explained how my father had been subjected to Presbyterian churches in his childhood and had an aversion to all institutionalized beliefs, that my mother had been an occasional Unitarian. She shook her head.

"They're the ones that I understand least of all. It's all so dull and clean. Nothing muddy in it, you know? I'm sorry about your mother. How she died."

For some reason I had assumed she did not know everything Michael knew about my history. I waited, but when I looked up and saw how she was blushing, I knew my silence was cruel.

"Thank you. It happened a long time ago."

"I know. In 1952. Dad told me. Not when, but what had happened. I asked him about your parents once. It must have been hard—your mother, I mean. I went and looked it up and found something in a newspaper. I'm sorry if you think that was nosy. I guess it was, but I was doing a research paper for my history class and I was looking through old *Free Presses*. Did you know it was going to happen?"

What is it that brings relationships through moments like that? More than restraint, although I breathed in slowly, deeply, looking for every emotional handhold to keep the whirlwind from tearing me away from that table. How could she know, if I scarcely knew it then myself, that she was probing into areas I had barely permitted myself to enter? I like now to think that it was not just for Michael and myself that I persevered, but that some intuition in both Melissa and me had projected the possibility of our future love far beyond where we were presently sitting.

"I did not," I answered slowly. "Or maybe if I knew it, I did not believe it."

She nodded. "I know what you mean. They're different feelings. I knew Mom and Dad would get divorced, but I never really believed they would." She breathed deeply, then looked at me again. "Sometimes I think it's as if my mother died. That's why I asked."

I shook my head vehemently. "It's not at all. You can see your mother, and you will."

"But something did die when she left. When I made up my mind."

"Something dying is not someone dying. If she is still alive, you can make a new something."

I could see she was pondering that, would undoubtedly ask another question, and I was learning that the only way to forestall Melissa was to check her question with one of my own.

"Do you miss your mother?"

"Sometimes. I'm glad I didn't go with her. We'd be arguing all the time. I can do that, but I get tired. You know what? I wish Dad had really thrashed her once or twice."

I could not help recalling Bessy and Art. "I don't think you mean that literally. It's awful when it really happens. And never a very fair way for a man to settle his differences with a woman."

She blinked. "I guess I meant just blew up in some way. Yelled. Threw things. Got really angry with her. I did all the time. He just let it all sit inside and eat at him. Does he get angry at you?"

"Not yet."

"Don't you sometimes know you want someone to get angry at you? I can do something and know afterward I was just testing. I think I'm a lot like my mother, an awful bitch. I could never be around Billy very much because when I get bitchy with him he just contemplates his stigmata."

I could not help laughing. "I don't think you're a bitch, Melissa."

She pouted and countered with, "Do you think you're a little too young for my father?"

Our waitress delivered me again from stammering into a hasty response. No dessert, we said quickly as if trying to block any tempting list. I ordered coffee, Melissa, tea.

"No." She was obviously still waiting. "Not if neither of us thinks so."

"Do you think he knows what he's doing?"

"I hope so."

"Are you sure he's not on the rebound?"

Now the actress was there, and the self-consciousness when she used that word told me she was less sure of what she was saying.

"Where did you come across that idea?"

The mask of sophistication collapsed into embarrassment. "I've been reading up. I started taking out books on divorce about a year ago." She leaned forward eagerly. "Listen, you really ought to be very careful, you know. What Dad is doing is right down the line. It happens when one of the persons has been holding on for a long time and trying hard and then he lets go, but ends up clutching at the first thing that comes along and he really doesn't know what he's doing. And . . ."

The waitress set down the tea and coffee, but I am sure my own expression must have halted Melissa.

"That came out all wrong."

"Not if you really think I'm a 'thing' or if you know me so little as to think I would care much for someone who was clutching at me like a thing."

She was staring at the tea, hunched over the cup. The bag was steeping in hot water, the water was turning darker and darker, but she did not move. Then she raised her hands to her face and leaned into them, elbows on the table, and she was weeping. I panicked, looked around at the other booths, the waitresses. But Melissa was crying soundlessly and no one seemed to notice. I came around the table, put my hand on her shoulder, and pushed gently.

"Move over please."

She slid in, nearly knocking over the teacup. "I'm sorry." Her voice came muffled from the hands. "I'll be all right." But her body was shaking again.

"Would you like to leave?" I asked in a few moments, my hand now trying to soothe up and down her back. I felt useless.

The head shook. "Do you have any Kleenex?"

I groped some from my raincoat pocket. She took the tissues

without looking at me. Her eyes were swollen, face puffed and wet, altered toward a simple, childlike appearance far younger than at any time I had ever known her.

"That's not fair."

I took that as just accusation. "I'm afraid I was heavy-handed again. What you said could be right, Melissa, but sometimes you make me very defensive."

"I mean 'not fair' because now I have you at a disadvantage. Crying is too easy a way to win."

"Win what?"

"Oh, I don't know. I can't figure it all out."

She pulled out the teabag. I dragged my cooled coffee over and we both sipped.

"Are you going to ask me not to see your father? You don't really think we're in some sort of battle or game over him, do you?"

She shook her head. "This tastes like varnish."

"Want another?"

"No. I guess all I mean is I was going to ask you one thing and I want to win that."

"Tell me."

"Please don't stay at our house with him. For just a little while."

"I guess that night wasn't too swift on my part."

"It made me feel cruddy. Like I'd forced my own father to get sneaky."

"Would you have felt better if you had been there and we'd just gone upstairs together?"

She looked at me quite helplessly now, and I was afraid she would cry again. "I don't know. I'm confused, that's all. I can't straighten it out, especially when I think maybe I'll come home and you guys will be upstairs, or sometimes I wake up at night and try to think about everything that happened in the last year or so and it's as though I can't think because I feel the house is all weird now."

I was glad that I had held back the anger that wanted to lash out when she first made her request, a gambit to separate Michael and me, a daughter's jealousy.

"Melissa, have you thought about getting help from someone who is not involved in all this?"

"A shrink, you mean?"

"Yes."

74

She had but decided not to now. Things had been working out all right until this started, her thinking was clear till recently.

"Are you as confused if Michael comes to my house?"

"Oh, no, no, that's fine. That's Dad's business, yours. I don't want you to stop, I don't think. I just want to understand." Her lips trembled again, but she held on. We sat in silence. A passing hand slipped our bill onto the tabletop.

"Isn't this something you and your father ought to settle?"

"I can't yet. Anyway, wouldn't you have hated me for that? If I talked him into it and you thought I was doing it behind your back?"

The fact that she did not want me to hate her was encouraging.

"How's this? We'll give you some space and time. I won't be staying at your house for a while. Under one condition."

"What?"

"That you talk to me. Tell me what you are understanding. Try to let me be your friend."

"I don't know."

"I said 'try,' not 'be.' "

She blew her nose into the ball of tissues. "OK."

I stood by my car in the lot to watch Melissa wheel off. The clouds had lifted, the sun was gleaming on the puddles. She had on her poncho but with the hood back, and as she left the lot, she waved, wobbled, regained her balance, and pumped up Pearl Street. Although nothing in those past hours had happened between Michael and me, I sensed our relationship was far more complex than it ever had been, and by that evening there was no question my intuition was right.

"*You've* decided?" Michael shook his head. "Pretty amazing, don't you think? A daughter and her father's lover making up their minds where the affair should be conducted?"

Our first hot argument, and we had no patterns yet for our anger to take, banging into thorny hedges at the end of blind passages, uncertain if there was a way out.

He sat on the edge of the couch, his jacket collar still turned up against a chilly night. He had called that evening and asked me to come, but I had said no, would he mind coming to my house—I would explain. At that point no anger, just bafflement. But unfortunately Melissa had been at home to send him on his way. When he arrived, hands thrust in the side pockets of his tweed jacket, head slightly forward and face scowling under his windblown hair, he had not taken his hands from those pockets as I kissed him. He stalked to his precarious perch on the couch. I sat with what must have been equal unease on the nearby chair and tried to explain.

At the end I said lamely, "I wish she hadn't told you. I wanted to talk to you, but it didn't seem like something for the phone, or your office."

"Or anywhere. What the hell are you doing? A sixteen-year-old girl telling her father how to behave?"

"Seventeen."

"You can't seriously think that your acquiescing to that is good for her at all."

"Are you being hasty?"

"About what? I am leaving my house when Melissa comes up to me with that cat-that-swallowed-the-canary look of hers and says, 'Going to see Julie?' That in itself is surprising. I mean she's hardly ever referred to you unless I do first."

"That's progress, then."

"And I say, 'Yes,' and then she says, 'Please thank her and tell her I feel much better already.' " He jammed his hands farther into the pockets. "So she has banished you from my bed."

I sat back into the wings of the easy chair, trying to put one hand casually on an arm, but my fingers arched there as tensely as a spider about to leap and shake out its web. He was not going to leave me to silence, though.

"Well?"

"I hope you didn't barge around with Melissa the way you are with me. The matter is more delicate than your perception."

"Oh, c'mon. Let's not get gauzy about this. And no, I did not wipe my troll feet all over my daughter. I did look upset, I'm sure, and said something about how she and I would discuss it later. Frankly, I figured you were the one who ought to have known better."

"So I deserve this anger."

"I'm not angry!" he yelled, his face flushing. He hunched back into the couch. "For God's sake, don't you think you've left me in a bizarre position?"

I tried again to describe my meeting with Melissa. He did not interrupt, but I could also see I was not finding the right words to express the twists of her feelings. My problem was compounded by the fact that I knew it was wrong of me not to talk with him immediately. But his reaction seemed unjust, and that was enough to make me stubborn. He glanced at me or shook his head. My jaw clenched, words died in my throat. I put out both my hands, palms up, and shrugged.

"I should have known better," he said.

"Known what?"

"Oh, to let you and Melissa go off conferring together like that without a warning. You simply don't know her well enough. I think she's gotten exactly what she wanted."

"I guess that says something about how perceptive you think I am."

"I've lived with her all her life. There's something of Fran in her, and this was certainly a clear case of powers—yours against hers. She won the skirmish. She's made you retreat to your own territory again. Now she has her home intact, father to herself inside those boundaries, and she's in a good position to take the next move."

"Which is?"

"Keep me in her own territory."

Again I was at a disadvantage. Surely what he described was no new thought to me.

"You have a wonderfully positive view of your daughter's motives, don't you? And do you always blame things you don't like in her on Fran's nature?"

His hands came out now, but only to let his arms fold tightly. "I'm really not very interested in discussing her nature as much as the situation."

"You brought it up. Maybe there are some things I can see that you can't because Melissa and I are both daughters. Anyway, for the sake of my relationship with her, I'd rather have her do some choosing."

His scowl was easing.

"Are you afraid she'll take a stand and you'll have to choose? You sound so defensive, Mike. You'd rather bull through at this point and try a father's authority, make her feel like she's got no choice, because you're afraid she'll say no if you give her a choice? No, that's not quite right. You're afraid you'll say no if she says no."

He unfolded his arms, put one along the couch, and began tracing the ridged pattern with a finger. His voice was quiet now. "I feel

I owe her so much, Julie. It isn't simply the divorce. That's only the final gesture for all those years of presenting her with a fractured home, one that kept shattering in her presence—those weeks of tension and silence, the ways Fran and I must have used her without even knowing half of how we did. How can I possibly deal with a situation now in which she tells me I'm betraying her once again?''

"But is she?"

He shook his head. "No, I guess not." Suddenly he arched his back, both hands flung up to comb through the sides of his curling hair. "Christ, it's just too complicated."

He swiped through his hair a few more times. The tension was leaving us. To my alarm, in its place came a desire to weep, and that would be the worst thing to do now. Later, I said, and clenched my teeth.

"Do you want to call it all off, Michael? Now?"

"No. I don't know what we're getting into, but I couldn't do that even if at times a very careful voice in me says that's the only sensible thing."

I was going to let that hurt but admitted, "Me, too," and he smiled for the first time.

"Oh, Michael. Please let me try this way. Don't you see? You have a relationship with Melissa. You can say how much you've hurt her and fear losing her, but you're her father, and even on the other side of more hurt or anger, you'll both be there. She has to deal with you all her life, and even after yours. But me? I'm starting from scratch, and I'm scratching in some of the worst places. If I had to fight for you against her wishes, I might win. Who knows? If I wanted to. I don't know that because it might not be worth it in the end. But if she never accepts me, I'll never be as wholly with you as I'd want."

He stood slowly, looked at me for a moment. "Let's start the evening over."

He walked to the front door, opened it, turned as if he had just walked in, and slammed it shut.

"Hello," he said quietly.

I met him in the middle of the room.

6

At first for Melissa's sake, then for the sake of my own soul, which wants to believe something can be done more than rototilling one's own garden, I attempted to suspend my doubt of political gestures or the ability of institutions to turn aside our violence. I find politics so tainted with unreality that its practitioners seem like actors on a stage that trundles by every two or four years to receive our applause or catcalls. I can argue as vehemently as anyone else at a party when someone is promoting Right or Left or Reformed Mugwump. But afterward I will stand in my naked, showered flesh, dimly shaped in the fogged bathroom mirror, and taste ashes in my mouth, the residue of heated discussion whose emotions have been consumed to no purpose. Nothing was solved. Nothing was really said. But we were at times on the verge of extreme insult, even physical violence. I vote as religiously as if going to confession, grateful to the ballot for at least the illusion of solid action, but after such nights of abstract tantrum I am eager to sleep and have dreams in which truths are waiting to be revealed again.

Is that why November 1963 shook me and others like me so roughly? If politicians are only the actors blown here and there by the tattering winds of our desire, then why every so often must we take their lives? The illusion assumes a dreadful reality when bone is crushed, blood spattered over a woman's dress. The audience rises. Surely there has been a mistake. This is only a play about a witty, ambitious senator from Massachusetts in his countinghouse of power accompanied by a woman more elegant than any American queen should be. Why are we being shown an ugly brick warehouse, the disheveled scraps of fried chicken by a window where a runt has waited with a gun and the first luck of his life, since he is not even skilled enough to be that fine a marksman? We want out. But the doors are locked. Those events were terrifying to me because of their meaningless, misbegotten shape. Ever since, I have not trusted the things I have thought to be most safely illusory. Nothing can be taken for granted, and in my lifetime such events have revealed a pattern too often reenacted.

We shared part of what Melissa suffered, but her grief was more pervasive because for her, politics were not illusion and Kennedy was a great hope. I never argued with her about the figures who helped to structure her beliefs, those patron saints—Gandhi, Kennedy, King. She tried to know all of what they had said or done. I came to her house for dinner that night. The television was never turned off. We did not really eat. She wept relentlessly, and none of it was acting. Already Melissa was bringing that world of history closer to me, urging me to step out into it.

I recall Friday evening that week, vivid because suddenly all details had the jagged clarity of broken pieces. Melissa's school had an evening of performances called Stunt Night in which each class presented a skit judged by a panel of faculty and parents. There was talk of canceling the show because of the recent events, but no, the children had put such effort into it, the show must go on. There would be a moment of silence instead, a brief prayer by Father Paquette, the principal. I went because Michael had to. Melissa was a senior and for all the other years he had evaded going, usually letting Fran perform that duty. He loved his daughter's acting and encouraged it, went to all her performances in plays or local musicals. "But listening to a bunch of screeching kids, amateur night at the gym with cheerleaders?" and he shook his head.

The old auditorium downtown was used as a gym at other times, or a concert hall, a boxing arena, a polling place. Because it was used for all things, it suited none, but it was all that Burlington could afford. The basketball hoops had been swung up, the heat was on—a stifling density of air produced by pipes that beat and rattled whenever the furnace below threw one of its tantrums—and we all moved restlessly on folding chairs designed to bruise the insufficient flesh between bone and wood. Her class performed last after three intermissions prolonged by stage crews struggling with overelaborate scenery. Most of the people there participated with all the partisan intensity of spectators at a football game, and very few of them left, even by eleven o'clock, when the seniors were thumping their act together behind the curtain. As partisan as they were, however, they were kind, applauding actors who forgot their lines, undaunted by singers who plunged ahead in any key but the one the pianist had chosen. I caught Mike nodding and slumping a few times, and during the last intermission we walked out into harsh November air to breathe deeply and stare at the street until we trembled uncontrollably with welcome shivers. "I wish seniors came first," he said glumly, but he was doing penance for all the years he had missed.

Their director had obviously decided that Melissa was the seniors' best hope, and he used her both as featured performer and as linchpin to hold large scenes together. When she was not alone or in small groups singing or reciting, she was in the center of some chorus placed so everyone could hear her voice or see her when she kicked a leg. And if I had thought of Melissa before as a plain but attractive girl, I was bewildered to see how she knew instinctively to turn that to advantage, becoming whatever the scene demanded—vampish, stodgy, lithe and bubbly, old and weary. But through it all there was also awkwardness because she was still Melissa Gardner, only a senior, and I knew that what often moved me most in watching her was that gap between the display of a talent's shimmering potentiality and an adolescent's uncertainty whether the talent was real, or for that matter what was real in any of the disordered life around her.

Each class's performance had some overall theme that was supposed to provide structure, although often the parodies referred to school matters I did not know, so I could not follow the design. The seniors had chosen *The Wizard of Oz* to impose some order on their antics, and I could at least see the references to that work even when I was baffled by the laughter and applause of the audience. And then, toward the end, Melissa came on alone. She was, of course, their Dorothy when she was not doing something else, and now the lights narrowed down to her, she stood on a stage where all the shaky scenery had disappeared for a moment, and even the pianist far to one side was only a hunched figure in a dim point of light. She was there to sing "Somewhere over the Rainbow." The audience grew very quiet, except for the occasional slap of wooden seat as some child stirred far beyond bedtime, and even the heat was randomly cooperative, being in one of its dormant phases. It was the first time all evening I had been nervous for her, and I could sense Michael

stiffening too, wide awake, hands in his lap no longer lying abandoned but clasped tightly. I reached over and put one of mine on his,
but it did not break his concentration. Even though I would never know
that tension or parental pride and fear, my own heart lifted its beat.

She sang. At first her voice was preternaturally like Judy
Garland's. Even her face took on that wide-eyed glow, somewhere
between innocence and the vision of too much knowledge. My first
response was one of respect for all the time she must have spent
listening, watching, to get those inflections so right, even the
gestures, and her performance explained the reasons for frequent
absences from her home in the past month. I wondered if anyone
who did not know her well would understand how this was almost a
form of possession.

Halfway through, all that wobbled and fell away. I could almost
see the spirit leave. She did not falter or forget her lines, she simply
left Judy Garland behind and everything that had been done with
that song. In the pause where the piano took over for a moment, her
face became the one I had known in her house or mine or at the
restaurant. Then she sang again.

Maybe that song belongs so much to one person's voice that we
cannot hear it in any other, or any other will be only a transcription.
But I loved it because I was hearing Melissa sing, putting all of
whoever she thought she was into it. If it faltered at times, it was
because her knowledge of herself did, and when I shivered here or
there, it was not to the beauty of the music, which, if anything, had
been revealed now as pleasant but banal. It was simply that Melissa
Gardener was standing there alone, no matter what I knew of her.
When everyone started to applaud, neither Michael nor I did for a
while, his hands clenched under my own tight grip. I could not draw
a magic circle around that night to keep out the world around us. She
was a Dorothy in a world where witches did not always melt and
wizards behind their flashing lights were not always benevolent, and
she was Melissa, whose own story was just beginning but was already
deeply marred by a history that had killed some of her hopes.

That evening ended with a short prayer, and once again we were
plunged back into our imperial world of murders and state funerals.
We went backstage after it was all over, including the judging. Of
course, the seniors won. Everyone looked weary, sober, even a little

ashamed, as if they were afraid that others would know how for a few hours they had forgotten. She was surrounded but saw us and broke loose. Michael hugged her and she clung, closed her eyes, then stood back with a smile a little too glittering, made some introductions to friends that were too bubbling. She included me in them all, we chatted briefly, turned to go, and she moved with us to the wings, leaving her friends for a moment. Yes, she would be late. A class party. But she had more to say.

"Please stay at our house," she said to me. "That's all over now."

I did not wait to hear what Michael was going to say. He looked a little annoyed. "Are you sure?"

"Very."

The photographer from the newspaper wanted some group shots. She pecked quickly at her father's cheek and was gone.

"Permission granted," Michael said as we drove home. "Why is being a father never what you think it's going to be like?"

Melissa and I did not fully discuss her decision for a long time—in fact, not until we were so used to living with each other in her house that our discussion was more like a reminiscence. I did not want to press. After that evening I had moved into a new way of looking at her, but I did not express it. I assumed something must have shifted in her too. But we talked a great deal about everything else. Suddenly breakfast after a night with Mike was no longer a quiet interval in which the two of us drank coffee, shared the paper, woke slowly to our separate days. Melissa rose now when we did. She joined us. She sat beside me and wanted to talk about what had happened yesterday, what Sister Martha had said about morality and politics and had I ever read much Ibsen? Did I think the Beatles were the true music of our times rather than those classical musicians with their ugly tone rows and incomprehensible computers? On the evenings when I was there she would take me up to her room, perhaps to show me a paper she was working on, or did I think this skirt made her dumpy? I *must* watch *Star Trek* with her and tell her whether I liked it too. We began our inconclusive discussions of issues, and sometimes her voice was raised against me in frustration: How could I say that? Didn't I see that attitude was the very reason for this or that? In the beginning I was daunted by those impassioned outbursts, watching myself being shunted forever along the sluiceway with the damned. But the issues never were solved, and the judgment always was forgotten, and I came to see that whether she knew it or not, having me to break against was what she wanted. In fact, her inclusion of me in her home had released so much need in her that sometimes Michael was only on the periphery, someone whose bed I shared.

"Is this what it's like to be a mother?" I asked him on one of the few evenings we had spent alone for more than a month.

"Maybe Melissa's making up for lost time. Sometimes she talks to you like I think she wishes she could talk to Fran."

Melissa wanted to know about my work, too, made me try to articulate what I was doing in stone or wood, became a watchful presence sometimes in my studio, and I tried hard to include her without impatience. I was grateful for all that new attention but guiltily admitted to myself that I treasured those times when I could have Michael in my house, or even the occasional nights, more and more rare now, when I would sleep alone. At such times I would ponder the confusion of wishes, finding certainty only in the fact that always some other state would be desired in the present. When Melissa had banished us, I had hoped to gain her affection, to persuade her to trust us enough to give us back our freedom of movement. Now I seemed to be so thoroughly accepted that I yearned for some distance and wondered whether there was enough of me to give. Or to accept, because I am putting this too partially. What Melissa was also doing was trying to give me an enormous amount of affection, and I did not know what to do with such abundance. The one thing, however, that became increasingly absurd to all three of us was our physical situation—two houses, two little squares of the city that we hopped back and forth on, to some extent neglecting both, beginning to feel more and more like itinerants living in mobile homes. Melissa called it "our game of musical houses."

That winter I read from my father's books to Sheldon, in between some Dickens, some Whitman. He would make tea for me, the wind battering at the walls, or bright squares of reflections from the snow cutting sharp patterns on the ceiling. I read four of Hob's books as I never had before, and if I came to him eagerly it was both from the excitement of understanding them in a wholly new way and from the pleasure of being with Sheldon, watching those words draw expression from his unmasked face. Sometimes Michael would come and I would make him sit through the end of a chapter.

Finally we could stand our restless way of life no longer, and we found a house to buy in the country. Michael's house was sold first, but our new home was not yet vacated, so he and Melissa had to move into mine. They packed. I helped them, and one Saturday the van came and took everything down the road to temporary storage. Then we put a bed together for Melissa at my house.

Michael had led her around her new home. She had chosen her room, luckily not the one I had imagined as Sheldon's because at this point I could not have argued with her. I stepped by her as if the floor in her immediate presence were randomly scattered with eggs. How could she help but resent me no matter how hard Michael worked at portraying the move as his decision? None of this seemed to be happening to her advantage—the home she had lived in all her life sold before she could even adjust to the fact that it might be, then having to camp out in mine in those final weeks of school and graduation. Everything must have seemed at an end for her. I hoped she would talk but did not probe, and now when I needed her words, she became nearly mute. She was much too polite, too narrowly defining paths in my house that were limited to the necessities of sleeping, washing, eating. I longed to have my house sold so that I could hold up my own empty hands to her and say "See, I too have suffered."

In my bleak moments I am apt to forget how continuity is firmly in consciousness and does not have to reside in places or things. I had chosen the move from our separate homes to a single house as a symbol of a new life, as if we both had decided to burn the past in two pyres on the hillside of Burlington. But I forgot the vacancy of transition, a gap in which we all tumbled weightlessly. I could not see us as still fully alive. Impatiently I lowered the price of my house. My agent herded prospective buyers through and we learned to look up from our meals to see them standing in the living room, or measuring the height of the arch to the dining room. I locked the door whenever I took a shower. Once I heard a shriek, a slammed door, and a very apologetic woman descended. She had not known my sister was upstairs. Terribly sorry. Lovely place but needed painting. When she left, Melissa stood on the stairs glaring at me, her nostrils flared in anger. She turned and plunged at the front door. Later her voice over the phone informed me icily that she was spending the night with Adele, where at least she could have a small amount of privacy. I listened, my own weary anger rising back. Fine. We hung up. How could I tell her I was only a wraith myself?

As if the household gods would not forgive me, a letter came from my mother's brother in Oklahoma. He thought I would be interested. Did I know my brother Tim was married and living in Colorado? The rest of the mail slipped from my hands, but I kept on reading. He had not actually met with him, but been in Denver for a convention and seen his name in the phone book. T. Randolph Cobb. Too odd to be coincidence. Called him. Yes, he was the same. No, would rather not see his uncle just now. Yes, he had read a small article in the *L.A. Times* when his father died. Was sorry. Frankly, he did not care if others in the family knew about him. He remembered his sister with affection but that too was long ago. The uncle spent the rest of the letter saying he found "the boy" uncommunicative and cold and wasn't that just like the reprobate? Would not forget the pain he had caused my father by disappearing like that and never making contact again. Especially so soon after my mother's tragic death. He had almost laid into him over the phone but decided no, better to go easy, establish contact rather than putting him off. Anyway, here was his address. Tim did seem more responsive about me than anyone else. Maybe I'd come see them in Oklahoma someday? A colored snapshot fluttered out. Three teenagers in swimming suits, grinning, braces, gangly limbs, two girls and a boy and a stretch of parched, brown lawn. His grandchildren.

I folded the letter, put it back in the envelope, and went to stand on the porch and stare down over the rooftops at a lake glinting hotly, our first humid day that might even be drifting toward a storm. I sat on the railing. My agent's car was advancing slowly along the avenue, her arm out the window to point at features of the neighborhood. I would write. But not now. My heart clenched and released, thudding in my ears as if the valves were stone lids. When I closed my eyes I saw him—tall, lean, the dark-haired member of the family, stumbling into tables with the new long reach of his legs, those ratty Keds that smelled up his bedroom. My uncle's letter brought Tim to mind more vividly than Hob's had, perhaps because it did not come in my father's quiet but pained voice. When the visitors left I put that letter carefully in my address book. I went to the room that had been Tim's. But it had been totally refurnished as a guest room so long ago that I could not find what I wanted there. I did not show the letter to Michael and made myself forget it for a while.

On the afternoon that my house was sold, I took Sheldon to see our new home in the nearby town of Charlotte, his too although he had not wanted to move until Melissa said stubbornly that she would not go without him. I saw the house better than I ever had before, turning it into words for him room by room. We entered by the back, pausing to brush through the leaves on the willow, and he touched the trunk, reached up to the first limb, and said it was a good climbing tree. He held my arm more tightly than usual, listened closely, let me leave his cane at the door so that he could pass his other hand along a wall, a doorjamb, the mantelpiece, the cherry paneling. I could not hold back the excitement from my voice, tried to keep my description accurate but once he interrupted, "I can't imagine *beautiful*. Tell me the color." From time to time I found my own hand touching the molding, doorknobs, reducing everything to his world of shapes, as if my hand could tell me what words were needed. Finally we were in his room and we walked around the walls to the window seat and he sat there. He fluttered one hand against the pane and flattened it as if meeting the sunlight palm to palm. His voice was quiet, speaking toward the field.

"Melissa likes it, you know. She always wanted to live in the country. She won't tell you that for a long time because she's feeling a little pushed now."

"And you like it?"

"It's very big, isn't it?"

"Yes."

"And empty."

"We can fill it."

The movers came after they had picked up their load at Sheldon's apartment. They heaved and trundled, eased ungainly objects down the stairwell, and then they were gone. I closed the screen door at last and chased the bumbling flies from room to room as I walked slowly over the floors more bare than they had been in my lifetime. Their scars and scratches showed a large ink stain in my brother's room that an old bureau had covered, patches of matted, undisturbed dust. I had thought there would be some neatly defined moment when I would stand alone in my room or my parents' and hear a cadence, perhaps no glorious repetition of dominant to tonic, but at least a muted progression to a rest, a double bar. Wasn't I beginning a whole new movement in my life? I walked slowly up the stairs, paused at the landing to look across the narrow strip of lilac bushes, profusely purple and white, to the neighbor's abandoned car. Mrs. Hanson was hanging her laundry. In each room I paused to glance at the floor, through the windows, and to listen. Nothing. Just an empty house. Oh, there was a certain nostalgic sadness I could easily raise. But that was too easy. I felt vaguely mocked.

A small, curved object lay on the floor in my father's room. I thought at first it was a dead insect, but I stooped and lifted an old barrette made of tortoiseshell and a bent clasp. It must have clung for years to some angle of bureau or bed. I took it to the window and light. Plastic never succeeds in imitating that complex grain and layers of natural shell, the way light flows through translucent veins to shine beneath the darker layers. My mother had worn it for years, and I could recall taking it from her hair when she would lead me upstairs for my afternoon rest in a bed so crammed with crayons and coloring books and dolls that there was barely room for me. I would clasp it as I worked, and if I grew drowsy, I would lie on my side and hold it in my opened hand, perhaps running my thumb across that polished surface, or gazing so long at the layers that I passed into them—safe because, almost as if I held a hostage, I possessed some part of my mother that she would have to come back to reclaim.

Michael's voice. I glanced out the window to see his car below. We would drive our cars and arrive together, this flotilla of Gardeners and one Cobb. I balanced the barrette in my hand, thought of leaving it on the floor for the cleaners to dispose of, but dropped it into my pocket instead.

"I'm coming!" I yelled finally when his voice began to call more urgently.

One look around the kitchen. Empty. Was I forgetting a last item that I had to bring? I paused at the window looking out onto the backyard. The grass unmown. A green time of year. New growth on the hedge was tangled in a low branch of the maple. The horn honking now. Coming, coming. I turned from the window with the absurd desire to take that whole yard with me. But I did, forever. In Charlotte we arrived to the heaped chaos of our lives, to confusions of boxes and bedframes and dishes that could within a fairly short period be relegated to areas of the house but that were only truly sorted and placed months later.

A hot and hazy Saturday in July 1964. I was sitting on the patio in the shade of the willow knowing that I should return to an attempt I had been delaying for weeks to sort the most obdurate boxes. But with all of the necessary unpacking done, weariness was showing itself at last in all of us. I slumped in a high-backed Adirondack chair, letting my head rest against the wood. My eyes were closing when I was startled by a noise, turned my head to see two bare legs dangling off the ground under the fringe of willow leaves, the branch trembling with weight, and then Melissa dropped into sight. She was dressed in shorts and halter, her body well tanned from weekend visits to the lake with friends. She looked at me curiously. "I didn't know you were up there."

I tried to settle back but was wide awake now.

She stood where she could comb her hands through the leaves, reluctant to let go of the tree entirely. "Julie, will you do me a favor?"

"Certainly."

She was breathing quickly. "Please get off my back."

At first I was merely puzzled. Then hurt. "What do you mean?"

"You're always staring at me, and when I try to talk with Dad and you're there, you aren't listening to what I'm saying. It's like you're listening with earphones, trying to translate it all or something."

"Am I around too much? With your father, I mean."

She shook her head vehemently. "I don't care about that. But you make me very self-conscious all the time. What are you looking for?"

"I'm sorry."

She tore away some leaves. "I don't mean you to be sorry. Just tell me what you want. Say it." Her frustration was shifting now toward tears.

"Your love, I guess."

"But you have that."

"I do?"

"What do I have to say? Am I supposed to do something? Pass a test? Walk on hot coals?"

I stood.

"Don't go away."

"I'm not."

"But sometimes, Julie, I think you are. Sometimes I feel you're like some weird bird on a branch looking down at all of us and you could stop turning your head this way and that and just fly off. Don't you know what I mean?"

"Maybe you're saying I make you self-conscious because I am?"

She shook her head. "It's like you want us to love you but you keep most of yourself somewhere else, shut away. What will I do if I look around some afternoon and you have flown away? What will my father do?"

"I won't, Melissa."

"Don't you know we all love you? Can't you make up your mind and stop watching us? Do you trust us?"

She threw down the handful of crushed leaves, turned, and padded in her bare feet across the stones to the lawn. She stumbled slightly, arms stiff at her sides as she kept walking out of the burdocked, hay-strewn field toward the fence and horizon where the land dipped away.

I wanted to run after that stalking figure, to cry out, "What do you mean? What do you mean?" But I did not. I too felt tears pressing at me, the surface response of insult and injury. But even as she stopped by the fence to put both arms stiffly to the top rail and lean, her shoulders trembling, I fell away into that shocked blank space where a steadier voice than the yelp of self-pity said, "You are learning something that you did not know or want to know. Pay attention."

And I did—not moving out of that dappled shade, staring across the dusty green of a much-neglected lawn, wondering what new self-deception I was wrapped in and if love can ever shine out of us in clear white light. Did I stand and watch, doing exactly what she had accused me of, or was I doing it because she had helped to make that scene be what she expected it to be?

I did what I thought was best then. I waited a moment to see if she would calm, and she lifted her head to stare toward Camel's Hump, the stiffness leaving her back as she leaned into the fence rather than against it. I walked back into the house, leaving her to what I thought was her private grief. But I know now that she was trying to describe my relationship not just to them but also to my own carefully guarded sorrow.

Maybe she believed how much I cared for her only after I had begun to care for her own concerns. Commitment was what she wanted from me, in every aspect of my life. Five years after that afternoon, not long before she journeyed to Bo Hassler's wedding and I to Boston, she was jailed after demonstrating in Boston. It was 1969 and a jowly, mumble-mouthed Nixonite had recently puffed onto our screens saying that at last we had "turned the corner" in Vietnam, or some other such gross cliché, those anesthetized metaphors they loved to flop at us, as if the flaccid language could conceal what that "corner" represented to suffering people and to shattered landscapes, acts disfiguring the body of time itself, since generation after generation would relive the wounds. No such bland face as Melvin Laird's could cancel the image of a child running down a dirt road, her face distorted with pain and terror, seeing no comfort ahead of her in a camera's lens or the hunched photographer. She was running from the fragments of home, family, a now unrecognizable portion of earth, and her own burned skin.

Michael was no help if Melissa and I argued after dinner when she came to retreat from being an ex-student in Burlington. She had graduated from the university but not gone on to anything more than working as a clerk in a department store. I would try to calm her by agreeing. "If you think that way, do something!" she finally cried out at me on the evening before she went to Boston, and with her mouth trembling, she rose from the couch and drove back to her apartment, leaving two bare patches in the driveway as mute testimony to her spurning.

"She'll get over all this." Michael put his glasses on again but did not open his book. "I know it's not just Vietnam that troubles her. But this war will end too."

Did he pause because he heard his words as I did? My mind leaped toward Melissa, and if she had been there then, I might have considered going with her to Boston, where she was joining a demonstration the next day. Michael's words toppled me into a new space. I do not mean this critically of him. They were the words for the situation—a father assessing the emotional life of his daughter. But I heard that phrase go off into the far larger space we were all floating in so numbly. If we had an ultimate knowledge of good and evil, we would not "get over all this," no matter how remotely we did our killing. Sweating and holding our ears against the blast of a gun, we sent the wreckage so far away that we barely heard the muffled landing between motions of our hasty loading and firing. Listening to the high whine and hiss of our jets, we computed the absolute moment to release bombs we would never even see burst, or in a cozy living room we expended emotional energy in a search for explanations while the last cool measure of Riesling was sweating the bottle on the table. But we should suddenly have known exactly what circle of hell we would occupy forever. We didn't. We'd get over it. The species could not have survived long without a memory as fluid as Lethe, a place to wash the hands.

The next evening, when Melissa called after her arrest, Michael was away at a conference in Atlanta. I called our lawyer for advice, then decided to drive to Boston. It was early morning when I arrived. The total shabbiness of the jailhouse settled on me—walls painted in muck-brown about three quarters up, then a strip of dirtier brown that carried over to the ceiling, cracks and siftings of plaster under the benches, lights in cages, a floor unswept, and the room filled with the odor of unemptied ashtrays, acrid sweat. I was told to wait and I sat on a bench, hard, chipped, and battered on its thick edge as if the people waiting in frustration had kneeled on the crazed linoleum to gnaw. I leaned against an even harder, colder wall, let the back of my head touch it also. I tried not to look at the officer behind the counter. If my first reaction in seeing the place had been disgust it had plummeted into fear, for Melissa's sake. I had to get her out of there. Silence and craft. And I did not want to think what might be going on beyond that barred door through which I could hear occasional voices, footsteps on steel stairs, the laughter of crows.

An hour later the door swung open and people began to file through. The line was too long and had to pause when the front of it reached the opening in the grillwork. I could not see her yet and they seemed to move with terrible slowness. The protesters were the only people talking to each other, were disheveled but awake and mostly young.

Melissa was framed in the doorway, tired, her hair wisping out around her neck and cheeks. She was a little overweight then, her dungarees too tight against a waist she obviously wanted to believe was smaller. The woman in front of her, sturdy and scowling, was haranguing her. I could tell by the way Melissa's eyes moved that she had hoped someone would be there. She saw me, and her eyes held still.

The expression of her face hardly changed. Perhaps if it had been simply relief or irritation at me for being there or even annoyance that I was not and could not be Michael since she knew he was in Atlanta, nothing in me might have happened at that moment. But her look had none of those stock defenses. It was a clear recognition and greeting, and I felt it to be an understanding. Sometimes as a child I would say my own name over and over until suddenly the sound of those syllables that had identified me lifted me up outside myself and I was no longer a name or a history but a portion of all that is human, as simple as a hand. She was no longer Melissa Gardener, or Michael's daughter, or Fran's kid, or my undefined relative. She was a woman, someone who might be a friend, someone who would go on in ways beyond any power of knowing I might have, and I loved her. I held still. Then we both raised our hands tentatively at the same time, a gesture that might have been in a mirror, and just as fragile as glass. I could not help recalling that moment years before when she had stood on a stage in Burlington and sung her way deeply into my life, but that moment had not been mutually recognized.

In the car she said, "Thank you for coming."

"I wasn't sure you wanted me to."

"I wasn't either. Until I saw you. I would have felt awful if you weren't there."

She was sleeping with her head lolling on the back of the seat long before we left the city. I kept glancing at her face, impatient to have her wake and talk to me. She alone could help me understand what I had been through in the past hours—because I began to wonder whether maybe I had been through something as much as she had. But I could not grasp it. We stopped, ate, she was still groggy, but she began to wake up when we were back in the car.

"Are you going to Philadelphia for that next demonstration?" I asked her as we neared Burlington.

"I don't know."

This much I did understand: I did not want Melissa to change. I was counting on her, maybe other people like her.

"What if I came too?"

She sat up. "Do you mean that?"

I did not answer at first. I was listening to what I had said. "Yes."

She clapped her hands like a child. "Julie. How wonderful."

She talked excitedly. I tried to listen, tried to be interested. I was, but I also was not ready to join her to the extent she anticipated. And maybe I never did. But we did go to Philadelphia together, I was with her in Burlington, and I helped stuff envelopes here and there. But how many of us were totally present anyway? Oh, there were the zealots, equal in their rage to their opposites. But for most of the people I came across, there was only half a heart at best to give—the rest was puzzled or numbed or shattered. We suffered little violence. Words were thrown at us, gestures, sometimes one of us was spat on, or when we were hauled into vans we were not dropped softly. I never felt I was a victim. I had chosen whatever hate or anger I saw. But once I had walked down Church Street in the city where I had grown up and seen that hate or indifference in the postures of quiet observers, some of whom I had known from childhood, I knew in ways photographs or television could never prove to me that what we were living through was real.

If only Melissa and I could have talked more about all this. We were much closer, but the part of me that could not completely join her prevented me from finding all the questions. But I will say this, even if it seems a small betrayal: We were always safely framed by curbstones, by lines of policemen, by committed lawyers. We chose freely to be where we were. Past College Street, past Bank, turning left on Pearl to walk to Battery Park and speeches. But I wondered as we trudged through our own July Fourth parade, what if we were there not by choice but were running frightened, bewildered, down a road away from one hate toward another?

7

When I woke in Boston imagining that I was Julie Cobb in possession of such facts and decisions as made my story, my slow waking and careful reentry were due only to too much wine with dinner the night before, a glass that my companion never let stand empty for long. He owned a gallery, was making promises, but all too clearly as the evening veered on, his motives were less for art than for some simple pleasures he had in mind. Which I rejected, and in doing so, had one less possibility of a show. He was offended, of course. The wine was Chateau Latour, and he had expected great things from it.

But I was lucky and had escaped the punishment I deserved. No headache, no queasiness, only the dull, internal ache of being somewhere I did not want to be. A shower was running beyond the wall. I closed my eyes again. As I often did, I imagined Sheldon sitting up in his perpetual dark, ruled by his own clock and the persistence of sound. In winter he listened for the milk truck, for the slight increase in traffic, for the muffled thumps we made in bedroom or kitchen. From spring on, he accepted the promptings of birdsong, happy to lie and listen to their earliest twitterings. But he insisted there was more than that, a residual sensitivity to light. "I know I can't see, Julie, but something is different. I can feel it," and watching his hands curl open on his lap, those careful, gentle palms and long fingers forming an open-latticed cup, I believed him. He had his rhythms like any of us, and the worst for him were moments when he lost contact with his sense of external time, waking bewildered in the middle of the night. His hands then were tense and nervous, and more than once when he called out to us, I had come to hold them. But I lay in Boston, and the late July sun was already well up. Oh, Michael, another wasted day.

I sat on the edge of the bed, then lurched to the bathroom and plunged my wrists under cold water. My mother would hold an ice cube wrapped in a washcloth against the inside of her wrist when she was hot, from time to time lifting it to wipe slowly across her forehead. "It cools the blood," she would say. Cooling her delicate wrists, the corded, bluish veins. And sometimes, on those rare, lazy summer afternoons, she would reach across the widest imaginable space to rest that chilled wrist against my forehead, and I would close my eyes and smile and ask for more.

Almost noon, but I stretched out and dozed again. The house in Charlotte would be still and cool. Perhaps the wind was stirring the willow slightly, a thunderstorm flashing and grumbling distantly over the northern spread of the lake. The storm rolled toward the house with slow and crushing weight. All the land behind it was covered forever with suffocating darkness. Trees began to bend, the barn leaned with them, my mother kneeled on the dusky lawn, her back to me. "Don't don't." My voice would not leave my throat. She held her hands out, urging the storm onto us.

What else did I dream? Or did I dream? There is another whole life during that third of our time in which our bodies inhabit one room, one bed. I have seen time-lapse photographs of sleepers. He twists and turns, curls and uncurls, groans, moves his eyes, erects, and subsides. The woman beside him dances, too. They touch from time to time, bodies adjusting to the space cut out by the other. Light grows in the room. She sits up slowly, hair disheveled, stretches her arms upward, curves over her crossed legs, head bent downward. For one moment she slips back into that country of sleep, of death, but she is on the riverbank now, not across, and the landscape she has walked through is only the furtive shapes of trees and high grass beyond the opaque screen of fog. Another life. What if it is the real one, the life these cells were gathered for? Only because of an anomaly of the brain, its self-aggrandizing and aggressive layer of waking consciousness, are we led to think the sleeper is a form of life at rest. The Tyrant of Wakefulness churns out his propaganda of sense impressions. Standing by a maple I see its birds, the leaves unfurling, full canopy combed by the winds, the burst of fall red, and gray sticks of winter. Because I walk above the ground, I define that tree's life by the cycle in my eyes. But under the surface my feet have come to trust as the limits to descent, the real tree burrows and sucks and grips against the frenzied motions of its upper self. What if the roots are what the tree is all about?

I woke to a life that for a long time was as altered as if I had been turned upside down. The sky darkened, grew solid, and far away on the other side of the line I had crossed I was dimly aware of leaves and branches doing their seasonal things. But first I crossed numbly through a cold river. In truth I was awake, but in desperate moments I tried to hope that the life of impenetrable sleep was the real one. Who was it who said, "Waking to find our nightmares real, is tragedy"?

The phone was ringing me awake, although in my confusion as I picked it up, I groped over its surface trying to find a button to push and turn it off. But it was not telling me the time of day. I heard the static of distance, then a voice at first unrecognizable.

"Mike, is that you? It doesn't sound like you."

He had not said anything since he had said, "Julie. I want to talk with Julie Cobb." Finally the voice answered, "Yes, it's me."

I was being pulled out and away by that voice. I tried to grip the bank, scrabbling at small roots, the loose stones. "You sound terrible. What is it? What's wrong?"

"Melissa." The phone filled with a wave of static that broke over us, then the voice said, "She's dead."

As he talked I kept repeating the simple phrase "I am coming home," a magic charm to get me there immediately. I heard him say she had been beaten to death. She had been sitting on the lawn of the Unitarian Church. She had gone with a friend during an early-morning break from work. A man crossed the lawn. He had a lead pipe. He walked up to her and began beating her with it. Someone tried to intervene. She died before reaching the hospital. There had been no hope. She did not know the man. He was insane. No one knew why he did it. He was arrested, had not struggled. A man had done this but it was as random as a truck without a driver rolling down a hill and jumping the curb. Melissa was dead. "I am coming home."

Would he be all right? Was there someone there? What about Sheldon?

Michael could not talk anymore. He was very confused. He did not know what else to say. I told him I loved him. His voice said he would be all right. The phone call was over.

Although my plane did not leave until that evening and they could find me no seat on the earlier flight, I decided to wait at the airport. On the way there the traffic was heavy. We stopped on a bridge, jerked a few yards forward, stopped again. I was beginning to feel sick. I was repeating to myself, "This isn't my story," which for a while helped to distance the immediate present. But nothing altered that pulse of underlying pain. I could see the dull river, its channeled banks and hazy, scorched land of concrete beyond. Near the height of the bridge hunched the form of a man, and his broad-brimmed hat concealed his bowed head. His clothes were tattered, shoes splitting at the toes. What was he doing there? Did he crouch for a moment on his way across, overcome by fumes and heat, gathering some strength for the trip down or back? Or had he given up at last, perhaps about to climb the rail and leap? We moved and stopped, moved and stopped. We were almost past him when the head raised. The brim was low on the forehead of his wide face. His mouth did not move, indifferent eyes were on me directly as if he had lifted his head because he could sense my gaze. I stared back at him. The taxi moved and stopped. I craned to keep our eyes in contact. He continued to stare without expression. Then he was gone. I sat back and closed my eyes.

"Oh, God," I said and started weeping.

8

What was real about a vacant terminal, a taxi ride through the outskirts of a town that had all the guise of familiarity but was utterly changed? With the windows down to give me the motion of humid air, through a landscape burgeoning into dark lushness with trees and shrubs, the smell of green again, I was driven to Charlotte, up that stretch of Mt. Philo Road toward the house that at a distance blazed with lights as if some grand party were in progress. Pebbles cracked under the tires. A strange car in the driveway. I paid and watched the taxi leave and then I stared at the dim outline of the willow that halted in its droop above the ground like some floating haystack. The field stretched toward a sky of faint stars.

Michael walked slowly around the corner of the house, I stumbled to him, and we held each other without speaking, still not talking when we turned and walked together into the house. I blinked in the bright lights of the living room. Two men I had never seen before were standing by the couch. Michael introduced me to the district attorney and a police officer, and I tried to be Miss Cobb. One of them asked me a question. They were all looking at me, but I had not understood.

"Sorry. I'm a little confused."

Michael was thanking them, they both turned to us again to say good-bye, and he went with them onto the patio, I stared after him, unwilling to lose sight of his figure beyond the screen. The car started. Lights struck the field, exaggerating its shaggy hummocks, and swung in arcs across the trees. Still Mike stood with his back to me, slightly stooped. He stepped once as if to stride into the field, but he swiveled and straight-armed the door. I reached for him again, clinging as tightly as I could because for a moment even this most familiar of rooms was strange. Far inside the cage of his chest I could hear his heartbeat, the muffled voice say, "Julie, Julie." I stood back, took him by the arm to the couch. He sat forward, his face held in his hands. When he pulled them away, he stared at his palms.

"Tell me," I said, unable to bear the silence anymore.

"I can't understand yet, Julie. I have not been to see Melissa. I can't. I don't want to believe." He closed his eyes. "Leroy Haines. He's nineteen. They say probably he'll be judged insane and not stand trial. He and Melissa were total strangers. He's a local loony. No one knows him well. Even his family lost contact with him recently."

"Why, if he was crazy, was he wandering around?"

His voice was almost expressionless, and I could tell he was saying things he had already said over to himself, or perhaps to Fran, who was on her way from Chicago. But he was accomplishing what I had needed, if that is the term, because each new phrase struck into me sharply, and it was all too real.

"What they tell me is you can't arrest someone until they have done something, and walking around muttering or being out of touch is no crime. And you can't help anyone until they ask for it. The last year or so he lived where he could. On coldest nights he'd find doorways, halls. They had him for trespassing once and tried to take him in for treatment but he wouldn't cooperate and there was not enough to prosecute."

I could not bear the way his hands hung loosely from the wrists over the end of the cushion. The hands twitched from time to time less to express some point than as if he were dreaming, his mind somewhere other than what he was telling me.

"What about his family? Why couldn't they do something?"

"I don't know much about them. He has a sister, older, his father is dead, mother's an invalid. Poor. Bissette says they're bitter. Angry at the city."

"Please," I said quietly. "What happened?"

He opened his eyes and stared down at the rug. "I keep seeing it over and over again. I step in front of Haines. I beat him back."

His face returned to his hands and he was weeping and I held him. When he could speak he did not wait for me to ask my question again.

"They decided to take Cokes and go sit on the church lawn. Melissa was talking about how glad she would be to turn in her resignation soon." He swallowed, drew both hands back through his hair. "Her friend Ann Harper doesn't know where he came from, if he was watching them or what. But she looked up and saw a young man in odd-fitting clothes—too heavily dressed, like one of those bums who travels with all his clothes on because he has no suit-case—and he had a piece of pipe in his hand. He was walking toward them, not fast. They watched him and Melissa was turning to Ann, saying, 'Friend of yours?' when he reached them. He didn't pause or say anything. He stopped a foot away. Melissa was looking up when he started beating her, very slowly. Hard.''

I closed my eyes but opened them quickly because I would rather stare at his grief than anything on the screen of my mind.

"Ann thought it must be a practical joke, a clown act with a rubber or plastic tube. But Melissa fell over and was bleeding and someone who had been standing in the parking lot was running at them saying, 'Hey, stop that,' and Ann ran away certain Haines was chasing her. But he wasn't. He was standing there swinging, and when the man, then two or three others got there, he quit and handed them the pipe and didn't say a word.''

I kneeled in front of him and put my arms around his bent neck. He looked up, face vacant.

"She was dead before the ambulance arrived.''

I kept stroking my hand down his cheek, waiting to see if he had more to say.

"I called you as soon as I could.''

I nodded.

"She said nothing, you understand?'' Again he was looking through me. "Ann says she did not even cry out. She may not have seen him well enough to understand what was happening. The sun was directly behind him and Melissa was raising her hand to her eyes in order to shade them when he struck.''

I put my head down onto his knees, and he stroked over my hair absentmindedly. But I lifted my head, looked quickly around. "Where's Sheldon?''

"His room.'' His hands jerked up, palms out. "I didn't know what to do. He's sitting there and won't talk to me. As if he blames me.''

"Alone?''

He nodded. I bumped the couch as I turned and then I was running through the kitchen to the stairs, missing one step on the narrow turn, and twisting my ankle. Every lamp in his room was on.

Sheldon was sitting on the edge of his bed, hands loosely clasped. He turned his face to the door and must have heard the quick steps because he had an arm stretched out already and I held on to him tightly while that hand patted my shoulder.

"It was on the news tonight, too. A crazy. Michael says there was nothing anybody could do at the time. All happened too fast. Oh, my poor Melissa." Then very calmly he said, "Don't turn out the lights, please. I like to know they're on."

That was one thing Michael had been able to do. At first he had thought Sheldon meant only his own room, but when he had walked around to all the lamps and had come back to stand by his father, Sheldon had said curtly, "I can do that. I meant in the rest of the house. I can feel the dark in the air. Turn them on." All that night the house blazed festively, and if I woke in our one unlit space to rise and carefully walk to the window, I could see the lawn, the shaking tree, and empty road washed with our glow. But I need not have been so careful, because always Michael was awake, although he rarely spoke to me when I returned to bed. The lights were on for only that one night, and Sheldon did not even seem to recall his order the next day.

I sat with him for some time. We hardly talked at all. But now where was Michael? I was a rope not long enough to stretch between two diverging weights. I wanted to hold on to both men.

"This sort of thing happens all the time now, out there," and Sheldon's hand waved at a brute world beyond the windows. "But I guess I always thought it was far away. New York. Boston. Never in Vermont."

Finally Michael appeared at the door. "I'm going to lie down for a while."

At least I knew where he was and could let my mind follow him down the hallway to our bedroom.

"Son?"

"Yes."

"You'll let me know everything, won't you?"

"Yes."

"I'm sorry I . . ."

"Don't be."

Michael glanced at us, and the expression was so numbed I could not help wondering if he was on some tranquilizer. But he was not. It was only the body's shocked retreat. He turned and was gone. Sheldon and I listened to his footsteps.

"You don't need to sit with me. How was Boston?"

"Terrible."

"Here." He pulled his arm loose. "I'm going to stretch out for a while. You'll have to tell me about it all tomorrow. Now you go. Mike will need you."

He pushed off his slippers and lay out on the bed, stretched full length on his back with his hands clasped loosely. His gestures were like a small child trying to demonstrate that he will be good, will rest, will not get out of his bed.

"You'll be all right?"

"As much as any of us can be." He frowned. "I'm trying to face down an idea that keeps coming to me, which is that maybe one can live too long, maybe it's better to have a shorter life if the price for longevity is having to go through the deaths of others."

"Don't, please."

"I'm trying not to. Good night. Come when you wake. We'll need each other."

I promised I would and left him in the bright room, his puzzled face with wide, unseeing eyes turned to the ceiling.

I had not lived a night like this since my mother's death and had thought I never would again. Hob's death had not affected me this way, perhaps because I had known for some time that he was not entirely well. I lived the next few days as if thrashing my way through the delirium and confusion of a high fever, uncertain if I had fallen into a doze in which bewildering images of strangers rose to say inexplicable things to me, or if I was waking to an even stranger world. But there were too many things I could not acknowledge then. I had been struck on the blind side, and that side remained blind but raging against the blow. Seventeen years before Melissa's death I had not been old enough to see clearly, and now a new wound opened up an old one that had never healed. But for a while I had no time to understand that. Again and again what secured my hold to the world around me was the fear of losing Michael, of not being there to help him when I could, or if I could. Someone close had died, and suddenly I kept seeing that any of us could drop through the fragile surface of the day.

From time to time that night I would whisper his name to know if he was asleep, and always he would touch me in reply, rarely speaking, as if to use his voice would cost him too much. I wanted him to know that he could talk and did not need to fear waking me. He took off his shoes and lay on his back, still in his shirt and slacks, and I dreamed in one of my dozes that he was a fireman, that when I stood over him and ordered him to undress he refused angrily, saying it was his duty to be ready. Twice that night I thought I woke to the shock of bells ringing, certain the house or the barn was blazing, that Mike had sat up, pulling on his boots, telling me triumphantly that he had been right. I woke to the blanched windows of dawn and cursed my mind for such inventions. The water was running in the shower as it might on any other morning, the limbs of the trees were familiarly warped by the old glass. My dream sank away.

But those were the last hours any of us had much time to think for a few days. The fact of death rushed past us like a tumbling comet, dragging and whirling us in its wake. When it was gone, there was that one night of absolute silence, a vacuum of passage that had sucked out our own lives. Then came all the debris torn loose in the world around us, and we had no time to struggle with our grief, hardly to mourn, because we were fending off reporters, friends, distant relatives, well-wishers, sensationalists, professional mourners, strangers with numbed or mutilated lives drawn to us by the politics and power of violence. The last were the hardest to deal with because dying for them was some twisted image of vitality. At first Michael answered the phone that began ringing shortly after we rose. Fran would reach us as soon as she could. The president of the university offered condolences. The police wanted to know more of Melissa's patterns in her daily life. Finally the phone rang fifteen times and no one answered it. I found Mike standing in front of the TV watching some flickering, heavily lined diagrams of stocks and bonds.

"Would you answer the phone for a while?" he asked.

It was already ringing again. A reporter. Could he speak to Mr. Gardener, the father? No. Who was I? A friend. Fine. Perhaps he could explain.

"We're trying to go a little further than the headlines now. The human-interest angle. Were there any immediate reactions from Mr. Gardener?"

I held still. I could hear the clack of typewriters. "Grief."

"No, no. I mean words. Today. Anything that could be quoted?

Any thoughts about Leroy Haines or the social problem it represents, you know?''

"None. Sorry."

"Well, is he angry, bitter? What if Haines pleads innocent by reason of insanity? Does Mr. Gardener believe in the death penalty? We'd like any domestic details you might have about Melissa. We've talked to friends who seem to think she may have been involved in some Christian sect at one point."

I hung up. The next day the headlines would read, "Father Speechless with Grief and Shock," and there would be listings of all Melissa's school activities, her courses in college, a smiling picture of her as Dorothy with bows in her hair, quotations from teachers who remembered her, all the bland and pulpy phrases of well-meaning sorrow so conventional that they could serve for anyone's tombstone. She became "a local girl," suddenly everyone's daughter, sister, a cypher for the fear of sudden loss. When that sort of sluice gate to public fantasy is opened, the sludge flows through as well, and that night a voice, breathless with its own tension, asked me, "She ever been raped before, you know, did she go back in the woods with Leroy and get her pants pulled down?" The voice broke into nervous laughter and I did not even have a chance to speak my anger, since I threw the receiver onto its hook in reflex.

Sheldon and I worked on funeral arrangements, relieved to have something to do. He was good at that, knew what to ask the funeral homes, how to call to arrange a plot near Liz. I sat by the phone with him, looking up numbers, finding something comforting in the steady, clear tones of voice he used with everyone. And for those few hours, we did not leave enough space for the phone to ring. We had selected the funeral home and chosen the plot when we called to Michael. He didn't answer and I began to look for him throughout the house, panic growing as I passed the television still on, the sound off, but a picture of Agnew sneering into the camera. Finally I heard the steady thumping of ax and found him splitting wood by the edge of the cornfield, his shirt soaked with sweat.

"No." He shook his head slowly. "That won't do. All she ever mentioned was cremation and having her ashes spread."

"Where?"

He wiped the blade of his hand across his eyebrows, shook the sweat off. "Camel's Hump."

It took us another slow hour to unravel everything, but Sheldon and I canceled the plot, reduced our order to the funeral home, whose director was disappointed. The service would be in a room of the funeral home before a table with flowers and Melissa's urn and some simple words of ritual. We did not let ourselves imagine how the rest would be done, the hike up Camel's Hump.

Late afternoon. I was stooping in the corner garden, weeding marigolds and chrysanthemums, my hands muddied. I could concentrate on that, a narrow focus of crabgrass, chickweed, and straggling sweet grass. The sun was low enough so that I was in shade, and for a few moments I could forget, breathing deeply that rot of humus, some mint I had inadvertently torn. When I had worked over a large enough area, I stayed on my knees and turned the soil with a trowel, avoiding roots of the flowers. It was a fine summer for slugs and snails, and the earthworms were fat, writhing away from sudden light. I was glad I had neglected the beds all summer. Days could be spent like this. On the other side of the house were rose bushes to tend.

Michael's slow footsteps crossed the patio behind me, the ax head chinked as he set it down. Would he be planning dinner or would I be cooking for a while now, trying to manage well enough to lure Sheldon down from his room? For a moment I hunched there, hands flat on the damp, torn earth, and he must have been pausing too. I remembered the aftermath of the other deaths and how the hardest part is lifting oneself up again and again in those first few days, up out of that pit of grief where one wants only to lie curled, unspeaking, staring at whatever dumb object is nearest at hand.

I pushed up, stood, a little dizzy as the blood rushed, and he was standing by the doorway staring ruefully at his hands.

"I guess I should have stopped sooner."

His palms had blistered and the blisters had broken and blistered again until the flesh was worn raw.

"It's been a while since I've used the ax. It honestly didn't hurt, Julie. Felt so good to be in the rhythm of splitting. I'm sure I did more than a cord."

His shirt and pants were soaked with sweat, hair straggling on his neck and brow as if he had been swimming. I took him to the sink and made him wash his hands. While he went for some bandages I washed too, blackening the bowl. I wound his hands as best I could with gauze and tape, covering them as much to have them out of sight as to protect them from infection. We hardly spoke. But as he turned, some bowstring in me, drawn back for too long, let go.

"Don't do that."

"What?"

"Take it out on yourself like that. Do I have to watch you maim yourself?"

He stood stiffly, those bound hands at his sides.

"You don't have to watch anything." He spoke very clearly, as if reading the words. "I'm sorry about the blisters."

"You should have worn gloves. You usually do."

"Too hot for gloves."

I put my hands to my head. "What the hell are we talking about?"

"Michael?" Sheldon's voice came muted down the kitchen stairway. "Hello? Mike? You down there?"

Michael still was not looking at me, and one hand made the unconscious gesture of trying to stick itself in a pocket where it would not fit.

"Answer him," I said with a hiss.

"Dad?"

The phone rang. Sheldon's voice began but the ringing garbled his words. ". . . bring up . . . and could you just . . . and I don't understand . . ."

The phone would not stop ringing, Sheldon's voice continued, Michael stared at the ceiling. I don't know which it was, a glass, a peanut butter jar, maybe an empty pot from some replanting I had been doing a week before in another life. But I grabbed it off the counter, whirled, threw it at the wall behind me, and turned again to his startled face.

"Answer it, talk to him, do something!" I yelled.

The phone cut off in midring. Sheldon's voice finished the phrase ". . . on your way up," then stopped. Michael and I stared at each other. Whatever nerves our emotions flow through, discharging into cells that thrust us into love or fury, must have been as cauterized in him as in myself because I felt nothing, his face merely a human mask uninvested with our years together.

"What was that?" Sheldon asked.

I spoke in a voice someone else might have been projecting

through me, it seemed so calm. "I am going for a drive now. I'll be back soon and cook some dinner for us."

Michael nodded and I walked away, crunching over the shards of my anger. All that was swept away when I returned.

I drove slowly, no clear destination in mind at first, although I would not turn toward the mountains, wanted to stand by the lake. If I had missed anything by having moved out of Burlington it was that pervasive view of water, showing even if only in glints and patches through trees and gaps between houses. I turned through fields of hay, kept angling at the sun, then chose the road to a little public beach. Some cars were clustered together in the lot, and on the sloping field that ended in a fringe of sand and stones before the water and its bobbing float was a group of young men and women. Someone was fluting idly on a recorder, clear notes as random as wind chimes. They paid no attention to me and I walked to the farther edge of the field to sit, leaning my back against the stone wall. The sun hung low above the mountains, and a steady breeze was blowing in, breaking the glittering water all the way to the distant shore. Three white sails slanted in various directions across patches of blue and gold. I breathed slowly, deeply, closed my eyes. The flecks of light and sails held still in a darkened frame.

I thought again of Melissa up her tree, staring at that lake, choosing to stay, and of the way such choosing unravels. She could not know then for all her willingness to believe in clairvoyance that she had chosen to stay with me as well as her father, had chosen also to sit on a lawn in front of a church in July. My mind was beginning to ask, "What if?" Only the smallest shearing away in time and space made all the difference, and that awful voice would not keep still. How could I believe in any pattern, continuity of one thing growing out of another when, if Ann Harper had been sitting on the other side, Melissa Gardener might have been the one running in terror across the lawn, scarred forever but alive?

The sun was low enough to be looked at directly. The breeze kept churning the small waves, fluttering grasses, lifting along the tilt of land so that leaves above me rushed upward. Everything wanted to rise into a pale blue sky. The voices came in gusts, high sounds like calls of gulls. Some of the figures were throwing a large ball, and one woman had started to fly a kite, its paper making tearing sounds across the wooden frame. She tugged, staggering back on bare legs into the water. I was angry with myself now to think of what I had just done to Michael. Whatever I was going through, how could it even approximate their grief? I needed us to mourn and yet have Sheldon be as whole as he ever was, have Michael sit down to dinner with me, rail at his latest encounter with some dean, then say, "on the other hand." I was throwing that shattered object at the wall between Melissa and us. If only I could have been angry at her for changing all of us, have blamed it all on her. The sun was being eclipsed by a line of low, western peaks. For a moment I groped toward another time and place when death and anger erupted, scattering ash and stripping the trees of my inner landscape to frayed sticks. I saw myself standing in the kitchen, phone to my ear, my mother in the lawnchair and my father commanding me to go to her.

My companions on the beach were swimming now. At first I did not even notice, then I saw they were naked, bodies flushed with gold. A man and woman were running toward the water where they splashed and toppled in, and on a flat rock three women were circling hand in hand, laughing, kicking their legs across each other in an elaborate pattern. By the grill, a small boy was staring up at the kite so high no sound reached us, an orange point that wove and tugged against an invisible string.

I walked down across the hummocked grass to the edge of coarse sand and took off my clothes, folding them neatly. They paid no attention to me, distantly absorbed in their own games. The water was chill, the breeze mild, and I walked until the waves lapped my thighs and then I plunged in a shallow dive, began stroking out hard, stopping finally to catch my breath. I swam deliberately then, passing through patches of warm and cold, water defining my body like indifferent hands. I stroked and pulled until arms and legs ached, and still the sun and distant shore never seemed closer, and finally only sky and horizon were there. I could swim and swim, night would come, and I would still not be on the other side, stroking into the dark, uncertain of which shore I was heading toward. But I did not panic. This time such a thought was vaguely quieting. I turned finally on my back and floated, waves washing over me, a long trail of a jet slowly widening and vanishing. I did that for a long time, letting the water carry and numb me. I made my vow to go home, to help them through in any way I could. But as I turned and slowly breaststroked back, some uneasiness would not let go, as if a sinewy creature far under me were trailing along through layers of much colder water, turning aside only when the land began again to shelve upward.

All my companions were gone, but the faint char of extinguished coals proved I had not imagined them. The light was dying fast. Before I left I walked back to the edge of the lot and sat in the un-mown grass, hunching my knees close to my chest, facing the gray water, gray sky. The first stars were out, pale pockmarks above my unturned face. I wished the naked swimmers were still there, if only for their voices, and if I stared without blinking I could see those three nude women dancing like northern lights toward the zenith. All day, off and on, suppressing it whenever the idea rose, I had thought of that evening with Melissa so long ago when she and Michael and I had made our pact to communicate if one of us should die, and if I stood quickly, turning my back on the rising breeze and uneven slap of waves lifting against the rocks, it was because of fear that she might really come to me now. If such a thing was possible, I was not ready. I retreated to my car and drove home, the headlights flowing over the twists of landscape. I was no longer numb or disbelieving. Melissa was dead. That could not be comprehended, but from the deep, wide space she had come to fill in my life her presence was ripped out, and in its place was pain.

That night I insisted they let me take phone calls, but finally there was one I could not handle.

"Who is this?"

"Julie Cobb."

"I'd like to speak to Gardener. Melissa's father."

"He's not taking any calls now. Would you like to leave a message?"

By now I could deliver those words without thinking, and automatically I picked up the pencil. It was eleven o'clock. I wanted the phone to stop ringing, and it had for half an hour. Michael was watching television, and Sheldon was sitting with him in the living room. Clad in his bathrobe and sandals, holding his cane, Sheldon looked like some forbidding prophet in the desert.

The woman paused. She breathed unevenly, and I tensed. Would it be another crank?

"I have to. Isn't he there?"

"Yes, but he's not . . ."

"Who are you, anyway?"

Slowly that question, or a tone of voice that implied it, was beginning to twist into me. Few of the callers were that aggressive, but even some of Michael's or Sheldon's friends seemed to hesitate before proceeding. And who, after all, was I? I had remembered earlier that night the final lines of a Roethke poem, *I with no rights in this matter, neither father nor lover.* Like a child who has found a charm to repeat in the dark against the rattling of a night house, I would say it over to myself, amended—I with no rights in this matter, neither mother nor sister.

"Julie Cobb. Now if you'd like to leave a message . . ."

"I mean is this some kind of phone service? A relative?"

"Perhaps you'd like to tell me who you are?"

Silence. "That's the problem. I really don't want to talk to anyone but Gardener."

"Would you leave a number where he could call you?"

"Look—" The voice choked off, a deep breath. "My name is Mindy Haines. I'm Leroy Haines's sister. I've got to talk to him. We've got to, my mother and me. Talk to someone."

"His sister?"

"Don't hang up. Let me talk to him. We didn't do this, you know. It's not our fault. I never hurt anyone. But everyone's making us feel like we did it. We don't even know her. You can't blame Leroy. It's their fault. We tried to tell them."

"Wait a minute, please."

She was saying something when I pulled the receiver away from my ear and let it dangle on its cord from the wall. I walked slowly to the back of the couch and leaned there between them. Maybe if I took my time, she would go away.

"That one took longer than usual." Sheldon turned his head.

"It's not over," I said.

"Maybe we should leave the receiver off the hook tonight." Sheldon was rubbing the crook of his cane against his neck.

"I mean she's still on the phone. She wants to talk to you, Michael."

"Who?"

"Leroy Haines's sister."

"Jesus." Mike jerked his head back.

Sheldon struck the floor with the end of his cane. "What next?"

"Shall I hang up?"

Michael shook his head. "I'll handle it."

The desperation in me was more than wanting to protect him. Did I want him to rise in fury, fling himself at the phone, deliver a scorching curse? If we bent these ends together, made the parallel rails of Gardener and Haines touch again, wouldn't we only descend into greater confusion? I kept leaning, could hear a pause without footsteps or voice, then the words, "Yes, this is Michael Gardener," before the television returned to its voices. The muscles along Sheldon's jaw were working, his hand gripped the cane so hard his knuckles shone white. I touched his shoulder.

"What the hell," he muttered sideways toward the wall, "what the hell," and I had no response. We stayed that way until Michael returned.

"Bed?" he asked.

"Well?" Sheldon stood and turned, his knees against the couch, cane in hand.

"She'll drop by tomorrow afternoon."

"What? Here?" He flourished his cane, then poked it into the sagging cushions, a swift gesture that startled us into imagining a Mindy Haines there, now.

"Yes."

"For God's sake, son. They're probably all crazy. It's not our business to help them live with what they've done."

"Dad." This time he hammered the word.

The cane whipped against the arm. "Not here, though."

"Careful with that thing. You'll hurt someone."

"Bed?" I asked.

"I don't want to be in this house with her. Not under the same roof."

"Then take a walk with Julie. A drive. Hide in the barn." His voice rose. "For God's sake, what am I supposed to do?"

"Not let the filthy murdering bastards of the world off easy, that's what." His face mottled. All that evening I had sensed rage gathering in him, but he always choked it back. And even as I watched him now, he did it again, swallowing, his jaw working. He lifted his crooked elbow like the stub of a wing. "Bed. I'm sorry. We should stick together."

Michael walked away. After I had flicked off the lights and television, I took Sheldon's arm but he said he wanted to stay down for a while.

"I should keep my mouth shut, but sometimes I feel like all I've got is what I can say. And I don't really even want to use words. I just want to go out on the lawn and yowl. Good night."

I kissed him and went to join Mike.

"You've never really met Fran, have you?"

The room was dark. I lay on my side, curled around him where he sat on the edge of the bed. We were both naked and from time to time the curtains billowed on a breeze, pale streamers of white bearing the dim light from a moon.

"I've seen her."

"Not the same. She can play rough."

I stroked my hand along his back. "So can I." Far inside I was weary, needing long sleep. The problem was not only physical exhaustion. Like entering a state of hypothermia, I was using up my reserves from the inside out and at some point the outer consciousness would flicker because there would be nothing down there left to fuel it.

"She didn't like the idea of the service, of course. Especially cremation. 'I don't care if it was Melissa's idea,' she said to me. 'We don't have to do it her way. It's for us, now. But you always spoiled her.' "

"Sometimes you did."

"Not for me to judge. Fran has her own idea of how to bring up a child. You squeeze character out of her. Well, it doesn't matter anymore." He lay back on the bed. "Tina Bushey called. Wanted me to know the sweet corn is coming in very early."

"She hadn't heard?"

He even laughed briefly. "Oh, no. That was just her way to ease in. She wanted to bring over some dishes of food. Said she knew how we probably didn't feel like eating, how when her boy died she hadn't even wanted to cook. But you have to eat, she said."

"They're kind."

"Very."

But by the tone of his voice I could tell he was thinking.

"Go on."

"Have you thought of it too? How we made that pact together?"

"Yes."

His face turned to me, a white disk. "You know I don't believe in those things. But I promised."

"Yes."

The gauze curtains hissed when they rubbed against the frame in a breeze.

"I don't think I can," he said quietly.

In the next pause, when I knew I should be the one finding something to say, I felt a quiet motion in my breathing, a hitch of expectation as if I would hear something inside myself if I let it sound, but I did not want it to. "I know. I can't either. Partly because I can't bear to think of her that closely. Yet."

Some notes from the piano sounded distantly, muffled by the floors.

"Dad. He started earlier this evening, then quit. Tuning the piano."

We listened for a while. He had begun with "A" again, was working outward through basic intervals, and I could imagine him sitting in the dark room, head turned to one side, elbow on the frame, slipping the wedges between the strings and feeling for the right key before pressing it down.

"Will he be all right, Michael?"

"At times today he's been very angry."

"Should I go down?"

"He's doing what he wants to do."

"Can you sleep now?"

"I can try."

"Have you forgiven me for my tantrum?"

"Sleep."

Miraculously we slipped off. For hours, waking from time to time, I would hear the distant quaver of chords and intervals moving outward, outward in the slowest ripple toward the ultimate shores of treble and bass until he tuned into silence and I heard his doorlatch shut.

The next morning he walked the house like Ahab, the slow approach of his cane and shuffling slippers sending me out into the garden to retreat under the canopy of willow before coming back to take his arm, ask him to sit and talk.

Shortly after Fran arrived she turned to me and said, "I suppose you won't mind if I speak to Michael alone?"

I wanted to tell her that she already was, since she paid no attention to my presence and even now her eyes merely grazed indifferently over the side of my face, as if words tossed vaguely in my direction were landing somewhere at my feet. To answer was first to have to stoop and pick them up.

"Certainly." I left them standing in the shed, Michael saying, "Sit down, sit down."

"I'd rather stand, but could we at least sit outside? This place makes me nervous."

I stalked into the cellar. Nervous? I took momentary pleasure in thinking maybe we had made something in this house, a core of peace, that would be opposed to her kind of magic. But had this Queen of the Night ever been calm? That thin, sharp, but delicately featured face, for all its leanly perfect proportions, might never be completely at ease, as if even in sleep a watchfulness were just beneath the surface. Cats have that vigilant beauty. Her fingers played along the opals of her necklace, and her whole body preserved its own space. I stood by the row of chisels wondering what Fran would be like in a site where the space did not make her nervous. Would she ever submit herself to location, or would she simply incorporate it into her own? I could see how for a man that inclusion could be very attractive. She was beautiful. She obviously flashed a wired intensity of being. When she rejected me like that, I was tempted simply to be angry, but under that washed a slow tug of attraction. What a sleepwalking relief to be accepted, to have the eyes settle, the sharp edge of her body turn aside so that I could walk safely into the field of her persence. Mike's voice carried to me down the open hatchway, but hers rarely did, as if her words licked straight upward, the tips of flames.

A thunderstorm broke itself across the landscape at two, a sudden wave of thickening air, an eclipse swiftly followed by a bright wash of sunshine, steam rising from road and rocks spreading an odor of crushed green. I stood upstairs by a window for a while, not closing it even though wind dashed rain against my thighs. I was beginning to feel trapped. We inhabited a waiting room—waiting for Mindy Haines, waiting for the phone to ring, waiting to climb into the car and journey to the funeral home, but above all waiting for something that seemed impossible to me now, forgetfulness, the ability not to wake or turn away from the window and run flat into the impenetrable wall of loss. Was Melissa's killer incarcerated, or were we? In the immense boredom of grief, time had become so sluggish that I felt I had been wandering from room to vacant room for months.

9

Perhaps a little older than Melissa, Mindy Haines was a stocky woman, and her flesh was not contained comfortably by the blue jeans or the loose work shirt deeply unbottoned. She paused as if daunted by the rise of the ceiling beyond the small projection of balcony.

"I'm Mindy." When her foot slipped off the step down into the main room, she lurched against me and grabbed my arm to keep balance. "Damn."

Most of what pressed against her clothes was muscle.

"Are you all right?"

"Just twisted it." She hobbled to the couch.

"Dangerous," Mike said ruefully as he stepped down.

Her face was doughy with no prominence of features, but the eyes were alert and sometimes she could not hold back flickers of expression. I could not bear that immobility and caught myself exaggerating my own gestures to draw her out.

"Tried to hitch a ride. You'd think with a storm coming on like that they wouldn't leave you standing out in the rain. People who have cars forget what it's like when you don't."

Michael hesitated to sit beside her, so I did, and he eased himself into the chair across the coffee table from us. She kneaded one hand along her boot.

"Hurt that ankle in a motorcycle accident once. I'm always turning it." She shoved her hands against the edge of the couch and leaned on stiff arms with her shoulders hunched. "Thing I really don't understand is, if you have a car, and you have room, why you don't help someone out?" She squinted at the beams overhead. "Bet this was a barn once."

"A shed," Michael said. "Probably for carriages."

"That figures."

I wanted to argue back, "What figures?" The resentment in all her words was abrasive and challenging. The situation was charged enough, but Burlington also had its class differences that I knew well from childhood, and she would be edgy from that. I was becoming self-conscious in an attempt not to judge her but knew she would have been one of those tough girls who played on the basketball team, smoked aggressively in sixth grade, probably dropped out of tenth grade pregnant, came back for a few tries until she reached an age to be free of truant officers, and if she ever had that baby she gave it up fast. All of which would have nothing to do with her intelligence and a great deal to do with belligerence.

"You didn't say who you were." She was looking at me flatly.

"Julie Cobb."

"You're the one I talked to."

"Yes."

"None of my business, but you guys married?"

"No."

I thought she was going to say, "That figures," but for the first time she relaxed and leaned back into the couch after lifting her hip enough to pull out a battered pack of cigarettes. She set an ashtray on her lap and lit her cigarette with cupped hands as if in a gusty wind. She was missing the last joints from two fingers on her left hand.

"You wanted to talk to us." Michael had been watching her without expression, his fingers tented in front of his face.

She blew her first cloud of smoke straight up. "My mom and I are pretty broken up about this. I know. It must be nothing like what you're going through. I'm sorry."

"Thank you."

She frowned at him. "No, I mean I'm sorry about what Leroy did. Sorry about Leroy. Sorry about the whole fucking mess."

She shifted the ashtray into her left hand and tapped the cigarette against the side. Her fingers trembled slightly. "Mom and me, we've known something terrible had to happen. We've lived with it for a long time, and it's kind of ruined things for us for years, but we never figured on this." When she dragged, the gesture was a retreat to a world of her cigarette, lungs, the immediate space of her body. Michael was staring at the floor. I could tell he had discovered he was trapped in a place he did not want to be.

"We only know a little," I said. "I guess your brother wasn't well."

"I'll say. But it got so much worse. We didn't know what to do. I'm three years older. When he was little I just about brought him up. My mom was sick lots then, still is, but in those days we thought she was really sick. Now everyone but her understands she just thinks she's sick. I mean my dad died three years ago and he always looked to be the healthy one, and probably she'll live longer than Leroy and me, be still tiptoeing around the edge of her grave and talking sick by the time we're pushing sod."

She ground the long butt emphatically and set the ashtray on the floor by her feet.

"I don't mean to sound so down on Mom. She never did anything hard to Leroy. If anything, she spoiled him. It was Dad who used to whale the shit out of him. He and Leroy were like that from the start." She lifted her fists and rammed the knuckles together. "What we don't get is why he would hurt someone. I mean, he had temper, but he never used it on people. Leroy never talked much. In school he kept getting kicked out because he *wouldn't* talk, not because he made noise. The teacher would call on him and he'd sit there and stare until the guy would get so mad he'd send him off to the principal's. Most of the time he wouldn't even get to school and then the truant officer would be after us. When Dad was alive, he bruised Leroy up pretty bad for that. Dad said he expected Leroy to do good in school, go on and be better than he was. We didn't know for a few years before he died how he had this tumor in his brain that was fucking up all his emotions. But he'd do things like trying to get Leroy to pray with him and Leroy wouldn't open his mouth, and then he'd get the strap and go at him. Jesus, I don't know." She turned the pack of cigarettes around but only tapped the ends back in place. "I couldn't bear it. I went for Dad once that final year. He'd begun treatments, had his head all shaved and these little target marks on the skin where they pointed their machines. Leroy never fought back. He'd stand there clenched and taking it, but by then Dad wasn't too strong. I came between them and started holding Dad's arms and told Leroy to get out, and Dad broke loose and started flailing me and that was the first time I'd seen Leroy do anything. I mean directly to Dad. He grabbed the belt away and held it by one end and started beating at the windows with the buckle end. Busted every damn pane of glass in the kitchen.''

"Wait." We both jerked our heads to Michael, whose face was pale, lips set. "You wanted to talk to us. But I don't think I want to hear your family miseries. What's all this about?''

"I didn't mean to do that." She paused as if trying to decide what she did mean, and I was surprised at how easily she took Michael's anger. But she had no way to know how unusual it was. "All I'm trying to tell you is Leroy never stood a chance. After that he took to having these fits where he'd break things up. We'd think he was fine and then he'd pick up a chair and start smashing it against the wall. He'd keep it up till there was only splinters and maybe his hands all torn. Especially after Dad died. But never people, always things. He got quieter and quieter. I was about the only one left he talked to much. He started staying away from home, bumming around here and there, but always alone. Folks around town got to know him. They'd joke with him, give him drinks maybe. Some people told me once they were surprised to find he could talk.''

"Melissa never had much of a chance, either.''

"Jesus, mister, don't I know." Her look toward me was almost helpless. But what could I do? I too could not see what she was getting at. She shook her head. "Look. I always thought we stood a chance with Leroy, even though he was pretty crazy. Especially when he started hearing the voice. Dad's voice. Or voices. He took me down to that place he built in the swamp past the tracks. Made it out of old boxes and crates and that's where he mostly lived when he wasn't home or in some hallway. Beginning, I thought maybe he was shacking up for real, I mean with some girl he knew from school or something. But Leroy didn't pay attention to women. I don't mean he was queer, he just didn't get too close. Surprised me. He was good-looking, you know? Wrestler's build, nice face, never had zits or anything.''

Michael stood slowly, and I guess we both expected him to leave, but he walked over to the windows looking toward the willow and field, his back to us.

"He said the voices sounded like all sorts of different people but he knew they were all really Dad. He showed me some of the places they came from. Stumps, an old car engine, a big chunk of cement that had been dumped there. I asked what the voices said, but he wouldn't tell me. 'If I told you, I'd have to pay attention,' he said, 'and I'm not paying attention. They won't get to me.' But once I found him in the bathroom at home, all curled up on the floor with his hands over his ears, and he was staring at the wall. I couldn't get him to move. He didn't know I was there. A few hours later he just got up and walked out."

"Why the hell wasn't he put away?" Michael said to the window, his back straightening.

"That's what I was getting to. Listen, can you understand what it was like for him? It wasn't that the voices were coming out of things anymore. They started coming out around other people's voices, music, sounds. I came home from work once—Mom was downstate visiting relatives—and all the way along the street I could hear this big noise of voices and music."

She focused on me because Michael kept his back turned, his hands clasped and kneading behind him.

"Coming out of our house, the radio. Neighbor started yelling at me, said he'd call the cops if I didn't stop it. Leroy was hunched in the chair all clutched up, staring at the floor. I had to hold my hands over my ears to get to the switch."

She laid her head back, stretched her legs out. She was wearing cowboy boots, battered at the toes, the heels worn lopsidedly.

"He begged me to turn it on again, he was trembling. But I didn't want cops. I'd been in some trouble that year already. So I grabbed some scissors and cut the cord."

She stared at her toes as if sighting along her legs at a target.

"Here's the point: That was the only way he could blow back the voices. If someone talked to him, he'd get tricked into listening, and then suddenly, while their mouths were moving, there'd be another voice, a sort of voice-over, using their mouths to say something, or he'd turn on the radio and the DJ would be selling cars and this other voice would say, 'Leroy. Now listen to me. These are your instructions.' It was getting so there wasn't any such thing as silence, or sleep."

"You haven't answered my question. Why didn't you get him some help? At least put him away?"

She turned a dismayed face to Michael's back. "Turn in your own brother? Do you know what they do to people like Leroy at

Waterbury? How they treat loonies there? Leroy needed help, but he's my brother. Would you turn in your own brother to the cops?''

I answered for Michael. ''Doctors aren't cops, Mindy. And I don't think what you're saying about Waterbury is true.''

She gave a harsh laugh. ''You kidding? You know what they do in Russia? Change your head all around if they don't like you or think you're bad. That's the way it is here, too. I've had friends be sent up there. Guys who got into drugs, also someone they sent over to inspect before putting him up for trial. He's been in rotten jails but he said he'd rather be off in maximum somewhere and get him a smart-ass lawyer than get stuffed in the bin where they run prods into your brain and stuff. Friend of his had his balls cut off there.''

''Like hell.'' Michael swiveled.

She half-smiled, flicked a hand. ''Well, he could tell some pretty rotten ones, and I never wanted to investigate. But you get the idea.''

''I'm beginning to.'' He perched against the windowsill. The light from sky and field behind him blurred his face and figure.

''Look. My kid brother never hurt a person. You know? He'd blow up like I said, but I never seen him hit anyone, even say anything mean to another person. He was sick but not crazy or criminal. I tried like hell to get help for him.'' Now she looked at both of us with wide eyes. She had made her big point, I think. ''That afternoon, right then, I went over and I took Leroy's face in my hands and then I held his head close up against me and I made a promise to him, I told him that I'd get people to work with him who could make the voices go away. Problem was he was too scared of those places to go with me, and I'd have to tell them about it on my own. I went to all the places we could. They wouldn't do a goddamn thing. First off, they said they had too many cases, then they'd ask me, 'Well, what has he done?' and I'd say, 'That's not the point, it's what's being done to him, what's going on in his head you've got to help him with,' and they'd all say, 'Well, we can't get treatment for him unless he's done something, shown how he's hurt. If he won't come in himself, 'specially.' We got him to go once but never again.''

''But you and your mother could have committed him.''

She glared at Mike, then shook her head and lit another cigarette. ''Mister, you really don't get it. Listen. What I'm trying to help you understand because it's helped Mom and me too is that this wasn't anybody's fault. It sure as hell wasn't Leroy's. I mean, we tried everything we could." Now her voice broke out of its sullenness into emotion I could smell—the rank, acrid taint of bitterness. "I mean what the hell kind of world is it when you try to get help, when you turn to the city you live in and warn them, and they won't listen? If it's anybody's fault, it's theirs."

She stood and walked to the opposite end of the long window from Michael, her back to us, and she jammed her hands in the pockets over her broad, hard butt. Her knees locked back with a jerk. "That was my fucking brother. They could have helped him, and now it's too late. Christ, I'll get over it. But you ought to see Mom. She's wrecked. Too old to come off this one. She'll never be the same."

When Michael lifted his face, staring at me with no anger left, only a deeply helpless look, I knew I had to get her away, soon. But he was not going to be silenced.

"We accused you of nothing," he said slowly. "Your brother killed my daughter. I'm sure he was sick. That goes without saying about anyone who kills. In a way, I don't care anymore how or why. But he did do it, and that is his fault."

Her head shook slowly. "Here's the way I can't help seeing it. That friend I told you about, the one who was put away after they tried him out at Waterbury? He was up for murder because he killed an old lady, his landlady. She was a mean biddy. Everybody said so, and lots of people came to the trial to tell how mean she was. She'd get on your case if you didn't pay the rent, then she'd start doing things like locking you out, or taking your furniture, or beating on your pipes in the middle of the night. Well, one day she came to his door and started nagging at him. He was real hung over. He told her to fuck off. Closed the door. She kept at it. He tried to leave, went out, and she followed him onto the street. He wanted to drive away, got in his car, and goddamn if the battery wasn't dead. She hung on to his window and kept cackling at him, calling him all sorts of bad things, bad-mouthing his mother too 'cause she'd known her. He kept telling her to back off. Well, finally he blew. He had a wrench, was working under the hood trying to loosen the battery cable, and he lost control, that's all, started beating her with the wrench. Killed her."

She whirled. The flesh around her wildly blinking eyes was tensed into wrinkles. She was jabbing her finger at both of us.

"Now, who the hell's fault was that? She asked for it. If she hadn't kept at him like that, he wouldn't have had to kill her. I tell you this: If it was Leroy's fault, it was everyone's fault, too. They're to blame for letting him go on suffering like that. He had to blow, but it wasn't any more his fault that yours or mine or your daughter's, so don't you go saying we're to blame."

"Who do you think you are?" Sheldon was on the balcony. He lifted his cane and smacked it down across the railing.

"Who the fuck is he?" She leaned forward to see him more clearly.

"I'm Melissa's grandfather, and who do you think you are coming here to dump all that kind of sewerage? Don't you think we've got enough misery without someone trying to tell us Melissa's to blame for being killed by some madman?"

She kept her face forward, but the straining look settled into a sulk. "I didn't say that. I don't know how long you've been there, mister, and I can't help it if you don't see it my way, but you don't hear good."

"I don't see anything, but I hear better than most, and what I hear is that you can't face the fact there was plenty you could do, you and your mother, but you didn't do it because you've come to think it's everybody else's business to do what you ought to do. I can hear you don't know right from wrong, can't, because where you stand there is nothing but the muck of wrongs you think the world has done you, and you can't see out of the swamp."

She swung partway to Michael. "I don't have to take that kind of crap from him or anyone. Tell him to lay off."

Michael looked wearily toward his father. "It's all right, Dad. She's going now."

"Frigging right I'm going."

"It's one of the first times I've ever been glad I'm blind. I don't want to see you, and if I could, I'd probably be up for murder myself now."

She turned to me, and her eyes had a drugged look. "Show me how to get out."

"I'm yelling for Melissa," he continued. "For Melissa. Do you hear her name?"

I walked toward the balcony, the door beneath it, and she followed. Over us Sheldon began to thwack his cane down on the banister.

"Melissa, Melissa, Melissa," he chanted to the beat of the cane, and all the way through the kitchen, the dining room, dimly into the hallway, his voice pursued us. As I pulled the door open and stepped out on the front porch, it stopped abruptly, and I knew Michael had reached him. They would turn together to his room, probably not speaking, not needing to.

"Is he nuts?" She still looked drained, was staring out into the road.

"No. full of sorrow."

Her hand had reached out to grip my arm before I could draw back.

"Listen. I know you understood what I was trying to say, didn't you? I kept watching your face. And she wasn't your kid, like them, so maybe it's easier for you. Someone's got to understand. Leroy was my brother. It's like he's dead now too, don't you see? We lost Leroy, probably forever. I mean if he wasn't crazy, he is now. But he never had a chance. He wanted help but didn't even know. I can't say it all, but when he killed her, he was trying to kill himself. I always thought that would be what would happen, that he'd kill himself, not someone else."

She drew back, perhaps sensing my own arm recovering its ability to pull away. Maybe what she was saying was right, but I did not want to hear it, to think about it anymore. She had become more and more repugnant to me.

"Please go," I muttered, and then I heard the phone ringing.

Her eyes were wide with eagerness. "Come with me. Sometime soon. Let me show you the place he lived last year. The places he showed me. You'd understand then. He was my brother. I loved Leroy. I about brought him up like he was my own kid."

"No." The ringing was urgent, unanswered. Neither Michael nor Sheldon would pick it up. "I have to answer the phone."

I turned, glimpsed her only briefly as I slammed the door, her body still leaning toward the place I had stood.

I lifted the receiver too late. Only a steady buzz. I watched Mindy standing by the road. She raised her arm, a car sped by, then she turned and strolled a few steps toward Shelburne. I ran through the hallway, out the door. Ed Bushey's pickup shuddered and slowed. Mindy stepped up into the cab. I was running across the lawn. The door closed. I called once, "Mindy!" then was ahead of them as Ed ground into gear. The pale ovals of their wide-eyed faces, the front of the truck jerked to a stop. Mindy's hand flattened to catch herself on the windshield.

"I about run you over, Julie."

I stood by his window and looked past him to her craning face. "Tomorrow. Where do you live?"

She told me. "When?"

"Ten o'clock."

"This a friend of yours? I didn't know. Figured she was from up to the Streeters. How you folks doing?"

"Fine, thanks. Thank Tina for calling."

"Watch it." He pulled me tight to the door. A car swung out and around us with a bleat.

"Tomorrow!" she yelled as I went across the road to stand by the barn.

Ed started the stalled engine, let out the clutch, looking both ways as if anything might jump out, and all the way down the road her white face hung in the back window, staring at me.

I had to sit down in the hallway. My head was giddy, the room floating. Either I or the rest of the world had become weightless. I closed my eyes. Mindy, Ed, a truck tottering down a darkening road, twisting in slow circles into a black drain. I opened my eyes to the floor patched with afternoon sun, the heavy compression of July heat on a watery air. I wanted Michael so badly that I could feel a ghostly arm extending from my shoulder, its hand touching his imagined body sitting beside me. His arm curved to my waist, drawing me to him. But he was not there, and my palms were wedged together between my knees.

Father and son were on some other planet in the room upstairs. Even if I walked to them, I would not be there, because I could not tell Michael about what I would be doing tomorrow. That had been clear to me as I ran across the lawn, and the voice that finally called her name made its own decision, cutting down like an ax on the rope that bound us all together. "Wait! Wait! Think!" some other voice had been wailing to me as their two faces floated in the screen of glass, but I had no time. I had a lifetime to think about not doing it but only moments to act. I tried now to push it all away. I would think later, think later. But even as I stood, steadied myself on the arm of the bench, and trudged step by step to the kitchen, I knew there were too many reasons why I would not tell Michael until later but the primary one was that somehow it was none of his business, this was something as private to my own life as a nightmare.

The Haines's house in the north end was on a side street, squeezed between two larger boxes with a strip of scuffed soil on each side. The siding had begun to peel back on the second floor, and a motorcycle without one wheel tilted forward, stabbed into the earth. Across the street a large gray dog began to bark and tried to leap off its porch, but the rattle of a chain pursued it and choked off the yelp each time it lunged. The door opened before I had negotiated the gaps in the porch where boards had rotted through. Mindy was dressed as she had been the day before, only her face was puffier. The sleepy look made her flesh even more immobile.

"I didn't think you'd really come." Her eyes moved up and down the street behind me. "Come in. Buggers don't know how to mind their business around here."

I glanced back but saw nothing.

"Oh, you can bet a bunch of the dimwits are staring out their windows at us. Most of them never gave us the time of day, and now all they can do is sit on their porches or walk up and down the street staring at us like we're an animal act."

She slammed the door. All the shades were drawn, and in the dim, stuffy room I could barely see lumps of furniture, lamps, shelves of bric-a-brac, a bicycle propped against the radiator.

"This is my mother."

Someone stood up from a chair, and as my eyes adjusted, I made out the splotched print of her dress, her long and very shining arms and legs as pale and shapeless as wooden spokes. She walked toward me slowly as if the floor were uneven flagstone, and as she neared I could see how her ankles swelled out over the tops of her black shoes.

"I don't move as fast. Arthritis." Her hand came out, and it too was crippled in its joints.

I touched it gingerly, and she managed a slanted squeeze.

"Mindy said you was the only one who understood. It's been something terrible."

Her perfectly round face craned at me, but I could not make out any features except her eyes because heavy, thick lenses magnified the pupils enormously.

"It has been for all of us."

Her eyes, the dimly crowded room pressed on me. "My boy was always gentle and good and promised to look after me. His father was mean. He about drove us all crazy. Look at me," and she flapped both arms a few times straight up from her sides, sticks that were the remnants of plucked wings. "I'm older than I should be, my joints are gone, and all my days are pain because of the worry and misery he put me through for years." She held up a twisted finger. "Mindy knows." The thin lips twitched upward in a brief smile. "But I stayed with him through thick and thin. I took the burden of holy matrimony on me and when he was wild and crazy I held firm and when he was sick and dying I nursed him. Now they've taken my boy. Was she a relative of yours?"

"A friend."

"Not blood?"

"No."

She sighed as if I had confirmed her position, turned, and began her shuffle back to the chair. "Don't mind me. I can't bear weight for long." At the chair she took three little steps to turn in place, started to lower herself, then plummeted the rest of the way. "You don't really know. It hurts more when it's blood. I believe in family, I believe in holding together and doing by your blood. It's all we've got left in a world full of crooked politicians. I'm bleeding inside for Leroy day and night. I'm lonely for him sitting in a cell somewhere with them voices in his head and the awful thing he done to your friend. Looks like she was a pretty girl."

The muscles in my sides, my thighs and shoulders, began to contract, my lungs narrow as if weights were pressing in on me from every side. I tried to answer but could only shift my glance helplessly to Mindy.

"We're going out now for a while, Mother." She yanked open the door.

Her voice rose plaintively. "But we've not had a chance to talk, Mindy, and I wanted so much to show her some of Leroy's things, to tell her about my boy. The photo albums."

"We'll be back, Mom."

I thought she was going to get up but she was only leaning forward as if to leap, two hands on the armrests, and bent elbows rising like grasshopper legs. The voice had turned suspicious. "Where are you going? Are you going to see Leroy without me? You said we'd go together when they'd let us visit."

"Just for a drive."

She leaned back. "Oh. That's real nice of your friend. You own a car?" But the tone was aggrieved, as if she should have been invited.

I did not want Mindy to follow, but as I walked over the holes and onto the lawn, breathing deeply, startled again by the rattle of chain and snarl across the street, the door slammed and footsteps crossed the porch behind me. Mindy came around the other side of the car and tried the handle. The door was locked. I could start, drive away. She was peering at me, pulling the handle impatiently. I unlocked it.

We paused at the end of the road because I did not know where we were going. She was hunched down, her heels on the seat and knees drawn up.

"Yesterday I thought I knew what I wanted you to see. But that was yesterday. Today I feel like what's the use?"

"We could forget about it."

She jerked her face to me. "You want to see Leroy?"

I shook my head.

"That figures. I should've sprung that on you later. I got to go see him today."

"I thought your mother wanted to."

"She wants, but not yet. I know Leroy. She's part of the problem. Maybe I am, too, but not as much. Look, the main thing is I don't want to sit in there with her anymore today. All right? Let's go." She lowered her feet and sat up straight.

"Where?"

"Park at Perkins Pier. You know where that is?"

I smiled. "I think so."

"What's so funny? Lots of people who moved to Vermont don't know which way the sun sets."

"I was born here."

"You? In Burlington? How come you talk like you're from somewhere else?"

"Where?"

"I don't know. Anywhere, I guess."

True. People like me kept no birthright in their accents. Our tongues had been transubstantiated into the wide, flat bubble of Standard American.

"I'm sorry about Mom. I mean how she lays it on so thick about Leroy being the good boy. She sees what she wants to see, mostly. He is gentle, but he's always been in one kind of trouble or another. Far as Mom was concerned, it was always other kids who put him up to it."

We drove in silence for a while along North Avenue. I glanced at her from time to time and knew that even though she was staring straight ahead, her lips pursed, she was watching me out of the corners of her eyes.

"How did you hurt your hand?"

The fingers curled under slightly and she frowned. "Accident."

In Battery Park a group of tourists were strung along the parapet with their cameras, a chartered bus waiting in the lot.

"Only thing about leaving Mom alone like that is, I don't like the idea of her having to take the calls. Except most of the mean ones are at night."

"What calls?"

"They never give their names. Some of them are dirty, but most are angry. Guys who want to bad-mouth us, say Leroy ought to be taken out and beat to death, say the rest of us should be put in cages or hung up or treated like mad dogs."

"We get some of those, too. The dirty ones."

"Doesn't surprise me. I mean, that's the way people are, isn't it? They like to do their stomping on you when you're down."

We drove in silence, but I found it eerie to think how much we were sharing that week. At Perkins Pier the waves were choppy and flashing, lifted by a wind that gusted but never ceased. I waited for her to move, but she was staring toward New York State, that green and uneven haze of land beyond the water.

"They took me out to Williston, this one girl whose boyfriend I'd messed around with, and four friends in her brother's car. They grabbed me after school on a Friday and one of them had a knife so I couldn't do anything. I was pissed and didn't care anyway. I sort of wanted to get them somewhere and see what I could do if they'd put away the knife. They acted tough, but a couple of them were woosies. Judy Carter, she's the one was in charge because of her boyfriend, Jerry. She was tough, but I knew I had a chance with her one-on-one. Halfway there I told her I didn't give a damn about Jerry anyway. He was nothing so great. I told her he was the kind that comes in his pants before he can even whip it out, but that made her more pissed because then she thought we'd gone all the way. We hadn't. He'd took me out on one date and tried to feel me up and I'd made him take me home. I mean where did he get off thinking he could pull that stuff on the first date? Besides, he was zitty."

She pulled at the cellophane and held a new pack of cigarettes out to me, but I refused. She pushed in the dashboard lighter.

"Doesn't work," I said, and she found her matches.

"They never do, except in new cars." She inhaled deeply. "Anyway, they drove back up in a field and we got out. I gave it a good try, but there was too many and they wore me out. I give them credit, though. They put away the knife, said they'd let me go if I could hold them off. She was a mean pussy, that one. They did it with the car." She paused, eyes squinting against a backdraft of smoke. "They took my hand and put it on the doorframe and then she slammed it hard as she could and kicked when it didn't close all the way. Nothing's ever hurt that bad. Broke up the joints on two fingers, skinned them to the bones. They dropped me off at the emergency room. Had to have those joints cut off. At least that's what they said. I've read since about people having fingers stuck back on, but I guess those were clean cuts."

I had to look out the side window, past the two or three parked cars. "Did they get caught?"

She snorted. "Caught? What do you think this is? Cops and robbers? I said it was an accident. Said a big stone had fallen over on my hand where I was working. What did they care at the hospital?"

I turned quickly to catch her eyes and did. "Are you telling me the truth?"

She stared, then smiled that furtive grin, the child in the back of the room who would have put a hand across her mouth if she had time.

"Maybe."

"How can I tell?"

"Why should I lie about this?"

She held up the hand between us, and her eyes were sighting me through the gap where joints had been. I would not turn away, she stared for awhile, then lowered her hand slowly, and as with a staring cat, I was never quite certain when her gaze turned away.

"Let's walk." She opened the door.

We strolled to the railroad crossing and along the tracks. For a while I followed behind her. She was too short to take the ties in a comfortable stride but stretched for each one in a determined gait, arms swinging stiffly. I took my chances with the uneven crushed rock. We passed gaping doors of splintered boxcars, the sour mash of spilled feed, passed backs of old brick warehouses, some still in use in spite of smashed windows and charred doorframes. As we moved farther away from the pier and into that area of swamp and field and dumps along the lake between Maple Street and Lakeside, my uneasiness increased. The tracks were clear ahead and back to the old station and depot, and the boxcars were empty.

That whole area reeked of neglect, the backside of a city that has surrendered to the automobile so that water and rail are only choked and nearly unfunctioning arteries. Even in my childhood the place had been derelict and cut off. On fall evenings when the wind blew over the lake, the whine and thump of shuttling boxcars or occasional hoot of a diesel would carry in a rush up the hill. There were places in my childhood that we were warned never to go—warned by parents, by teachers, by letters in the newspaper. Bums inhabited the caves of boxcars. They lurked over small fires of driftwood by the sandy fringe of beach. Ragged and devouring, they rushed out to seize young girls, drag them into the ooze, rape them, bury them in muck, wiping their slavering mouths with the backs of their hands as they loped off toward the jostling line of tank cars headed south. Or young boys had been crushed by the sudden motion of a caboose, the last domino in a jerk started half a mile away. We never knew the victims. How could we? They were dead or mutilated or kidnapped, but someone always knew someone who knew someone who did. No matter. Those legless boys, the wide-eyed girls who lay under fallen cattails, mouths gagged with mud, inhabited our dreams, especially on the nights after we had ventured along the tracks, taking the short-cut to sneak downtown to the movies.

"Where are we going?" I drew alongside her swinging strides.

"You know this area?"

"Yes."

The warehouses ended and soon there was a strip of scruffy woods, the water of swampland glinting here and there. The lake was close to the right, slapping at sand, and in places the gnarled roots of drowned trees lumped out of water and muck. She stopped, breathing quickly, hands in her back pockets.

"This was Leroy's real home. All around this place. He loved it. Ever since we were kids he'd come here to hide, or just be by himself. I could always find him here, 'specially after the old man took it out on him. He said it was his, hated it when people walked through for a shortcut, and if he found someone who'd gotten off a boxcar and camped, he'd come down to the fire and sit and not talk till they got so nervous they'd go or start throwing rocks at him. The guys on the engines got to know him. They'd wave, call to him out the windows. He liked to watch the birds. Big ones off in the swamp, herons and ducks. And he had a pet raccoon, or at least it was so used to him that it would come up when he was eating and he'd give it the can to lick."

She stepped off the ties and we walked more slowly.

"Look. You promise."

"What?"

"I'm going to show you his shack and I don't want you to tell them. They know he lived somewhere along the lake but they never found it. I don't want them taking pictures and all that. He's got a right to some secrets."

She accepted my nod as sufficient and now we were walking down a small bank, across a muddy gap, then up and into the spit of woods. The undergrowth was thick, vines and pricker bushes growing in the cindered soil between poplars and bony spruce. She knew her way along vague paths skirting pools of brackish water. Away from the lake breeze, the air was hot and thick with the taint of rot, sewage, acrid chemicals, and tars. A deep tongue of water with tall cattails made us swerve in a wide switchback, then we pushed through the low branches of a clump of white pine on higher ground and I almost walked into her when she stopped abruptly at the edge of a small clearing.

"There."

At first I saw nothing but tree trunks, scuffed earth, a heap of discarded trash. Then the stacked boxes and crates covered with rusted sheet metal shaped themselves into a shack. She stood ahead of me, only her front foot into the clearing, as if the place preserved some magic she did not want to violate and it might vanish if we stepped inside the circle. She pushed past the last branches, they swung against me, long needles pricking my bare arms, and I followed her. The place was quiet and remote, partly an effect of smooth gray trunks, branches thickly puffed with clusters of needles, a pine grove stretching tall and interwoven in its untended competition for sun. She kneeled by the opening to the shack.

"You wouldn't think looking at it, but it's dry in there even when it rains hard. He'd drag away wood or metal he'd find back by the tracks and keep pieces hidden here or there for when he needed them."

A small ring of charred stones and earth was near my feet. For a moment I was lifted out of any context, did not see the place as belonging to Melissa's killer but felt only what I would have if I had been a child exploring forbidden land on some Saturday afternoon, had wandered away from my brother's hand or the voices of playmates to stumble into the grove and see a place I and my friends would have coveted, shelter from the world of parents and schools and chores nearly as perfect as owning that ring we dreamed of that could make us invisible if we slipped it over the proper finger.

She leaned at the dark opening. "In the last months when the voices followed him even here, he kind of lost touch with everything. Look in."

I put my hand on the ground beyond the opening and eased my head and shoulders in. I saw nothing at first. The air was thick but cool, as if some dampness far under the ground constantly seeped upward, and I could smell the presence of someone else, not rank but like opening a person's closet and smelling the essential odor of his flesh as particular as a fingerprint. Was it from the heaped blanket, or the small square of canvas stretched along one wall, or that torn wool jacket hanging on a nail? Or had he spent so much time there for years that even the earth had absorbed his scent? I tried not to breathe. But I had to, and breathing deliberately, my eyes staring at an old baseball cap that topped a small wooden box, I incorporated him in my cells beyond what the mind could ever accomplish with its fumbling imagination. I was dizzy, felt tricked.

"It was horrible for him when he found the voices here too. They'd always left him alone here. He told me again and again that once he stepped into this place and crawled into his shack, nothing could get to him. And then one day he had a bad time with Mom. They'd started pushing each other because she'd got on his case about lying over some money. They'd never argued like that—I mean physically. Dad, he couldn't stand lying, always beat the shit out of us both if he caught us. Leroy ran off for a few days, and when I saw him next, walking on St. Paul Street, he looked sick. Hadn't slept for three nights. That's when he told me how they wouldn't leave him alone even here.''

Her hand pushed on the small of my back. "Go in. I'll come too. Let me show you."

But my whole body went tight. Her pressure put me enough off balance so that I had to totter forward on my hands, but then I backed out and sat up again in light. I was sweating heavily. I wiped at my face.

"That's enough."

She shrugged. "You don't believe me, I guess."

"Believe what?"

"Listen, all this is true what I'm telling you about Leroy."

"I didn't say it wasn't."

"Shit. What's the use?" She stood. "You don't care. You're just spying on us."

She had started to walk away and I stood up to follow when she whirled and pointed that maimed hand at me.

"You tell any of this to anyone or show this place and I'll show you a thing or two."

I was not intimidated but remembered her own words in the car and gave them back. "Why should you lie about this?"

Her hand came down, she shook her head. "I don't even know anymore why I wanted to show it to you. Maybe I thought you'd understand. But you can't. Nobody can but me and Leroy."

"And Melissa." When I spoke her name in that place, anger tightened my throat beyond the possibility of speaking further.

But Mindy only looked at me as if I were crazed, and turned to brush through the limbs. I stood alone, the voice in my mind sounding her name in a chorus of my tones, Sheldon's, even Mike's—Melissa, Melissa, Melissa—and then I put my arms up to shield my face and stepped through. I never went back to that place again or heard anyone mention it, so that years later when some fragment of it rose as setting for a dream, I could hardly persuade myself to believe it was real.

Mindy flounced onto her seat in the car as if she had been dropped from a great height. "You can take me to the correctional center."

At the first stoplight I turned on the radio for music, voices, anything, even though I hated the idiot jabber of disc jockeys. She did not attempt to speak anyway, and when I had to glance toward her to check the traffic, she was always twisted to her window, hands jammed between her thighs.

In the parking lot I settled for a monotone of politeness. "Thank you for showing me."

But her hand flew up, palm toward me as if she were protecting herself from a thrown object, her face still turned.

"Listen." Her voice was so low I had to turn off the radio. "He beat us all the time. First only me, then both of us, then mostly Leroy. 'Tell the truth,' he kept saying, 'tell the truth,' and Leroy never saw it, but I did from the beginning, because in the beginning I told the truth, I told him everything, I'd do anything to please him, and even when I didn't know what he was beating me for I'd tell him everything I'd thought or done, and nothing was what he wanted, they were all lies to him. So after a while I learned to make up the lies and sometimes he'd hear what he wanted to hear and then he'd quit. But Leroy always thought he had the truth to tell Dad but didn't know how to say it." She swung her body toward me, her hand on the seat between us and those pale eyes were full. "Don't you know how awful that is? Why did we love him so much? Why did we both want so much to get it said? We should've hated him from the beginning and then it would've been easy and Leroy wouldn't have had to run off into a swamp, and I wouldn't still be lying my ass off every time I open my fucking mouth."

She sat back and started to fold her arms and then breathed deeply and brushed a hand back through her hair.

"I guess I'll go see brother Leroy." She looked at me again. "You want to come?"

I shook my head.

"Figures."

"No, Mindy. It doesn't. It's all too much. You're forgetting you're not the only one who's going through something."

She shrugged, again her face doughy, numbed. "Suit yourself. I guess you're sad, too, but after all, she wasn't your kid or sister or anything very important. It's not the same for you as it is for the rest of us."

"I with no rights in this matter."

She looked at me with a frown. "Come again?"

"Nothing. Just something from a poem."

"Jesus. What next?" She pulled the handle and swung out. She looked as if she might walk away, but instead she slammed the door, spun around, and thrust her head in. "Thanks for nothing." But her voice spoke in the gentlest tones I had heard her use, and she paused so long to stare with her mouth slightly open that I thought she would say more.

"Good-bye, Mindy."

I watched her stride off, up the curb and over the sidewalk to the front steps, ankles bowing slightly in her cowboy boots, her hips and shoulders held to a minimum of motion. She was bracing for a punch, but it was hard to tell if she was preparing to throw her own or block one coming at her.

10

Tim strides ahead of me and I am not fast enough to reach his side before he has clambered up the path to the tracks. I stop. He stands with one foot on the ties. The fall sun diffused by a cloudy sky is bright enough to silhouette his lean figure, but his features are blurred.

"Come on, Julie, we'll be late."

"We're not supposed to."

"You're not. But I'm old enough."

What I do not dare to tell him is that the fear is not of my parents or anything they can do to us. Their punishments are mild—dessert denied, an hour in a quiet bedroom spent in contemplation of one's evil. Anything they can inflict is comforting and known compared to the unnamed mutilations I will suffer at the hands of those tattered, skull-faced brutes hiding in swamps, their stench worse than our garbagemen, grappling me to them with harsh hands they keep in their pockets when they wander the city in disguise.

"You want to see the movie or not?"

"No fair. You have the money. I want mine."

"Make up your mind. I'm counting to ten."

His voice begins slowly. I think myself home past the empty factory of barred windows, past the park where some boys in helmets are battering themselves around a field in pursuit of a football, to home on a gray day, a house that my parents have abandoned to visit friends and help pick their apples. By *eight* I am starting my scramble up the path, slip once, scraping my hand on the stony soil, and by *ten* he has turned to walk toward town. I pause to sight along the rails cutting through all that danger they cannot hold back. I have to move my legs twice as fast, but I stay beside him, concentrating on putting my feet squarely on each tie, beginning the monotonous counting toward a number I will not remember but will recall in dreams as infinity, the tense rhythm that measures out my terror.

He is not speaking. Even now I think of my brother as mostly silent, and I make up the sound of his voice. Gestures of his body express him most of all—those long feet in battered Keds toeing in, a spring-footed walk that in our house looks too rangy, bony arms that might fling into tables or chairs and knock them over. But outside, that same stride is light and lithe, capable of carrying him perfectly to the resting point of some ball's trajectory.

I try not to see his feet, which can confuse my own count with their steps. The woods and lake pull closer at each side, and soon the battered freight cars will fill the second line. He is imprudent enough to let his hand swing close, and I have it in mine. Usually he avoids touch, or uses it in brusque gestures—a sudden ruffling of my hair that is meant to be reward for something funny or well done but that yanks the roots when his fingers snag, or a nudge with an elbow in my side when he wants to underline for me some moment of parental idiocy, leaving me breathless as I try to grin happily through my braces. This time he even speaks.

"See? No boogeymen. You shouldn't let people scare you like that."

"I'm not scared anyway," I can say now more truthfully because of the steady pressure of his hand.

The wail of the ferryboat leaving the dock, carried to us by almost imperceptible motions of a northern airflow, seems very close. The boxcars are on either side of us. He stops. I clutch his hand with both of mine. Grunting. Heavy blows from an open door. The figure of a man is hunched over his heels, back to us. He is lifting a hatchet. His arm rises slowly, then jerks downward, clenching his body toward the thing he strikes. He is wearing an overcoat ripped almost to his shoulders, a tattered khaki shirt beneath it, and the back of his head is unevenly patched with tufts of hair.

I want to run, but it is too late. The hand rises, then does not fall. The head jerks around to stare at us over one shoulder. His eyes are round, a nose flattened and shapeless. I close my eyes like a shutter so that what I remember with absolute clarity is the statuette of the man. In retrospect I am sure I can say he was as startled as we were, and he froze with that stare because we could have been anyone—rail guards, other bums, manifestations of his own fears swooping down on him. But he is in my mind forever bunched in fury before the downward stroke, his brute face watching me. It does not matter that the arm cannot reach me or that the hatchet falls with a clatter on boards he is splintering for a fire. His face is looking at me, and the stroke will be directed at everything I love.

The wood leaps under the blow, clatters, but he has not turned away to look at the target. Instead he stands, faces us with the hatchet hanging from his hand. The lower part of his face is twisted to one side as if his jaw shifted and never sprang back. He is saying something we cannot hear. The sleeves of his coat are too long, arms ending in cuffs, and only the hatchet's head on one side. When Tim begins to walk he almost drags me, my legs are so stiff with fear. The man raises an empty sleeve to wipe across his face. He is grinning now.

"Hey, girlie, c'mon back. C'mon back and play, girlie."

Tim yells at him, "Go to hell, you bum!"

The man is laughing. His sprung jaw hangs awry, his hatchet hand waves heavily in wide arcs, and the empty cuff makes loops to gather me in. "Hey, girlie, girlie!" he screams like circling gull. I look away toward the depot, certain he has risen on the flapping borders of his tattered coat. He will dive on us with a swoop as swift and vicious as his downstroking arm and cut our hands apart. I am running against a huge current because I will not let go of Tim with either of my hands and he will not run, so my legs churn uselessly and all I have done is lengthen his strides while he mutters, "Julie, quit that."

Finally, near Perkins Pier he jerks me to a stop. I dare to look back then. All I see is rails splitting two lines of freight cars, pointing back farther and farther. No figure. I search the sky. Only a few gulls, a clattering wheel of flapping pigeons from the warehouse. He stoops. His face is at my height. He is usually angry when I am too childish, but he slips his hand free of mine and instead of going away forever, which is the interval the lack of his gestures could make me feel, wider than memory but not longing, he lifts that hand to put it on my cheek.

"Hey, sis, he was only an old bum. No spook. Do you understand? That doesn't mean he won't hurt you, and that's why Mom and Dad don't want you there alone, but he's only a mean old man."

Every instinct in me calls for tears, but I hold back, press down and down. I know that if I cry, that hand, those eyes will turn away in disappointment. I make a smile.

"Hey, there you go. Now, step on it, or we'll miss the cartoons."

In the theater he sees my scraped hand, takes me to the water fountain to wash and wrap it with his handkerchief. "One thing more," he says as we hunch low in our seats, safe in the vast hubbub of excited kids and music and bursts of expectation whenever the curtain stirs. "That trip is our little secret. It would just get them upset, and nothing happened, really, so why worry them?"

"Yes," I swear, and only vaguely seeing Buck Rogers clinging to the mouth of a pit, one arm around the roots at its rim, the other around the waist of his dangling love, I say to myself, "Yes, yes, yes," because Tim and I are at last conspirators, clinging together on the edge of the same long drop.

And years from that afternoon, I stood in a shower of tepid water, my mind thrust back to those rails and boxcars by my visit with Mindy. Michael and Sheldon had gone to the funeral home to check on arrangements for tomorrow's service. I tilted my head back, letting the water soak and pull at my hair, held my breath against its rush, the warm slick down my neck and breasts and belly, and I could think only of Michael's naked body over mine, his breath on my closed eyes, that first moment of any night when he entered me, as intense as if it had never happened before, wanted by me as strongly as if it might never happen again. I stood away spluttering, wiping my hair back.

If thinking of my brother was a way not to think of Mindy, what would I think of to replace him? Because nothing more seemed to have come out of my wandering with Mindy than memories or imaginings I did not want, and I sensed that there might be even more to follow if my mind was left to drift. My brother and I had corresponded briefly a few years after my uncle had sent me the address. It took me that long to write, not because I had forgotten but because I could not think of what to say, then how to say what I had decided to say. My drafts would sound stiff, or cute and flippant, or as serious as a deathbed confession, but most were as devoid of emotion as a form letter. What I finally sent drew a response from him a month later, a page probably as reworked as mine had been because it was typed without errors, double-spaced, and friendly but impersonal. Yes, it was a relief to know I was alive and well also. He too had often wondered about me and hoped for the best. He wanted to reassure me that he had no regrets about his earlier life, the past was past, and his life was now very fortunate and unexceptional. Of course, time heals. And he hoped I would have the opportunity to visit Colorado someday when he could show me lovely places (in fact, they often reminded him of Vermont) and introduce me to his family. It was signed, "Affectionately, Randy Cobb."

At first I had been furious, had to retrieve the balled-up letter from the trashbasket, smoothing it out on the desktop, reading again to see if I had missed some subtle tone. How could he be so indifferent? Didn't we owe it to each other not to let the past be past? I thought of that most aggressive weapon, the telephone. I would call him, make his voice go farther, catch him in that no-man's-land where revisions were not possible and unexpected tones or questions would have to draw out his life and mine. I was no longer his little sister, damn it, and he should not be allowed to run away again.

I went as far as talking with Directory Assistance, copying down a number in Denver. I never dialed it. Again, imaginings closer to reality paralyzed my impulse. He answers, I hear a voice as unfamiliar as all those years and the distortions of telephone can make it. And what do I demand of him? "Please, Tim, may I hold your hand again?" Pause. "Randy, not Tim. Aren't we a little old for that?" Pause. "You were always too old for that." Pause. "Well, I haven't gotten any younger."

Instead I took a copy of my own letter from the drawer. I placed it beside his. The only substantial difference was that his was ruffled and torn on one edge. I had been no more successful in expressing affection, and I wondered if he had tossed mine aside at first with the same impatience. We had given each other nothing in the first exchange. I wrote again. Certainly that letter too must have shown self-consciousness in the labor of revisions, and even I could tell it bore little resemblance to my own speaking voice. This was no rough-hewn, serviceable stool to step us higher to more inaccessible shelves, but an inlaid coffee table, polished and fluted, on which to place some formal vase filled with carefully arranged blossoms and leaves. But no less real. True, the memories I chose to remind him of were not humorous or sad at our expense, but what, I asked my inner accuser, is wrong with formality, the elegance of ceremony? Still, mailing it, I had to think of what Melissa, my constant conscience, would have said in scoffing at my evasions. Perhaps that was why I told her and Sheldon nothing about my brother.

But his response was brief, for all the world as brusque as when he would shoulder me slightly at the movie theater during a scene in which I had leaned to him for the slightest touch of reassurance, perhaps the sleeve of his jacket on my wrist. That shove, more like the twitch of a horse's haunch against a fly, told me not to be a baby, above all not to expect him to be a mother, because he could not compensate for what we had begun to lack. "I am sure you will understand if I say that I would prefer at this point in my life not to open these matters of the past to extensive review or discussion. I have much to do in the present and find myself happily engaged with all its concerns. However, perhaps if we do meet at some time, such an occasion will be more than appropriate to indulge in such pleasant memories as we can find. I have found it best in my own life to concentrate on its positive aspects, and that, too often, I fear, cannot include my earlier existence. Best wishes, again, Randy."

This time I did not rage. I grieved in some sunken chamber deep in my pyramid of fitted stones. Light, I suddenly realized, was all I wanted there. For me, or for my brother? I did not know and had to put that wish aside because there was no way to force him to come down to me. But somewhere in that place, never seen because it was dark layered with dark, hands were lifting and carefully testing the heft of a pickax.

I turned off the water, the pipe gave its usual thud, and I stood there, letting the breeze blow coolly over my wet skin, listening to the returning sounds of a July midday—cicadas in the nearby elms, the sputter of a small airplane descending to the local field. No time now to think of brother or family, and even if Mindy and my morning with her were an aspect of Michael's life, I could not help feeling a vague indulgence. I had turned it all to my own purposes in ways I could only partially understand. I bent to let my hair fall forward, rubbing it with the towel, wet strands of hair cool on my back. I ran my hands flatly over breasts and belly and thighs and then stood still thinking of those summer afternoons when Michael and I would make love in the heat of midafternoon, long and lazy hours of dozing and caresses and listening to each other's heavy breathing as we woke or slept. Would we ever be like children again, indulging our sense of private freedom and the sweet desires of our bodies? Or would Melissa, torn from us with such violence, always be with us now? Why did I believe so bitterly that the violent act could never be resolved?

That night we drank too much and returned to climb unsteadily to our bedrooms. I undressed quickly and lay under the sheet, watching Michael get ready for bed in his usual deliberate manner. Always he wore a preoccupied expression, balancing and measuring the last impressions of the day, perhaps sorting what his mind should ponder in that time beyond remembering that he was about to enter. The watch was unstrapped, wound tight as he stared at its face, then set flat on the table by his side of the bed. Each layer of clothing as it came off was either carefully hung in the closet or folded and draped over the chair. But since Melissa's death his motions were fitful or slow, and this time, stripped to the waist and sitting on the end of the bed to untie his shoes, he paused, leaning forward, face in his hands. When he looked up, his back to me, he continued to lean on his elbows but stared toward the open window. I did not want him to pause. I wanted that lean, taut body to lie naked beside me where I could touch his back and belly and hips, hold his face in both my hands as I settled astride him.

"What is it?" I spoke as quietly as if he were sleeping.

"Just remembering how Melissa and I went South once in her spring vacation. The two of us. Before we knew you. In Charleston we went out to see Fort Sumter because she had been studying the Civil War and then we walked along a stretch of beach at low tide and I kept digging down when I found the air holes of clams and she would try to hold back my hands and pretended to be angry because she said all the clams wanted to do was sleep. Finally she would see a blowhole coming and we'd race for it and we got to laughing so hard we fell down into the wash of a wave and were soaked. But I can't remember how long we stayed in Charleston, where else we went there. I keep trying." He leaned down, pulled off his shoes and socks, and again stayed bending forward. "I don't want to forget anything about Melissa. I want every single day to stay there and come back to me when I call for it. I will not lose a moment of her life."

Now his back was straight, arms held stiffly to the bed, and he stared at those windows as if he addressed some implacable force out there in the wind that gusted through the mesh, but his next words were spoken very softly.

144

"I miss her."

"Michael. Please. Come to bed. Come to me. I want you."

He stood slowly, unbuckling his pants. "Too much to drink. I shouldn't think of these things now. No control. But maybe that's also why I'm blanking out in places. Sorry. I shouldn't panic."

"Sometimes I think it's all panic, but I'm so numbed I can't feel the level anymore. This morning I . . ." and I held still. Will the mind always do that? Grinning, stumbling, foolish thing we have told to stay out of sight, it dresses in servant's clothes and appears at the most casual moment to serve hors d'oeuvres to the guests but drops the tray, head lolling, mouth spewing all the secrets of the house.

Michael turned out the light. "Yes?"

"Nothing. I don't remember."

I put my palm on his chest. He was lying on his back, hands behind his head.

"Speaking of which, where were you this morning?"

Not now, not now. My body at last in touch with him ached. But any secret would put a fine layer of dulled skin between us. My body would be dispossessed, the spirit at one remove still imagining how to tell him, when. What good would that be? As if he were rejecting me, I drew away.

"I was with Mindy Haines."

I waited, if only to hear him breathing, but even that stopped.

"Doing what?" His voice could have been coming from behind a screen.

"She wanted to show me some things about her brother."

"You went somewhere with her? Why?"

"I don't know exactly. I want to understand it all better."

"Do you?"

"Some things."

"Don't tell me, then." He turned slowly to lie facing me. "Because I know all I need to know, damn it. Mindy Haines has a brother. Her brother killed my daughter. My daughter is dead. Tomorrow we'll mourn her together and all my life I'll mourn her, sometimes alone, sometimes with others who remember—even if we reach the point where you and I can laugh at some of her silliness, as I almost could tonight, Julie, thinking of those clams. But the facts are stones." I did not move or speak when he paused to breathe deeply, and when he began again, his voice was calm. "I can't change them into loaves of bread or break them. There's nothing that Mindy Haines can do for me. Even having Leroy Haines executed or strait-jacketed forever won't change that ultimate stone of Melissa's death. I don't want to listen to you talk about them, or even know you have been with her. I want to forget."

I had held my arms so stiffly behind my head that when I changed positions they trembled as if I had been carrying heavy bags. "But what about later? What if by making yourself forget now, you are making it impossible to remember later?"

"What I need now is sleep more than anything."

So much more to say. But I held still, refusing to let words form into answers. What right did I have to tell him he was wrong? Why did I even think he was? Maybe like Scheherazade I only wanted to talk and talk to avoid tomorrow, dreading those ceremonies when I would more than ever be a bystander.

I let one hand wander along his arm to his side, his hip. "I want you."

His fingers combed my hair. "Sleep, Julie. I'm tired."

So I gave in to the simple truth of weariness.

But I was right about the funeral service. Even though the words the minister intoned at us were well-intentioned, they seemed applicable to anyone, spoken out of our wishes to mention only the best in someone. I was reminded in the simplest ways that I had no official standing there. I became Sheldon's companion because Mike and Fran had to sit together. Even by that evening when Fran joined us for a drink after dinner, an occasion for us to say good-bye and wish her well before her return to Chicago, I had not found my way back from the periphery. Perhaps that made it easier for me to wonder how conscious Mike and Fran were of the fact that now nothing existed to bring them together again.

Although she slumped low into the couch, fingering her beads, slim, sharp-shinned legs extending under the coffee table, she was alert and unrelaxed.

"How can anyone take the language of astronauts seriously? Splashdown. Retract cycle. As much gibberish in it as a football game."

If she was looking for reaction from us, none was aroused. Sheldon sat near me in the easy chair and already he had dozed once, head sinking forward, hands jerking to catch his balance in dreams. Michael was in the kitchen cleaning up the remains of a dinner at which we had eaten too little, drunk too much, and now Fran was doing her best to catch up, clutching a large planter's punch already nearly emptied.

"Space flights. What a bore." She was looking down along her slanted face at me, a lazy tone of conversation but watchful eyes. "We already know they can go to the outer limits and not find anything as alive as we are, because we've looked hard at the dead planets tumbling around and around. I can't get into it. No room for the imagination."

I wanted to answer in the silence she left us, and that was when I found her kinship to Melissa. Her statements contained a subtle temptation to argument. I longed to hear the water stop running, to have Michael rescue us since he alone had some nervous energy left.

"Well, I find it all quite wonderful, actually. Perhaps." Sheldon said more coolly as he proceeded, "your imagination just isn't interested in such things."

Breaking glass. The water shut off. Both Fran and I looked to the kitchen door.

"Everything all right?" I called, and Fran swung back to stare at me.

His aproned form in the doorway. "Just a glass. It slipped." He was gone, and the water flowed again.

"Just a glass," she said with a snort. "He went through a dozen Baccarat glasses in a few months once. Do you know how much they cost?"

Familiar territory. Costs, goods, the value of objects, lucky finds at sales. Melissa had described this side of her mother's obsessions, and I could easily say, "No. Expensive?" and listen to the rise in price since they had received three dozen glasses in various shapes at their wedding, and yet I rode beneath her words, entering their world—a wedding, celebration, Fran and Michael alone with presents they both touched, drank from, shared, then Fran and Michael and an infant Melissa. I wanted her to go back to the moon, to problems of the imagination.

No one refused when Michael poured more drinks. The rum was working out to my surfaces in a slow flush, so I lowered myself to the floor, where I felt more private. When Sheldon spoke, his face was turned to the one break in our circle where no one was sitting.

"I wanted to say something today, just stand up and say it."

"Now's your chance."

But he did not turn toward Fran or even seem to hear her.

"I'm the oldest. I ought to have tried to speak some words for all of us."

He brushed my leg with his cane and planted it gently in front of him to lean on it with both hands, his legs spread and face thrust forward. That pose was so characteristic of him when he was listening in those spaces he allowed for reply in midargument that I expected a voice to answer back and then for Sheldon to refute it. But when he spoke I could tell he had considered many of the things he was saying, truly had intended to say them at the service.

"I wanted to point out how you've all seen Melissa in ways I never have. I haven't seen her since she was very young, and only dimly then. Even when I knew she was a woman, I kept seeing her as a child. Never mind, though. We're all reduced to children now, aren't we? What can everything we know do for us? I lost sight of her and can only imagine what she became." He paused, but none of us could speak. He was almost reciting, a formality that transformed us into audience. "I don't need to imagine much because I know what she really became. She told me everything and let me give her useless advice. I guess I thought I was being wise and what I had to say helped, but one day after she'd gone I was thinking of what I'd said and how it was advice I'd want her to follow to keep her safe but was advice I'd never have followed myself. I thought about her tone of voice before she left and I knew she didn't come to me for the words but for having me to say her own mind to, having someone to tell it all to. Well, then I knew what to do. I stopped giving advice, although I'm old and useless enough so I couldn't always stop myself, but instead I gave her back my own tangles, a grandfather's worries or memories, and I didn't hold anything back. So that's what we had. We swapped all the secrets of the days and even nights. We swapped our lives. I wanted to tell everyone today about all that."

Now he was slipping quietly into a muted tone, talking more and more to himself. Fran did not shift posture, but her fingers clicked nervously through the beads of her necklace.

"There was plenty neither of us could understand. We'd ask questions and there would be explanations, but sometimes the explanations wouldn't make sense either. No matter. Telling and listening counted. I'd swap my life for hers now. Maybe you think that's easy to say because I'm an old man, and I'm not supposed to care as much. Well, I do. Because I'm a fortunate man. I've got Michael and Julie and friends and all the good memories. But I'm hurting now. Someone took an ax to the roots." He lifted one hand from the other where they were still resting on the top of his cane and held it palm up. "I wanted to hold the next generation in these hands." His voice stopped as if he had not known he would come to that point, the hand made a fist, and then moved uneasily in his chair and frowned, an expression I had seen when he woke on his bad nights. "Are you there, Julie?"

I took his elbow to reassure him. I did not remove my hand and he did not slip away from it. He sat perfectly still, breathing a little unevenly but his face impassive and pale.

"What," Fran said quietly but with a tightness that shocked me, "are you getting at, Sheldon?"

"Too many things to get straight. This afternoon I got to looking for things that last. We die, but there's memory. Except that starts to go, too. Then I thought of Liz and me and felt proud. We had our bad moments, but we endured. We came to each other as virgins, we had our family, she died, and I'll die having known only one woman all my life. I've missed out on nothing, but in this room I'm as curious a creature as a medieval monk. But so what? Maybe Julie and Mike will never be married and live together as faithfully or faithlessly as they want for much longer than Liz or I did. But Liz is dead, and I am alive, and a failure might be made out of that." He lifted his glass, took a large mouthful, and swallowed. "Melissa was twenty-three. Twenty-three years of our lives. Gone."

"Very helpful." I had never heard Fran's voice tremble or imagined her breaking in any way. Her face thrust forward, mouth turned down. "As usual, like father, like son, you have managed only to make something painful enough even more painful. Oh, how you Gardeners love to climb high over things and look down. Shall we sit on the mountaintop and count our failures? Don't you think all her life, when she was very much alive, I thought about the ways I failed my daughter? Shall I tell you all the ways her bitch of a mother damaged those brief twenty-three years? Do I need tonight to have her grandfather remind me of my inability to live as holy wife and mother to his long-suffering son? Are you happy, Sheldon, to prove once again how the tongue is mightier than any sword at opening wounds again and again? Gardeners, Gardeners, I'm sick of them."

She started to stand but slumped back, put both hands to her face, then drew them away and sat perfectly still, her head as set as the regal pose of a Nefertiti.

"I don't think that was what he meant," I murmured.

"I don't know what I meant." Sheldon kept shaking his head slowly from side to side.

Michael stood. He walked to Fran and put a hand on her shoulder. She did not look up at him. "I apologize for all that."

"Courtesy of Gardener and Son?" she snapped.

He held out his hand. "Would you like another drink?"

She stood as if something hot had spilled on her. Her nearly empty glass toppled from the arm of the couch, and she spun to face Michael. Her hands were in tight fists. When her arms rose I flinched, but she was holding him tightly, weeping with her face against his neck, a voice shattering against him whenever she could find the breath. Michael's hands moved up and down her back, over her hips. I picked up the glass and walked away to the kitchen, leaving Fran's voice now finding words, saying, "Michael, Michael, what can I do without her?"

A car turned into our driveway. Michael and Fran came through the kitchen. She was leaning into him, weeping quietly, and he was holding her tightly to guide her. Over her head he said to me, "Be right back." They were gone, and then I heard Ed Bushey at the patio door calling "Anyone home?" And Sheldon was saying, "Come in, come in. Is Tina with you?" I turned on the water and leaned against the sink's cool lip, closed my eyes, breathed deeply. In, out. One, two. Even if the Busheys were our friends I was not sure I could make more conversation. I stared at the screen, the dark night beyond. Fluff from the poplars had caught in clumps against the mesh. Somewhere down the road a dog had startled a skunk, and the sharp musk blew in with the breeze.

From the kitchen doorway I called to the Busheys. Ed started to stand, I urged him down. Could I get them something? Beer was fine. I found the last two bottles in the back of the refrigerator, popped their caps, and took two mugs from the shelf. No sounds from the front of the house, no lights were on. Had they gone to the front porch? The little sitting room off the hallway? Upstairs? When his hands had stroked her hips with the same unconscious and habitual gesture that he would use to soothe me or greet my own embrace, I had been jealous and did not try to deny it, but now I saw that same scene, I felt him holding me, and I wished I could stop at jealousy rather than such absolute loneliness. Because we all had become dangerously fragile, and I could not help thinking what if he had died and not Melissa? I faced into the dark threshold, wanting to call out to either of them, to hear their voices reply. Let them answer in tones annoying enough to return me to anger.

"Michael? Fran?" I spoke hardly above a whisper, and then my voice stuck. I swallowed.

"Hey, Julie. Lose those beers?" Sheldon was calling.

Ed stood and Tina let me pour her mug full and set the rest of her bottle by her husband.

"One glass is always enough for me or else I'm up all night." She smiled shyly.

Most of her gestures had that restraint. Ed too would have liked to control his expressions, but they came with too much force behind them. When he spoke or laughed his broad, fair-skinned face and heavy neck blushed as if he were blowing into a balloon, and the effort of holding his limbs in place tensed the broad muscles of his arms. They were quiet, gentle people whose four surviving children had grown up and scattered themselves successfully all over the country, one as far away as California. I had come to love the intense privacy out of which their unfailingly generous motions came to us. As I sat by Sheldon I took refuge in the vague sense of comfort they gave me, remembering they were the kind of people who would not expect me to make small talk for the sake of politeness. Tina and Ed had been to the service, and Ed began talking to Sheldon about the minister. She leaned to me.

"I put a little something for you folks on the table there." For the first time I noticed the wide pan with cake at the far end of the room. When I told her she shouldn't have, she waved a hand and sat back again. "Did you have some of our early corn yet, Mr. Gardener? Ed's never seen it come up so fast as it did this year."

"No, but I can hear it growing. Noisy damn stuff."

Ed laughed, one leg stuttered. "What you hear's the coons, Mr. Gardener. I've never seen them so bad as this year."

"I had a pet coon once." Sheldon leaned his shoulder against Tina's. "Right in the city."

They were talking easily now, and I listened for a long time until I let my concentration slip, recalling a firm, simple statement Tina had made to me recently from the memory of losing her own child, and more than any moment that day, more than the brief community the service had attempted, I had a glimpse that there might be some distant end to this constant slipping and tumbling down. Toward what? I could not concentrate on that either.

Michael was gesturing to me from the doorway. "Hello, Ed, Tina. Did you make this cake, Ed?"

"If I did, better not eat it."

I reached Mike as Tina was saying, "He makes some of the best wheat bread you've ever tasted. He could cook as well as anyone."

"Not cakes. It's not that they fall. They contract, is what."

"I put her in the guest room, Julie. She took some pills, and she's calmed down, but she shouldn't be completely alone."

What could I say? "Mr. Bushey thinks the coons are bad. The cake is for eating. Sheldon hears the corn. I am too tired to speak. Should I sleep in the barn? You are looking out for Fran. Fran looks at her dreams. Hello, Michael Gardener, I'm Julie Cobb, daughter of J. Howard Cobb. Come back some other time. I just left." How long did we stand there listening to all the voices in our heads? Maybe our frozen postures made Ed stand like a massive horse heaving up from a good roll.

"Come on, Tina. We've wheedled that beer you wanted."

Ed tried to say an easy good-bye to Sheldon, but he approached with the terror of a man who knows he might knock over something beyond the line of his vision.

"The worst will be over soon," Tina said to me.

We walked to the door together, and I murmured, "I hope so."

"If the newspaper would only pipe down. That must be very hard, seeing her name again and again. It's quite wonderful the way we recover from loss, but not when we don't give ourselves a chance."

Ed said something to me about more corn, and they both turned to wave and say good night again. Mike walked with them to their car, dim forms moving away through the faint aureole of the outside light.

"Fine people, the Busheys," Sheldon was saying behind me, and he began telling me something about the generations of Busheys who had worked land in this area. "Even this house was lived in briefly by some relatives through marriage."

The car started, lights caught the bright eyes of a startled cat in the field, then swung with slow arcs toward the trees and disappeared. I waited for Michael, but he did not appear. The slab of the patio ended in a dark fringe of grass that needed mowing, the path trailing dimly toward the driveway, the pale, sharp-edged wall of the house. Beyond those shapes I could see nothing until I looked toward the tops of the trees where the lighter sky and its stars showed in patches. I stepped out, abandoning Sheldon.

"Michael?" I called more loudly against the puff of a breeze, "Mike?"

"Here." His voice was in the black field.

"I can't see you." I began walking into the grass, and as I left the house lights behind, I began to distinguish various shades of darkness in the corners of my eyes.

"Over here."

I followed his voice. The grass damply brushed my ankles. He was standing with hands in his pockets. We were facing toward the willow, the extended shed, but from here we could see the long slope of land back toward Shelburne, the sharp little lights of some houses, then the reddish glow of Burlington.

"I want to do the ashes soon, Julie. Not tomorrow. Maybe the next day. If the weather's good."

"I didn't know how short the service would be today. You didn't tell me what to expect."

"I thought I had."

"Maybe you told Fran."

"I can't seem to remember what I've said to whom."

He was talking so remotely that I knew only part of his mind was with us. I wished I could say something to break the silence. I could hear Melissa berating me as she used to when we argued. "You've got to speak out." The blinking lights of a jet slanted down toward the city.

"What are you thinking about?" I searched out the Big Dipper, followed the line to the North Star. The Bear. The Wain. Call it what you will. Only a little more defined in shape than apparitions formed by clouds, and on a clear night revealing other possibilities.

"I worry about Fran. I think she depended on Melissa more than I knew."

I did not answer, perhaps afraid of my words if I did not sort them carefully. Hadn't there been enough damage for one night? I fixed on that star, tried to remember how much even it had shifted in the centuries since men had needed it for navigation.

"No more nor less than you," I said finally.

"I heard from the prosecutor this morning. There'll almost certainly be no trial."

"Insane?"

"Haines will be put away."

I kept the questions to myself. How long? Why should all of us pay to keep him alive all our lives? What if they "cure" him? Isn't all murder a form of insanity? Will they ever stop writing and talking about Leroy Haines? If he lives for years and years, will we have to pick up newspapers occasionally that have articles about him, show pictures of an aging Leroy in Waterbury, or on his front porch?

A dog was barking beyond the fields. "Come on." He began to walk away. "We'd better call it a day."

We strolled to the patio. "Michael."

He turned slightly.

"Do you love me?"

I could not see his face.

"Of course."

"Hey." Sheldon stood by the door, calling out loudly into the night. "I'm off to bed."

"We're here," I said, and he nodded before shuffling away toward the kitchen.

"I'll look in on Fran a moment." Michael held the door open. "Coming?"

"I'll be up."

I walked slowly around the empty room, turning out the lights, then stood in the dark. I could smell all of us there—that dash of some strong shaving lotion Ed used, Fran's L'Air du Temps, our muddle of drinks, the stale scent of the one cigarette Ed had allowed himself. I closed my eyes and walked Michael up the narrow kitchen stairs, the hall above, into the guest room. He steps into the dark room heavy with closed-in air since surely he has not remembered to open the windows. Maybe he does now, trying to pry one up without having to jar it too hard with the heels of his hands. Swollen, it lifts only a few inches, and he settles for that. She is drugged, breathes heavily on the bed. He walks to it, slipping one foot forward after the other until his knees touch the edge. He allows himself to think how his father's world is even darker, all motions dependent on touch and sound. He can see her curled form, leans toward the familiar shape of her pale face on a pillow, even the way she breathes not exactly like me or anyone else he has known. He does not want to wake her but needs to touch her skin and tousled hair. She is still dressed, her forehead slightly moist. If he leans and kisses that brow once, he does so for all his loss, their impossible future, and for the love he bears forever in everything the three of them have shared. I know she is as far beyond the waking of this prince's kiss as her daughter, but hovering close to them both, darker than any darkness in the room, I cannot help envying them.

11

A bright day, and wind hot from the south swirled our own dust forward when we slowed for the potholes and washboarding of the last mile before Burrows cottage. I saw my own fretful instability in the breeze lifting and shaking the leaves. An old maple would be seized with a frenzy to turn its canopy inside out, or a swath across the fields of hay paled in a gust. I sloughed off more and more numbness as we rose away from the lake. The body is its own barometer, and mine was registering the fact that this might be the last sunny day for a while, since that south wind scattering a few insubstantial clouds in a hazy blue inevitably would drive in banks of gray, and the air would turn spongy with water. But there was no dread in that. It was time for rain, and what was coming would not be wild bursts of storm but a long, slow downfall, cleansing the lowland leaves of dust, a time to rest and watch grass darken to green again.

Our terrible week was almost over. Fran had left for Chicago. She did not want even to discuss Melissa's ashes, much less climb Camel's Hump with us. Before taking her taxi she had formally shaken hands with each of us, even Michael. Sheldon began playing the piano, picking out Scott Joplin and listening to something else in the rests that we could not hear.

We parked the car at the edge of the clearing, and I helped Michael into the straps of the pack that held Melissa's ashes. As we walked, we glimpsed the brook to our right through the trees. Sometimes it was hard to distinguish water from the rush of wind. When the trail began to rise more steeply on the slope of Bald Hill, we both pointed to the glimpse of the summit looking deceptively close. How cruel that view seemed to me as a child when my parents first took me up. I was certain it was only a few skips away and had not believed Hob when he said no, it would take another two hours probably and I had better slow down. A half hour later I had begun

156

the lamenting refrain, "When will we get there?" until finally his patience had broken and holding me by the arm he had shaken me once, said, "Julie, I mean it. If you say that once more, we'll go home." I had stared blankly into his eyes. "Hob," my mother was saying, "she's never climbed it before." I closed my mouth tightly on the need to wail, put to work those feet that wanted to stamp with petulance. I trampled the lichen and adder's-tongue. If no one would tell me when we would arrive I would have to get there by my own estimates and I would not go down the mountain with that question unanswered. In fury, in clenched determination, I stood on the summit and triumphantly looked down upon the way we had come, deciding never to ask my father anything again. But I broke that an hour later when we had started down the Alpine Trail to see the remains of the Army plane that had crashed there in 1944. I put my hand in his. The parts of the wreck were twisted, already shapeless from rust and vandalism. "Why did they have to crash?" I asked, and his answers were as unsatisfactory as the previous ones even if he tried to blame it on weather or faulty machinery.

Le Lion Couchant. More dignity in that name than Camel's Hump. I had climbed it so often from every side and angle that on some trails I had memorized boulders or ancient trees. This was the place I sat to rest and left my canteen only to find it hung on a nearby limb when I returned a month later, or here my first boyfriend, as we were climbing on a school trip with an especially self-sacrificing young teacher named Trina Peacham, had tried to hold my hand and much to my chagrin I had rebuffed him because I saw Jane Beliveau looking at us. At some time in all of those trips, and even now, I mulled over those names like mantras—Couching Lion, Camel's Hump—until they became nonsense and I would imagine the mountain less worn and without a name, without human creatures to mark it in the territory of their consciousness with words. The water we climbed away from, the birches, the rocks with their deep rifts and black seams of soil would be so old but alive that all the burden of history, mine or that of my species, dissipated.

His feet lifted and trod down, the basket creaked, I was beginning to sweat, but the wind kept fanning us, finding its way even through the dense groves of small spruce. Sometimes when I looked straight ahead I could not help thinking of what he bore and my heart would beat back, my breath come short against more than the effort of our climbing. We hardly spoke at all until we reached the old clearing and juncture with the Long Trail.

He pulled at the straps and slipped them off, I helped lower the basket. The back of his shirt was patterned with sweat, and he mopped at his face with a handkerchief.

"Let me carry it?"

He shook his head. "I'm out of shape."

He usually did not like to sit when we climbed, said it was better to pause and stand to keep the legs from tightening up, but this time he joined me on a high clump of grass that had grown lushly over a rotted stump. I took his hand and held it on my knee and from time to time the wind burst down on us from the peak above. From here we would begin the ascent of the last ridge and summit, rising soon on rock and lichen and patches of Alpine grass. Even now something in me was rising toward a long-awaited freedom. But I could not find a specific image for it, and certainly whatever was ahead of us immediately was not pleasant.

"I was camping here, over by that rock, the night they were trying to find me. When Hob died."

He took his hands off the straps he had been adjusting, still leaning forward. I had never talked with him about those days. Now my remembered self seemed like a different person caught up in bewilderments, lying on the summit of Camel's Hump as the sun set and wondering what she would do with her life, and when, or if she would ever find some clarity.

"No one else was on the mountain all afternoon. I came back here and put my tarp up and had some supper and then I went to the top again for the sunset. Actually that was the whole point. I was a collector of mountain sunsets then. I was disappointed in myself when I got down and heard."

"But how could you have known?"

"I couldn't. But I kept thinking back over the whole day and that evening and felt hurt that I had not known. I went over and over it. I'd remember how I had paused to rearrange my pack, or how the first time when I was on top, earlier in the afternoon, I had stripped and lain in the sun behind some rocks, and I wanted to be able to say, 'Yes, right then, I felt a weird sense come over me, I sat up, I shivered.' I wanted premonition."

"But found none? Or did you invent it?"

"Zero. I had been thinking of Julie Cobb so hard, how could anything get through to me? That was the hardest moment for me. I kept accusing myself of preventing him from making some final contact. I would imagine that as I had lain on the top rocks, the sun down and wind picking up and I was watching so hard to see the first star, that then, at the very moment that Julie Cobb was saying to herself, 'I will change my life, I will come down from this mountain and tomorrow things will be different, clear, I will stop wasting my time,' just then my father was hovering nearby, calling me."

A white-throated sparrow broke into prolonged song, and farther up the ridge the answer came, inverting the original interval downward.

Was he as reluctant to finish the climb and perform the last act as I? His voice was quiet and slow. "How long did you keep accusing yourself of that?"

"Not long. Afterward I realized I was only holding on. How much worse to think that the universe is so indifferent that nothing registers. I wanted to believe that at least I *could* have received signals even if I was too flawed to."

"I think we've had this conversation before."

"I did not do that on purpose."

He shook his head. "I've had it on my mind."

I helped him into the straps and went first this time, knowing I would not be able to restrain myself. Always the climb up the last cone would accelerate my pace, no matter how tired I might be. I would move faster until I was nearly running, eyes fixed on the last curve of rock, body aching to stand still. I heard Michael behind me as we started, and for a while I kept a slow pace but soon I was taking wider steps. The trees were only hip high, sparse, then bushes. I did not hear him anymore, looked around quickly to see the slope falling away, Bald Hill below, the land's sweep in hazy green on every side. Loose flakes scrabbled under me, I stepped up from the worn path onto clear rock, clambering over the bare, upthrust hipbone of land, and the wind now did not cease but only raised or lowered the shove of its gusts. Hard dry moss crackled under one foot, I moved faster, faster, an ungainly, large-winged bird only needing enough momentum to lift free. The rock steepened, my heart beat back against it, my breath cut short, chest strapped and legs aching, and then no upward slant before me, only one last low curve and I stood with nowhere else to go but a blue updraft of air, my arms lifted into it, and I closed my eyes, body aching, believing I rolled and lolled and twisted in a frenzy of gliding upward toward the sun.

I took one deep breath and opened my eyes. I was facing the lake, and I sat down, clutching my knees to my chest, looking out and out through the valleys, across the plain, the long strip of lake to the jagged outlines of peaks beyond it. The air had thickened with damp haze since we had started, and already to the south the sky was gray with a lid of unbroken clouds. I longed to be alone for a few hours, not hearing Michael's bootsteps nearing. But in a rush I was glad. If it had to end, if it had to be done, better here than anywhere else I could think of, and whether or not that was what Melissa had known when she made her request, I blessed her for it.

Mike stood over me breathlessly, and then he moved to a depression below, took off the basket, and set it there upright. He turned away from it, his back to me, staring out over that same view. Perhaps we both needed to let our spirits descend slowly, our feet placed flat against rock, reminding ourselves of what it would be like to stand no less solidly far off near that water and look back to the humped form of mountain.

We sat for a while side by side in silence, and then he looked at his watch. "I guess that weather will be here before too long."

We both stared at the low gray line of clouds.

"I'm not quite sure how to do this, but I'm glad no one is here." He stooped, pulled up the urn, gripped it in both hands, and gestured with his head toward the summit. "Up there?"

I followed. He set the urn down, hunched over it to pry the lid.

"Are we supposed to say something? Just scatter them? I've imagined this far but I could never get any farther."

He was staring at the urn. I was afraid that we were both losing our nerve.

"Open it, scatter them. I'll help. Then we'll sit for a while and think of her."

We stared at each other like two conspirators only at the last moment understanding the implications of their plotting.

"I thought yesterday that there might be something I could read, say over her ashes or into the wind. I walked around the house and looked on all the bookshelves. I read in her books and poems or stories I knew she loved. I put my finger on random passages like I used to when I was a child and thought I would find answers that way. Nothing seemed right. Nothing seemed appropriate. There aren't any words."

His hands were open at his side but still stiffly curved to the shape of the urn. He kneeled and began prying at the lid.

"It must be sealed or something."

He pulled harder, straining, his arms shaking with the effort. I pointed out two small clasps on the sides, and when he released them, the lid loosened. He squinted toward the lake as if the sun were not directly overhead but shining up out of the water. He lifted the lid, dropped it by his side, and it wobbled and rolled down the rock, bounced high, and disappeared into a line of moss and low bushes. The urn contained some gray ash and white flecks of irreducible bone. He plunged his hand in, drew it out clenched in a fist, and let the ash go.

"Help me."

I reached in, not wanting to accept the texture of ash so light it powdered through my fingers or those fragments pressed in panic hard into my palm. He was dipping his hand and scattering, the quick motions of a sower, the urn cradled in his arm. The wind gusted, blew back on us, I tried to hold my breath but too late, could tell by his final motion of extending the urn in both hands away from himself and turning it over that he too had been caught by the swirl of updraft. He let go, the urn clattered dully on the rock, rolled out of sight. He was wiping his hands along his thighs. We stood there, braced against the wind.

We walked back to a hollow. The hand that tugged me along clenched mine so tightly that my fingers were numb when he let go. We sat beside each other, the wind passed over us, and I moved close enough so that our shoulders and hips touched.

"Sorry I panicked." He closed his eyes.

"We can think of her. That's a form of praying, isn't it?"

"I do that all the time anyway."

So I closed my eyes too and we were silent. The wind was stronger now, and I could imagine how it would be as we started down, shoving at our backs, billowing out our shirts to sail us off the rocks, and when we entered the tree line again our skins would seem burned, bodies heavier than their winged counterparts had been above. If only we could be sailplaning above all this again, soaring through such different lives. I drew back to where we were, concentrated on that touch of hip and shoulder moving slightly as he breathed. We might have been asleep together in our bed at home. I thought her name. My hands tightened against the memory of ash and fragments blown against my face. I looked for images of her but could not even bring to mind her face. "Melissa, Melissa." What I finally lifted and held was not simple enough to hold for long—the candles burning after our dinner, three of us talking about this possible moment although none of us really believed that vow would be called in, least of all that Michael and I would be survivors. I began at last to see her across the table, still so much a stranger to me then. But what was she wearing? How did she do her hair? Where had she been? It would all come back to me later that night with such clarity that I would sit up in bed, hands to my face, seeing her mouth slightly open, eyes wide as she leaned across the table.

Mike had not stirred, his face a mask of sleep. I looked across the skyline and again closed my eyes. Why when I wanted images, at least the concrete stuff of memory, did my mind go white, a place of abstractions as blank as uncarved, polished marble? All day and night I usually imagined too much, threw faces, events, both real and fantasized across that screen just behind the one the real eyes filled, and by doing so, I often shut out the world like a one-way mirror. I might be stooping to lift a fallen book and see the boy my father imagined sitting in that field and once again the fox would move into the light enough for both of us to see him, or I would be once again watching Michael from a tree I had never climbed, seeing him through Melissa's eyes, and these were only scenes placed in memory by the inner eye. "Melissa, Melissa." Her name was my chant now. I pushed against the polished surface, tried with eyes clenched tightly shut to roll away that stone.

But I do not break it, it dissolves, I am dragged into the whitened surface, not solid as I had thought, but soft, opaque, so shining with trapped light that my eyes ache, and yet I try to hold back from it, stay where I am only staring down onto the surface. Now I am tumbling in light, trying not to breathe it but I must, and when I do it fills my mouth, tasting like snow, that faint decay of earth mixed with ether, frozen air. I see with painfully dilated pupils, the white air is coagulating into forms, but none of them are ones I know. I try to hold onto anything that is familiar—a tree, a bush, a slant of roof, an impossible brook where water leaps up stones like struggling fish, and then at last a white chair sits still on a white lawn, a figure assembles under a wide hat, and shadows slowly rise out of darkening ground, coloring green across the lawn, mauve streaks of shade, the long spikes of late afternoon. As I move my shadow toward the figure I can see the white, polished shoes, thin legs, the edge of a skirt. I try to hold my shadow back. I do not want to see more of the figure under the hat. "Melissa, Melissa, Melissa," Sheldon chants above me, his cane breaking down against the stone. The figure does not move, the sun is now harsh on my back, the long knife of my body's shadow strikes the brim, the shoulder, and there is no white—the lap is pooled with blood, the gashed wrists lie facing upward, palms cupping dulled blood, my mother staring forever downward at what she has done, not breathing, face frozen in wonder.

I did not cry out. I turned and pressed hard against his chest, my voice saying into him, "She's dead, she's dead."

I heard his voice but did not even try to follow the words at first, listened closely to the steady beat of his heart in my ear and let my mind repeat those words in the rhythm of his pulse, "She's dead, she's dead." Finally I opened my eyes and tried to concentrate. But he was saying something incomprehensible about a child, so I drew away and watched his lips stop moving.

"Do you see?" he said.

I shook my head, leaned again so that his cheek rested against my forehead. Suddenly I was very depressed. I had seen again what I had known for many years. I had been chanting, "She's dead, she's dead" but had only put into words what I had been saying since I was thirteen, and if he mistook what I was saying, he had a right to.

"Let's get out of here before it rains." I stood, the wind whipped hair into my eyes, and I heard voices nearby. "Someone's here."

Before we could move a voice above said, "Hi, there," and a woman in a blue bandana was smiling down at us. "Windy, isn't it?"

I let Michael do the talking. Our basket had rolled and caught in a hollow near the peak. A boy and a girl were scampering around on the rocks.

"We're from Oregon," she was saying, still smiling, and at some distance on the spur of the ridge to the south a man was standing with another woman, each holding one end of a flapping map while they peered and pointed off toward the lake. "We've been climbing in the White Mountains, but this is really spectacular. You're from Vermont?"

I nodded. She was stocky, her worn slacks shapeless over her hips, a mother's constant watchfulness on her broad face even as she talked to us, and she called out, "Daniel, not down there, please. I hope we didn't chase you away."

"No, no." Michael was standing braced against the wind. "We were leaving."

The other two were coming slowly up the summit.

Michael said, "Have a good time," and I was furious at him for wasting words. Kind Michael. Always polite Michael. Gentle Michael. I wished he had told her to keep her brats off the mountains.

By the time I reached the clearing the wind was scattering a few drops of rain on the windshield even though the clouds had not yet covered the sky. I was ahead of Michael and sat alone in the front seat, my head back and eyes closed. In the space of a few short days I had incorporated into myself both Melissa and her killer. The odor of Leroy's cave, Melissa's ashes on my tongue. There is no spirit without the body. But I was too weary again for anything to seem strange. Mike appeared about ten minutes later, did not seem to mind that I had not waited for him.

"Did you see the deer back there?"

He described them, two standing completely still near the brook, and he was certain that only because of the noise of water, wind, and his own scent blown away had he been able to come so close. He took his hand off the gearshift and put it on mine where it lay on the seat.

"Thanks."

"For what?" I kept staring at our hands.

"For helping. I'm glad that's over."

"So am I." I looked out my window toward the opening in the woods, the sign explaining what trail this was. I wanted to strike at anything that could stink of the old circles of mood. The grief was dead, long live the grief.

"Are you there?"

"Yes," I said to the woods.

"Will you marry me?"

I jerked around, although my hand stayed under his. His face, to my surprise, was serious, but I could tell by the vague embarrassment beginning to show that mine must not have been.

"But why bother?"

"What if we wanted to have a child?"

"But we don't. And what difference would marriage make, anyway?"

He looked away now. "What if I did?"

"Isn't that what they call marrying on the rebound, Michael?"

He let off the brake. "I think they have something else in mind when they say that."

"Parenting on the rebound?"

We had drifted backward slightly and he eased on the foot brake. "Are you all right, Julie?"

"I can't say yes to what you are asking. Not now."

When we were driving slowly back down the pitted road, he said, "We need some rest, I think."

He said that too tensely. He deserved relief. But my words were locked away. I stared at his face, trying to read what could be going on behind it, how to take his words, uncertain how to understand my anger or why I blamed him for shifting and not taking me with him. I had to find something more to say, but more than ever I feared my ability to hurt before I knew what I was saying. He was vulnerable because I did not know him. He was watching the road ahead carefully, trying to steer around humps and craters, and briefly I could see him simply as Michael Gardener, a man who had buried his daughter in air, and those ashes now were washing down over stone into the scant soil. But that was only for a moment, because I could not see what else he was becoming, a face clearer to me than it had ever been before, but changed.

12

Disintegrations. Weeks in which each day was its own discrete entity, and in the beginning I did not even try to put the pieces together. As if to set a tone for that broken time, I met Arthur Sprague again. He had lost almost everything by then. His wife had divorced him, his shed and trailer had burned, and when I saw him he was bending to search through a trash barrel on Church Street. I waited for him to finish before I crossed over. He steadied himself with one hand on the mailbox and for a few moments we talked as if we had seen each other only yesterday. But it had been at least a year. Neither of us was good at discussing weather or local politics, but I could sense he did not want to let me go.

"How about a drink? If you're buying." He leaned at me, breath boozy, his flesh, his sweaty and disheveled clothes in ferment.

"Three in the afternoon is too early for me."

He attempted to draw up with dignity, but his hand grappled the box to catch him from tottering. I had forgotten how tall he was until he stood fully, lifting out of his perpetual stoop. He was even more gaunt now and very much his age, eyes rheumy, face so veined and splotched that even that craggy nose was subdued. Our accidental meetings usually were brief, but he seemed to know what I had been doing, as if he were a distant uncle who had heard the news from other relatives.

One hand slapped the blue metal. "If you won't buy an old pal a drink, let's sit in the shade somewhere and have a talk. Unless you're in some kind of rush to get your ass elsewhere." He grinned again.

"I'm not if you're not."

He looked at me with mawkish seriousness. "I used to be. Used to work hard at doing a good thing well and when I laid down at night if I felt like it I could roll over onto my woman, Bessy, and we'd have a good time. But that was before Annette got herself telling lies to social workers, and I can tell you that even if she maybe wished she could have what her momma got, I never stuck it to her, no matter what lies she told, and that's a fact. I'm crazy sometimes, what with the booze and all, but I'm not sick."

He let go, steadied himself with widened legs on the pitching deck, and then we plunged off together to the square of neglected green behind City Hall. He still took one step to my two, although sometimes he had to come down short to compensate for the reeling surface. He was so used to those sidesteps that I could tell he was not even conscious of them anymore. It was always rough weather for Art Sprague. For me, too, then. I had been unable to work for some time, starting on one thing, abandoning it for another, finally settling on a large piece in wood that kept refusing to find its space, restlessly insisting on jags and curves that would not reconcile themselves to each other. Worse than the tension in my studio was the silence growing between Michael and me, one that followed me in all the rooms of our house even when he was not there.

"I say she burned the trailer and my shed. That child of mine is sick."

Art glowered across splotches of shade to the bus terminal. We sat on the wide back steps of City Hall. A few people were scattered on the lawn, but it was midafternoon on a Saturday in August and most people with nothing to do were closer to the water, if not in it.

"But why would she do that? Make sense, Art. That left them with no home."

"You don't listen any better than you used to. I told you she was crazy, didn't I?"

"Was there insurance?"

"Hell, we never even owned that land, just set ourselves down on it and once the shed was up and the trailer slapped on blocks, we were fixed enough to be hard to get rid of. All belonged to some bugger from Connecticut anyway, and he didn't much care because he had land all over."

"Where did Bessy and Annette go?" I had seen Bessy only once, in Shelburne with Annette at a little store frequented mostly by tourists or suckers like myself looking for gifts that people outside of Vermont would think of as typical. They were even more bloated than I had remembered, Annette's broad face staring at me with that small, fixed smile, and Bessy, looking embarrassed, kept turning over and over in her hands a cellophaned package of maple sugar women that finally split under the pressure of her conversation, spilling figurines on the floor. "I feel sorry for him sometimes," she had been confessing although I had not asked, beads of perspiration on her brow and upper lip, "but I couldn't take the beatings no more." "I don't," Annette piped clearly, "he ought to be in jail," and then I had stooped to help gather the shattered, beheaded candies while the two women accused each other of clumsiness and the clerk was telling them it did not matter.

"Got themselves some rooms in North Ferrisburg. Can't be too far off to suit me. Except I've got nothing against Bessy. It was Annette started going off to get stroked by some state fellow and then she called the cops on me one night and first thing I knew, a judge was saying I couldn't even step on my own property." He looked sideways quickly. "Well, the place I'd lived for a long time, anyways."

I was going to argue, but my tongue held still, the breath I had taken came out wordless. What was the use?

"Worst of it was all my tools and work stuff was where I couldn't get to them. I locked the shed because I knew Annette would talk her mother into selling off my stuff to make some money. But I didn't have nothing to do while I waited. I told the judge, 'Lookit, you got to let me at least go there days to work in the shed. That's my job. I'm no fucking good without my tools.' But Annette and that social worker said I shouldn't be allowed because I'd get drunk and come down to the trailer and beat the shit out of them."

He was staring at his hands, and I looked too as they flexed and opened. His tone of voice toward the end led me to believe that Annette had been right, but I was shocked at the alteration in his hands. They trembled when they were not clenched, and the fingers were puffed and misshapen around the joints. I could not help thinking that even if he had his tools those hands would hardly be able to work, and more than anything I had seen or heard so far, the trembling fingers saddened me.

"But they finally said I could pick up some of my stuff. I got me a lawyer through Legal Aid and they proved I had to have tools for my work. That's when she done it, I know. She burned that shed sure as hell to keep me from having my tools, and then she burned out the trailer so's to make it look like it was all an accident. But it didn't fool me. I tell you what." He stared at me now. "I think she would've been even happier if she had me tied up or passed out drunk in that shed when she torched it. That's how crazy she came to be."

A bus was grinding into place at the station down the street.

"Listen, Julie." He swiveled, lurched back slightly with the effort. "You know I can be mean, you know how sometimes I can even get to wanting something from a woman and hardly control myself. I haven't forgot that day back in the woods. But let me ask you, I didn't force you now, did I? I mean, you think of it, and I could've done anything I wanted out there and no one'd known the difference. But you said no, and I stopped dead. Well, I tell you I couldn't because old Art Sprague would've known the difference, that's what." His hand poked a stiff finger in his chest. "So all I'm trying to say is, you don't believe none of it, do you? I mean that poison she put out in court about me and her, my own daughter saying I laid her and done it to her often." He shook his head, his voice choked for a second. "Say you don't believe that, Julie. She said all those lies right there in court and it was even in the newspaper and how could I prove it wasn't true? I tried to get Bessy to help. I asked her to tell how it was lies. That's what I can't understand. She went along with it. They were out to get me. They were out to rip my name all to hell and get everything they wanted." His voice was firm now, and he stared out toward the dead fountain glutted with old leaves, drab paper, broken bottles. "I forgive Bessy. She was scared, wanted out, and thought that was the best way. But that daughter of mine." His fist came up, shook at the bus station. "I wish to hell a child of hers could come along someday and done the same. I wish she could still have children so's they could all be born sick and crippled."

He was not seeing that stretch of trees and grass and crisscrossed sidewalks. His face was rapt as if Annette's deformed and suffering children were making their way toward our steps. I saw them myself and believed he could curse the leaves off the trees and sear the unmown grass.

His arm collapsed, back slumping again, and he jammed the hand into the pocket. I was glad he had forgotten to press his question. How could I know what to tell him? There must have been nights when he was so drunk that either woman looked the same to him, and if Annette had not struggled or made it clear she was the wrong one, she could have been paralyzed between a wish to have it so and a knowledge of what happened to her mother when she resisted.

"What are you doing, Art? For work."

"I'm retired. I'm old enough to be, aren't I?" We looked at each other, but he could not keep his grin. "Hell, Julie. When my tools and stuff burned up, I had nothing. They took it all away from me. I tried working for a while as a carpenter, but that's no way to do. I mean, putting up Sheetrock for some landlord or jacking up old porches. I'm better than that. You married yet?"

"No."

"Shacked up with that same fella Gardener? I heard about you two. Got friends in Charlotte, you know."

"We live together. Have for a long time now."

Again he snorted. "A long time. You got a long time to go before you know what a long time means." He looked down at his clasped, trembling hands. "I was real sorry, though, to read about his kid. Seemed like an awful thing to have happen."

"Yes."

"He must be pretty broke up. You too."

"It will take us some time to get over."

He nodded. "I seen that crazy from time to time, walking around. Jesus, I don't know what it's all coming to."

What I said next to Art was on my tongue since we had sat down, and even as I felt the unfairness of saying it to him, I acknowledged that we had always been as truthful to each other as our burdened minds would permit. "Why are you killing yourself, Art?"

He did not deny it, as I had expected. The clasped hands tightened a little, bobbed at the wrists.

"What's to live for?" He breathed a few times, puffing out his lips when he exhaled slowly. "I'm old enough and I've spent my time trying. No use thinking I can clean it up and start over somehow. I'm just waiting out my time now." Then he did turn sharply to me, and those eyes had some of their old insistence and clarity. "What about you, lady? What're you waiting for?"

"What do you mean?"

"What do you do for a living? How come you got no kids? How come you look and act about the way you did when we was working together? When're you going to make up your mind?"

"About what?" I laughed, but it was too sharp, and even I could hear the defense in it.

"None of my business. But I'm not so dumb. You look like one of those people over there to me, if you was to go into the station at late night. Someone sitting at the counter with a suitcase at her feet having a cup of coffee and waiting for the right bus. Why don't you get on and go somewhere?"

I might have argued with him, but what would have been the point? I was sitting on the steps of City Hall with Art Sprague staring at me and no words I could give him back.

"Oh, well. You're plenty young still. You making things?"

I tried to describe some recent sculptures, but he grunted, waved a palm.

"If you can't sit on it, it ain't worth a shit."

I stood and he shuffled stiffly down the steps, walked with me as far as Main Street.

"I'm going down to Perkins Pier and see if somebody wants to part with a fish." He started to say more, thought better of it, then did. "You spare me a buck?"

I had my wallet out of my pocket as fast as if it were full of little snakes and pulled out a five-dollar bill.

"That's too much." He folded it into his shirt pocket, staring at the taxi stand. "But better than nothing."

I turned once to see him stagger across the intersection, receiving the hoots of passing cars as if they were his due, celebrating a return to port.

After dinner I heard Michael and Sheldon talking upstairs, father and son. Parent and child. Who could I talk to? What if I called Tim? I considered not speaking to Michael for a while and wondered at the pleasure that gave me, a clear judgment deciding that he deserved my silence. For what? I scraped plates, plunged them in hot water, soap, scrubbed against the coagulated grease and fragments melted onto the stovetop. I looked at the last tilted pots in the cold, deflating suds and walked down into the cellar, slamming the door behind me.

Something scuttled away in the corner when I turned the light on. Probably another field rat, and I noticed with annoyance that I had left the hatchway to the yard ajar. I yanked the handle. The metal clanged. All my implements hung in perfect order. Fixed to its working pedestal, the uneasy sculpture hunched awkwardly. I could go back to it for a few hours. Concentration would banish everything else in my mind. But what right did sculpting have to obsess me like that? Why had I ever begun? I could recall only vaguely when I might have seen a sculptor as a child, perhaps in a studio at the university. When had this nonsense all started?

I leaned on the table, and my locked elbows began to ache. What good would that twisted chunk of wood do me now, or ever? What room would I clutter with it and its myriad of little spaces, its angles making the illusion of order? Upstairs in our room the bed was made and covers turned down as I would leave it every night before supper, the mirror on the closet door unsmudged, Michael's socks folded and stacked against each other on their sides in a drawer with underwear and his boxes of cuff links. The venetian blinds hung still on their straps in perfect order, each slip and bra and blouse was in its perpetual place; the hangers in the closet kept jackets and skirts and suits in unwrinkled rows.

I reached behind me to the rack where all the tools were so perfectly placed that I did not even have to look, and I seized the handle of a hatchet, brought it forward over my head to smash down on the sculpture. The blade imbedded deeply, I pulled it out and struck again and then kept swinging, my own voice moaning with each downthrust, smashing also on the struts of framework, the boxed pedestal. Chunks and splinters flew off, I left deep gashes across it, and the wood under the worn surface showed bright, new flesh. A fragment was flung against my cheek and I stopped, skin stinging. I put my hand to my face but there was no blood. Sharp chips of wood lay at my feet.

I ran my fingers along the raw seams, wanting to join the wood together again with my touch if only to erase the witness to my inexplicable and childish rage. I put my hands to my face and closed my eyes and tried to breathe deeply, evenly. What was I doing? Those hours of careful labor shattered. But I did not care, I did not want that work. I wished I could chisel a sculpture out of granite that represented every memory and secret and haul it down to the lake and row it out past Juniper Island to toss it in and watch it sink. I yearned for the weight of that plummet drawing my shoulders forward as I released the stone, my hands free as it turned slowly downward, losing the light.

I left that mess to go to the hatch and thrust it open. The drizzle, almost a warm fog, gusted at me under the metal canopy and I turned my face up into it, closing my eyes. "Julie," my mother would say, "that's enough now. Control yourself." But those tantrums were more like fits, and when she would finally come to the door of my room where I would be lying, sheets and blankets torn from the bed, the pillow stripped, all the clothes in my drawers and closet strewn in rumpled heaps around the room as if a pressure cooker had blown and spewed its contents everywhere, I would be far beyond the need for control, having reached my own final quiet of exhaustion. My mother would stand on the threshold, her hands tightly clasped, eyes wandering over the room in fear as if I had produced the semblance of her worst dream. Lying on my side, knees drawn tightly to my chest, I would look away from her face and hands to stare dully at her feet. Usually I was naked by then, whatever clothes I had been wearing indiscriminately heaped with all the others. "Move, come to me, walk over that line," I would think to the feet again and again, wishing them forward, one step at a time until the figure above them would be there, the hands that the figure possessed but now rarely used for touch would unclasp themselves and gently cup my head, fingers combing back through my hair as they used to, a face in front of mine, its lips on my forehead, voice saying, "Julie, Julie, Julie." I would let my cheek be pressed against her, hear her voice coming from deep within her chest, "Julie, Julie, Julie." But the feet never moved. The voice trembled to hold its monotone. "I want you to clean all that up before your father comes home. Do you hear me? Why do you have to let me down like this?" The feet would turn, the door close, footsteps tread once on the floor, then be muffled thumps on the carpet, the stairs. The refrigerator door would open. Rattle of ice cubes. A celebration for the absence of touch. A drink to silence. I would sleep until I was cold and then find refuge in my bed, dragging the covers with me. But even now, my face drenched, the water seeping back into my hair and down my neck, I could be angry with my own mind for bringing up that image of her, more convenient for my present indulgence in self-pity than for any understanding of who she was.

"Julie?"

I whirled, my hands involuntarily covering myself as if I were naked, but only Michael's voice came down to me.

"What?"

"Sheldon's ready for a game if you are."

"Coming."

I heard his footsteps move away toward the shed. He would put on some music, read *The Times* or a book. Sheldon would be waiting upstairs to play Scrabble with his Braille set. I looked at the wreckage but decided to leave it, even the hatchet lolling in the splinters. I paused with my hand on the light switch when I reached the top of the stairs. One clear fact to proceed on. I was going to sleep in the little bedroom under the eaves that we called Melissa's room. Alone, away from the pressure of Michael's body, his presence. I needed to think, undistracted.

Sheldon and I played to a draw, but I could tell he had something on his mind and was waiting for an opening to ask. I had come to him too puzzled myself to offer him much, so that before I left he had to make his beginning sternly.

"What's wrong with you two? I'm not up for any more grief this summer."

"We don't have much to say to each other."

"Don't let him fool you. When Mike was a boy Liz and I could worry. He had a way when something was on his mind of getting very wide-eyed, quiet. He'd sit and stare as you talked until you'd want to yell out, 'Blink, damn it!' I think that's when he and I started arguing. I found the only way was for me to get him to argue back, for me to be so ornery that he'd have to break out and come back at me."

"A form of making him blink?"

"Yes, but his mother had a better way, getting him to come sit while she ironed and asking him little things about school or his friends and then trying to pop a question in the door fast that asked something crucial she thought she'd seen. If she was right, he'd sometimes come back with a whole paragraph, as if behind those unblinking eyes he had been working it all out. If she was wrong, he'd get up and go. Not angry, but disappointed. She hadn't found it for him. You see, he didn't really know what he was thinking about until someone found a way of turning him around to see it. Then he would fall into a book. I mean far into a book. Read all of *Moby Dick* once in two days."

"Tell me about now. It's important."

"Can't tell. You find out. My ways won't work. We're all a little battered, aren't we?"

Time for bed. Time to tell Michael, but how to tell him was not clear. I found him in the shed as I expected, listening to the stereo. Bach. A violin partita.

"I'm moving into Melissa's room for a while, if you don't mind."

"I mind. Why do that?"

"I want some privacy."

"Don't we have enough of that? You've hardly spoken for days. What's this ritual entombment you're going through?"

"I want to be alone for a while."

"Fine. To hell with it." He swept both hands in front of him. "What do you want me to say? Do you want me to tell you how selfish and foolish I think you're being? How when I need your help you're hardly there?"

"Finished?"

"Yes. No. Listen. Go stay in another room. Do what you like. But don't expect me to sit around nodding and grinning and patting you on the back. I'm not your father."

"You certainly aren't."

He was rubbing his face with his hands. "I don't think I have the least sense anymore of what is or is not real." He brought down his hands, and now he was looking at me without jerking his eyes around the room as he had been before, watching invisible things thrown by his gesturing hands. "I love you, Julie. Sleep where you will, and I hope you'll be as lonely as I will be."

As he walked away, I looked for some hitch or hesitation in his step, but he showed no expectation of reply and I did not call after him. I was shocked at how quickly his anger had risen at me, forgetting that his mind too had been stumbling about for days in silent confusion.

The room was stuffy, its windows tightly closed, but clean and almost bare since I had put the few articles of Melissa's clothing into boxes. She had stayed over so infrequently in the past years that very little personal had been left. I opened the windows, small and high, looking out over the dark fields. The breeze gusted from the south and on this side of the house I could hear a monotonous dripping of water from the high eaves onto the metal of the cellar hatchway. I went to the hall, looked down the corridor, and saw Michael's lights go out.

On the bureau was Melissa's paperweight, one of her favorite objects, an antique globe that contained a scene with particles of snow that could be shaken into a blizzard. I had been going to throw it away but could not touch it. Sometimes I would come to her room or pass it and I would see her sitting on her bed, legs crossed, and she would be staring toward the bureau where the paperweight was placed by itself in front of the mirror, snowing gently on house and hill and carriage. "What do you see there?" I asked her once from the doorway. She turned her face, eyes unfocused and slightly dazed. She frowned and raised her finger to her lips. "Shh. It's my mantra."

I lifted it and the snow fluffed a layer of dense ground fog up to the doorway of the house. I shook it hard, put it back in its place, and went to sit on the bed as she had. Ahead I could see the landscape, a carriage full of warmly wrapped people drawn by horses through the blizzard I had made, and beyond that the reflection of the wall behind me, my neck and shoulders and the outline of my hair. But the globe filled the area of my face and I was looking at myself and the object as if I had become the thing I saw. I held my back straight as she had, let my hands fall limply from the wrists over my knees. Did she have words too, or did she time her slow descent into herself by the falling snow, the gradual clearing of that world within the world?

February in a winter of deep snow. I am twelve and it is not the first time I have run away from home. I am leaving because my father and brother have quarreled bitterly over the use of the car, and my mother, rising from the table with the quick certainty of someone having an appointment elsewhere, has effectively ended the argument by driving away from the house while they are both still glaring at each other over the half-eaten remains of our lunch. Because of my angle of vision, I am the only one who has seen her silent gesture in the kitchen, hands cupped over her ears. I know how she will come home, moving carefully with the concentrated bearing of a practiced drunk, her glance slow, emotions sunken far under the abandoned surface of her face. When I stand I do not leave with her graceful silence. I beat my fists down on the tabletop. One empty glass wobbles and falls on its side.

"Why don't you leave her alone?"

My father has lifted his fork to spear the soft cheese on his plate.

"Your brother and I were discussing the use of the car. Your mother has chosen to involve herself in our discussion by making our comments irrelevant."

They continue to eat because for either one of them to leave that table without cleaning his plate, perhaps having more, would be to acknowledge defeat. So all I can do is rush from the room and up the stairs, slamming my door in hope of bringing plaster down on their heads. But I cannot stay in that room. Under me I keep seeing, as if I am chained suspended from the ceiling above the, two trolls who are my father and brother saying nothing, each eating as slowly as possible but neither of them tasting anything they fork into their mouths.

I pack the small knapsack I use for carrying books to school, filling it with the bare essentials—a skirt in case I have to dress up somewhere to get a job, an extra sweater, some underwear and socks, two notebooks, and a sufficient number of pens, since I am uncertain how much ink there is in any of them. My journal, the record of why I left, the economies I made, the harsh spiritual journey leading upward to the transcendent light of martyrdom, will live long after me as a guide to other lives of quiet desperation and a rebuke to the brute insensitivity of father and brother, the passive cruelty of my mother. I dress warmly because I can see the first snowflakes of our almost daily storm. They do not hear me on the stairs, but I hear the oppressive clink and scrape of their stalemated feasting. I pause on the sidewalk. If I really want to lose them I must not go by road or walk in landward directions. I must head over the frozen lake, across the trackless water to freedom. I take my snowshoes from the garage, bear them on my shoulder down the hill toward Perkins Pier.

The snow is falling steadily now, flakes so small that when I look back I can barely make out the docks, the old warehouses by the tracks. I walk past the curve of jetty and the light on its tip, west toward the wide stretch of grayish white that is the invisible opposite shore. I concentrate on sweeping steps, loping forward in a steady rhythm of swing and thrust. The top few inches of snow give to webbing, then hold as firm as packed sand over the ice thick enough at this time of year for cars to be driven across it.

Eventually I stop and turn to get my bearings. What is ahead of me has also become what is behind. Nothing except snow falling and snow resting. I strain to hear any sound, but the silence is so absolute that I hear only the sound of my own hasty breathing. So I continue, let that rhythm become monotonous again, watching the curved tips of the snowshoes. The new snow pulls up as I kick into it. At some point the air begins its own motion, sending snow at a slant into my face to sting my opened eyes. When I pause after a long period to catch my breath again, I close my eyes because the sight of only snow makes me dizzy and I wonder if one could become so confused that up and down would also be impossible to distinguish. But in that darkness, snow pricking at my face, I believe gravity will not desert me. I go on, more slowly this time. The muscles in my thighs are tightening and for a while, until they warm up again, each step has a slight hesitation as it begins.

Once I am certain I hear the muffled stroke of a heavy dull object rolling its weight into another. I stop. But it is only that slight, ceaseless motion of the unfrozen depths shifting against the leaden mantle of ice, a boom traveling the long line of a crack. Once my father and I stood on the bare ice and he told me if I could move as fast as the crack I would hear nothing but that boom, living in the un-diminishing center of explosion, and he had tried to make me follow the crack of a whip, the thunder in the path of lightning, the seam of speed along the passage of a supersonic plane. But I made him stop, frightened, my hands over my ears, and when he laughed I could not hear him, his face a grimace of mirth that might be pain. I walk on.

The swing of arms and legs is an act of breathing, involuntary, never to stop until there is no one there in me to know it has stopped, and the only thing I have to do is pass through a world of snow. The real world is my own mind where images are rising, twisting, un-folding so fast that I cannot recognize most of them, and then I know that this is an extended form of sleep, but instead of limiting the body on its rectangle of bed and under the upper layer of sheets and blankets, I have a new freedom, an endless space to flick through as I dream. I stoop, think I will unbuckle my shoes to rest since I cannot sit comfortably with them on, but instead I scoop a handful of snow and put it to my mouth, and the pain of it on my teeth, my lips, stands me up again. I am wide awake. The snow is no longer in my face but slanting against the nape of my neck, and I realize that for some time it has been that way. I am lost.

What I imagine is very clear. I will wander in circles until I drop. I will sleep and not wake. For a moment I am somewhere beyond panic, a space as blank and quiet as the one I stand in. I am not afraid, but I know very clearly that I do not want to die. I think of home. My father will have gone back to his study. Wherever I might be in the house I would be able to hear the sporadic racket of his typewriter, a dull thudding through table legs to floorboards to rafters, his wooden Morse code. Tim would be hunched in front of the television, vengefully watching a basketball game, hoping the sound is high enough to disturb Hob. My mother. She has parked the car somewhere at Rock Point. She sits in a haze of cigarette smoke. The same snow is slowly building layers on the surface of fender and hood. The straight, unmoving bole of a dark tree slants to her left, the ground slopes away toward the shoreline, where cliffs are caked in their thick oozings of stained ice. I know she is in a place much worse than mine and if I start to walk again, one painful thrust after another of heels rubbed sore by boots, it is because I want to reach that small cove between high rocks and walk up the ravine, throwing my snowshoes behind me, to stumble out onto the drive and find that car, now so heaped with snow that it is almost buried. I will beat against the window with my fists, scream until she turns her dulled eyes to the window and sees I am not the wind or her own slow pulse.

I like to think my mother saves me, or that image of her trapped on a spit of land above the lake. At least I cannot pause again or be tempted to lie down and rest. I stumble onto the shore. My body, when it is safe, reduces its complaints, and I trudge in the gathering drifts, the muffled clanking of a loose tire chain passing nearby. And I let my anger return so that my mother seems absurdly safe, as safe as it might be to sit in some dingy bar downtown, cupping her glass of Bourbon between her hands and refusing the occasional attempts at conversation by some lonely salesman or bartender. She will come home for the next layer, a liquid dinner in front of an old movie, my brother will slam out the door to seize the car, late for a party in Jericho, my father will wander down from his study, still somewhere in midchapter but no longer interested in who does or does not have the car, more worried now to scavenge some food to cook for him and me. And I will take that consolation, hold what shred I can of dignity, keeping my secret, knowing there are worse things than helping my father turn hamburgers, than sitting with him in the kitchen, his whole expression now alert, happy his work is done for the day, happy I am there to take the affection my brother will not accept, fussing over me as if I have been away for months. I have been away. I have been lost and returned but not found.

The snow in the paperweight had settled again on house and lawn. Inside the glass ball, the gay people in their carriage could once more see over the heads of the prancing horses, show me again their lifted caps, the muff nestled in a lap. I didn't hear Michael or Sheldon stirring, so I switched off the light to lie down on top of the sheets in the warm, wet night, waiting for sleep. But it would not come. I heard every creak and groan of the settling house, the pipes running some water, and finally Michael lifting his window. In the other room, he was talking.

I stood on the threshold. "Michael?"

"Hello."

"Did you say something?"

"I don't think so."

"I heard your voice."

"Muttering, I guess."

"May I come in?"

No answer.

"Mike?"

"You banished yourself. Permission is yours to grant, not mine."

"Granted, then."

I walked in, slipped under the sheet. I did not touch him yet. I was not completely there. Even as I stepped into the room, I partly resented doing so. I needed to have his presence affirmed by touch and sound, overcoming a simple fear of death, but I also wanted to struggle with him, to push away and come back. No matter what, I could not proceed alone. Silence was my mother's trick.

At first we did not need words anyway. I reached for him. Even as I was crying out against him, the first time we had made love since Melissa's death, part of me pushed away in each thrust, but his hands on my hips tugged us together again. We lay in silence, drifted to sleep, and I woke for a moment in one of those involuntary jerks, knowing that he too must be feeling a countertug for his own reasons, our hands touching to be certain we were there, minds still struggling through formulas of an uncertain alchemy. What began that night was a strange life of darkness. By day we could only sense the thrust away and we fell into lives as routine as possible. But by night we lay and talked or held each other in a world where all the rules and constraints we imposed in sunlight were suspended. Sheldon had urged us to talk, but now too often he was left to silence not because we chose to ignore him but because for a while he and his room were on the periphery of our lives.

There is no way to recount the mere passage of time, and yet that was what we needed most of all. But at first time was apparent only in brief moments where some aspect of the season entered me—the overripe and decaying green of late August, the sudden burnished and cold blue of a morning in which every blade of grass, each leaf would be etched in an air without haze. But each day was only another sunrise, no sequence, and night did not link them but was there to draw a dark line along the edge of disconnections. What happened when?

I recall a phone call pushing me rudely back into time for a moment. The voice was familiarly truculent. "Is it you?"

"Excuse me?"

"Julie." She said my name as if she resented having to pronounce it. "That's you, isn't it?"

"Speaking."

"Don't pretend you don't know me."

By then I had the voice identified. "What do you want, Mindy?"

"You never called me or anything."

"Why are you calling?"

"Don't you want to talk?"

"About what?"

"Jesus. That's it? You just walk away? Don't you figure there's more to it?"

"I'm going to hang up. The answer is, that's it."

"Hold it. Look. Don't be a little snot. Do you think it was easy to call like this? I got some pride too, you know. You know what they're going to do to my brother? Put him away. Salt him off into the bin. Hush it all up and ship him off to Siberia. They're not going to give us a chance to show how bad they blew it. And you haven't even seen him."

"Good-bye, Mindy."

The voice did its old shift, the one that earlier I could barely evade. Now it only oppressed me more. "Please. Who else can I talk to about it all? If you could only see him, like I wanted you to before.

You'd understand then. That would help. Couldn't we meet somewhere, have a drink?''

''No.''

''Yes, you will. I saw you the other day. What if I just come up to you? Say hello. Start talking. You couldn't say no, then.''

I did the only thing left. I could not help imagining the scene—crisscrossing paths, a figure under a tree sidles toward me, her hands in her back pockets. I hung up. A few seconds later the phone rang. I counted until it stopped. She did not try again.

I would wake and ease out of our bed. We would talk so long and late that I would be certain toward the end some of our replies were spoken by dreaming selves, and I would not want Michael to wake to my restless tossing. We talked so hungrily. We kept finding we had so much to say that we could have talked simultaneously all night, and often his voice would begin before my phrase had ended, tumbling words of response or continuing what he had been saying before. Memories, speculations, as if in all the time we had known each other we had only been learning the language. My mother, my mother, my mother. His own words were obsessed with Melissa. I kept my bathrobe always on the floor by my side of the bed, accustomed to night walks through our quiet halls, sitting in the shed sometimes until the sky began to pale. So far our wakings and walks were out of phase. Or did we both simply give precedence to the first riser? Often I reached into the space where he should have been, settled for keeping my hand stretched into it until his returning body let me draw back. And all of this counterbalanced by the curt, even remote discourse and motions of our daytime selves.

Sometimes I mistrusted my memories. Was I right in thinking that when I was a child, she touched me only to make the simplest gestures of clothing or bathing, and even then she would rather not? Or was I reinterpreting that past through what I knew of our final years together? Her hands toward the end had a way of moving brusquely but with complete efficiency. Certainly by the time I was old enough to do things for myself, she usually kept her hands in the narrow confines of her own space. I learned not to sit close on benches or couches or to choose the seat next to her when we all traveled together. My body would only clench with the need for a casually extended hand, but if her arm was spread over me along the back of the couch, it never slipped down in unself-conscious affection. I would straighten up against it, nudge it with my shoulder blade, but within an almost calculable interval the arm would retract like the tentacles of a wounded anemone. Could that have been terrible shyness, a respect for the space of my person becoming more and more a separate identity? If she had lived, couldn't we have found a way across that reticence?

I think I stood once in the kitchen of a friend watching her mother braid her hair as they chattered about the Christmas cookies they were about to let me join in making. The sun glared brightly off snow heaped by the window, bright squares fell across the mother's auburn hair, her daughter's long, red plaits. I watched the hand pause, my friend was pointing excitedly at the bottles of colored sprits, the cutters in shapes of a tree and sled and Santa Claus. Her mother smiled down on the top of the brightly lit head, the hand kneaded gently at the neck and shoulder. "Oh, that feels so good," my friend said, closing her eyes and dropping her hand to her lap, and they did not understand why I turned and seized my coat and said I had to go, had to go, and backed away from her mother's startled reach, as if that hand were white with heat. Or did I make that up, my own melodrama to express the need after my mother died? I would tell this also to Michael, but where was the voice to answer my stories, saying with that firmness of knowledge, "No, Julie. You've imagined that. Here is how it happened."? Who could help me distinguish the history from the story in such intricate weavings of memory?

When Michael shifted, his bare foot coming to rest on my calf, I welcomed that simple, absentminded touch, often a gesture that was the prelude to something he wished to tell me. He described Melissa in her second-grade performance, a Thanksgiving *tableau vivant* in which she played the part of Demeter holding a pomegranate over the piled cornucopia of fall harvest, and Mike could never forget how still she stood. Her skinny, white arms hold the fruit out straight to the audience, hardly even trembling while some speaker reads a translated Greek hymn. But she weeps unconsolably afterward when, because the hall is cold and she is dressed only in a pleated sheet, she sneezes before the curtain can close. And in another tableau I see Melissa at twelve not knowing that her father stands in the doorway and observes. She is absolutely rigid, her mouth open in a strained, gaping manner. He rushes in, certain she is choking.

Furious and embarrassed, she has only been practicing a ventriloquism for which she sadly discovers she has no talent.

Sometimes Jane was divided in my mind, as if she were a two-faced playing card—two-dimensional only in the sense that two images were there, but never to be seen simultaneously. Or perhaps that was my image of her until I found myself gradually entering her mind and began to see that was her own image of herself, one she must have found even harder to pass through than I. At least two persons, but no matter how large the chorus, always singing back to back, never quite to the same beat. How could I help but find her muddled in my own mind? The hand that reached to touch me was full of passionate intensity, all the caring of her intelligence and emotion, but the same hand pulled back from me as if I were the fire it had touched rather than letting me know how the sudden thwarting disconnection from within herself had withered the gesture before it could be fully given. I do not have her books to read, I have only the book of my own memory, and I still try to find all that it can give to me.

The archaeology of our past. On the dig at the lost city of Jane Bentley. Sometimes a whole clear pattern of walls and rooms emerges, even a blocked chamber full of intimate objects undisturbed by my own fumbling maraudings in the past. But often only a small fragment just out of crumbling soil. I dig around it, mark it, sift the dust nearby, then ponder the meaning and function of a small curved piece of clay marked with faint designs. In such a Pompeii, one struggles constantly to see through the foreground of disaster, the terrible eruption that froze the quiet, daily life and left the body petrified in its last position, curled between fear and flight.

Her facts. The traceable record. The things chosen to record each of us, fingerprints that constitute a history. Born: November 11, 1903, in Lynchburg, Virginia. Graduated Sweet Briar College 1924. Married J. Howard Cobb 1929. Son, Timothy R. Cobb, born 1930; daughter, Julie Cobb, born 1939. Died July 12, 1952, by her own hand, Burlington, Vermont. But when I look at this record, I am gazing through the eye of a huge, indifferent dragonfly—a creature so prehistoric that its broken prisms have not yet been focused by some primordial brain behind it all. Birth. Marriage. Death. Between those large coordinates the small creature crossed through smaller squares and boxes. In the private city of my own life, its newspaper would have filled pages with words for my mother. In the city where I lived in recorded time ten lines sufficed to let acquaintances know, telling them there was no place for us to mourn together. "There are no plans for a service at the present time. The family asks that no flowers be sent. The family asks only that those who knew and loved Jane remember her well."

Some mornings I would wake uncertain whether I was recalling what Michael had told me recently, or what I had dreamed about Michael and Melissa from things he had told me long ago. Did it matter? More and more I began to imagine their lives as well as recall my own. For instance, I see them on the beach near Fort Sumter, where they had been visiting one spring. They chase across the sand and topple into waves. When they calm, each will wander quietly away alone over the glistening, smoothed sand of low tide. They do not even notice how their hands part, how they drift slowly away from each other as if in touching the sea, the sea has spun them lazily out into deep waters. To let go of such a handclasp does not matter, and dropping from it into private worlds does not seem harmful. They can come together again as easily as they let go.

But the raucous cry of a gull, the high slap of some wave makes him search for her as if the open water might have drawn her in. Far down the flat white glare of sand, her figure is standing, and for a moment he cannot tell in the wavering air whether she looks toward him or away. She bends in a perfect slow arc and touches the incoming wave that surrounds her feet, pauses, retreats, spreading itself in clots of light. "Melissa, Melissa, Melissa," he says to himself and wonders at the name as if he has never heard it before.

She stands and cups a skift of foam in one hand. She holds it out, letting the breeze scatter it, and when her gaze slips past the focus of her own hands, she sees the sloping sand, the distant fort, the figure of a man absolutely still and turned toward her. At that distance he is only a silhouette floating in air, water, melting sand. Her father. Why doesn't he wave? Why does the air move him? Like a skittish filly in a field, she skims along the firm sand, laughing, by her motions making her father break into his own run toward her.

But I remember visiting a landscape far away from Vermont where a basket is placed in my hand. I hold on. I will not move. Across the bright green lawn, the other children have scattered to the edges, a kaleidoscope of small bodies. They bend under fringes of hedge, soil their knees on roots, and the shrill cry of a boy lifting his hand toward the sun, "I found one! I found one!" only increases their furious burrowing.

My mother stoops. Her face is beside me, but I will not look at it directly, stare instead at the tight straw mesh of basket, its net of shredded green tissues.

"I can't come help. That's not allowed. You can find some, though. Look. I think your cousin Jinny has one."

"I won't win anyway," I whisper, wanting to push her away. If she really expects me to win she could help, and the eggs do not matter to me. They are only tokens that might admit me to the highest pleasure, ownership of the large white rabbit who even now hunches in his cage over a pile of lettuce and limp carrots, eating unconcerned. My rabbit, if my mother would only release her magic and help me to win. My rabbit, if winning was not itself an illusion no matter how many eggs I might find.

A voice over my head. "Won't she join them? Dear me. Too bad. Shy?" and I can see the crinkled black shoes of our hostess, the rich old lady who owns the estate on the hilltop.

"Please." My mother whispers in my ear. That voice pleads beyond the simple wish for my own pleasure. Even now I can hear the complicated needs—wanting me to do it for my own happiness lest I lie that night weeping again for wasted chances, wanting it for her sake lest my weeping remind her of her own losses, needing me to go now so she will not have to face Miss Simpson's analyzing stare at mother and daughter, the curious gazes of all the mothers. Her needs, my needs, inextricably wound together, each of us demanding the signs and symbols of love. Was that the magic after all? Her voice a charm to send me out, and once I have departed, nothing can keep me from my goal. I pause for a moment between those two women. My mother's hand has come to rest on the small of my back. Whatever her motives, the touch is solely for me, and no one else can give it. She is asking me to believe in this afternoon, its game, no matter what I know.

Head and shoulders are held stubbornly, small legs kick out, and arms swing to the music of my own angry march. At least I have a clear beginning destination, the egg in the bed of narcissi that any fool could see, but none of them has gathered. I bend and pluck it up. For a moment I hold it in my palm, struck by the intricate zigzag of its patterning, and suddenly Miss Simpson seems more acceptable than she ever has, credited with powers of design and execution I could never match. But now single-mindedly I hound out eggs, rooting in bush and flower bed, ruthless in snatching from the heels and elbows of competitors.

Bent low and burrowing through a particularly promising thicket, I look up to find myself alone in an inner garden. In its center is a circular sundial, a wide, low bench of marble with markings. High boxwood surrounds me, pressed by this lavishly sunny sky into lush perfume. Small birds rustle and flutter invisibly on inner branches. The voices are only distant, wordless cries. For a moment I do not move. I remember the story my mother has read me about the circle of dancing fairies, the girl walking in the woods who stepped inside. They took her away for hundreds of years and yet she never grew older and came back to a different world, a circle of mushrooms in a wood of decaying trees, a village of strangers. I set down my basket and hold still. I pray for only one thing. I do not pray to have all this stop or to be able simply to walk back because I know some price has to be paid and magic cannot be reversed; I pray only to have my mother enter now, quickly, before the rest of the world completely fades, so that I will not have to go and return alone, and we will journey there and back together.

She does not come. But neither do their voices fade, nor the sun turn black, nor the birds stop their intimate lives. I look at the sundial, the gnomon rising stiffly like a sword thrust into the stone. I walk over and climb onto the marble to look at the strange markings, pictures of smiling suns and planets. Miss Simpson's voice penetrates even through thick hedge. "Only ten more minutes, children, then time's up." But here, time is not kept by ticking wheels, only the slow and silent motion of shadows, and I sit there letting my own desire tell time.

Do I want the illusion of owning the rabbit? Do I want to return to the world of baskets and counting and my mother talking to women she scarcely knows in unrecognizable tones? But from that perch near the center of the dial I can see eggs scattered in flower beds and roots. Greed or the shadow of greed plunges me back toward their world and I jump down, pick up my basket, pluck eagerly until I have to hold up the edge of my skirt to form a sack.

Leaving that magic garden is not as simple as entering it because there are layers of hedge with twists and turns, but I brush through gaps and toil up the hill as all of us are called in, and I am not embarrassed that I must hold my skirt so high above my muddy knees. The other children's shocked and disappointed faces are reward for my shame.

"Sweetie, don't hold your skirt like that," my mother says, but I shirk her hand and go to the place for counting and tumble my eggs, my modesty regained. Some of their bright designs crack and shatter.

"Oh, dear," Miss Simpson says and laughs shrilly. "I'm afraid she may be the only one who went into the maze. The rabbit is certainly Julie's. Congratulations, Miss Cobb."

Laughter, applause. But I do not look up, or even try pleading with my mother because we have known what will happen, and now is my moment to step fully back into time, out of this hour of illusions we have invented together. My mother and I. Because I cannot own or keep it. We are visitors in a strange land of relatives with other places to go, and a rabbit cannot come with us. At that moment only she and I know, conspirators in these minutes of suffering. She is beside me as I kneel at the cage. I sense her hand nearby above me and clasp it and pull her down. Her face is near, I let my own turn to the delicate whorl of her ear, the wisps of hair. I will not talk to anyone but her and so I whisper, "Can I hold it for a minute, please?"

So this is how her magic works. We step together outside of time. The others fade away, banished by our dance. She unlatches the wire door, lifts the white fur, ears, twitching nose, and places it in my waiting hands. The creature does not struggle but lies close to my chest, letting my hand stroke, as if it knows how brief this possession is. My arm that cradles the rabbit feels the heart pulsing on the wrist, my mother's hand rests on the nape of my neck, and in that moment of a hundred years there is no grief because everything is ours.

13

"Michael?" I sat up in bed.

This time I did not want to wait for him to return. I was wide awake, alert as if I had heard a stranger moving furtively in the lowest level of the house. I followed the dark hallway past Sheldon's closed door. Lately parts of the house had begun to seem abandoned. Was it simply too large for Michael and Sheldon and me to fill? When Melissa was alive, her section of the house still seemed occupied, even if she came infrequently. Slowly the outer edges were pulling away from us. And Sheldon, hearing my footsteps pass his room one afternoon, had called out, "Hello, stranger. Would you share some words with me?"

A gust beat rain against the window, a damp draft winding in. Mike was standing by the windows in the far end of the shed, and the only light was close to the door where I stood and blinked.

"Michael."

He turned, hands in the pockets of his bathrobe. Words never convey the instantaneous syntax of consciousness. No gap in time opened between my pronouncing his name, his turning, the continuity into casual question and my reply. No translation of the moment of awareness into words occurs, and continuity is unbroken by perception. All I can say at this distance is that I saw Michael's lined face, his hands thrust in pockets, bare legs and feet below the bathrobe's hem, and knew I had never seen him before. Or maybe the gloss on that comment is this paradox: I saw him as a stranger would, but a stranger who cares infinitely about him, so the viewer is no stranger at all. His hair is disheveled, one ear lost in curls, the other naked where the hair tufts out, his shoulders rounded slightly forward as if the hands in his pockets are holding stones. The clarity of that moment makes it unforgettable, but then and afterward it does not surprise. The named existence stands utterly in his own space apart from mine, joined by that single, frail strand: love.

"Can't sleep?"

"Just watching the rain. Or listening to it."

I reached him and he turned back to the window. We stood side by side.

"Does it go on like this forever, Mike?"

"Depends."

"On what?"

"On what you mean by 'like this.' "

"The house getting emptier, neither of us sleeping very well. Both of us always thinking, thinking into ourselves so far that we can barely hoist ourselves back to the rim to ask someone to pass the salt."

"I don't think so. I'm waiting, Julie. But I don't know what I'm waiting for."

"Couldn't that go on and on?"

"I couldn't tolerate it. At one time I was like a little child whose parent has died. I was just waiting for Melissa to come home." His hand moved along my hipbone, up and down. "I'm sure someone has studied all this. There must be clear and fixed stages of grief. Maybe we skip some of them, or warp them to the person we are, but surely they must be similar. We should be able to retire with a few people we love to a quiet place and pass step by step from one stage to the next."

At times like this I knew his grief was very different from mine, and I would want to clutch at him because the differences between us might make it impossible for us to reach across.

"Where are you now, Michael?"

"I wish I were sailplaning. But I can't. I've tried twice. No space. The present seems too crowded with memories. But different than they used to be. Less sharp, less cutting with loss. At first it was picking up each fragment of something that had shattered. Every piece of her life that came back to me said, 'Never again.' Those pieces lived in time so clearly and there was no more time for her. Now they aren't just themselves. I see her as a small girl, running at me, her arms out, that downhill, falling run when a child knows you'll be there to catch her, a trapeze act. I can feel that final leap, legs gone rubbery, all her weight in my hands, and I am lifting her high up. But at the same time she is all the times I have touched or known her, and the strangest thing is she isn't just Melissa but any child, and even all the things I love to touch and hold, and they aren't lost at all. I'm shocked then, because instead of that terrible blankness I had, there's a joy. It aches intolerably, but from too much pressing on me, not too little.''

"Isn't that much better?"

His hand held still. "That's why I'm waiting. I don't know. I don't know what it means. Part of me does not want to lose even a fraction of my sense of loss. And whatever this new stage is, it's not without hurt. But I don't know what's next. I keep feeling that whatever happens next is up to me somehow.''

We walked back to the couch and sat together. We had spent some time talking about marriage, about his wanting us to have children. He had not abandoned that, but those ideas had lost intensity for both of us, as if first there was the surprise of overtly stating them, then the simple knowledge of possibilities we would accept or not. For me, still not. For him, puzzlement since he had never imagined wanting to go through all that again.

"I wonder if we should take a trip soon. Just you and me."

"Where?"

He waved a hand. "England?"

I smiled. "Not Greece?"

"You'd like England."

"You don't think we would be running away?"

"Is that bad? I would like to be with you. Alone and elsewhere."

I could not help recalling a very recent time when putting space between us seemed essential.

"Julie, for a while after Melissa died all I could think of was why. Why me? It all seemed to center on me. I don't blame you if you walked away from that. I wonder if I know how to love anymore. Or maybe it's all different. The question is not why me, it's what can I do about it?''

We were sitting back on the couch, our shoulders touching, heads lying close. The room began to pale, his breathing was very regular, and I longed to have this moment of peace be there for us to summon up and step into at any time. I thought of the house expanding, my incapacity to fill it. It was tempting to imagine leaving all that. But we would also have to return. His hand stirred where it lay on mine.

"I take it back," he said quietly. "I don't think I want to leave, or leave Sheldon alone yet."

"I was thinking that too. What if we became so much alike in our thoughts that we could never tell the difference?"

"Sometimes as a child I used to think Liz and Sheldon had a code, a set of eye signals or motions of their fingers, and I would feel left out. Do children always think that in good marriages?"

"I wouldn't know."

"But it's not signals. It's all the life a child has no part in, that never will be or can be understood."

"You don't sound upset by that."

"Lord, no. Wouldn't the reverse be much worse? To live with parents whose lives had to meet each other through the child?"

I thought of myself standing between Jane and Hob.

"Let me try to tell you something, Michael. That I've never told to anyone before, except myself—over and over again. But don't interrupt."

He turned his face to me and did not answer. So I began, turning my story into spoken words, letting them out with my breath.

"It seemed like any other day to me. Was I just being a child, or was I simply too insensitive? I suppose we were all so used to her unhappiness by then. I had been swimming with some friends, had bought a new bathing suit with money I earned helping my brother with his mowing jobs, and I was wearing it to impress the brother of a girlfriend, a boy named Chris Coates. You know how it is then. We'd gone down to Redrocks, and we swam from the flat rocks and for a while I thought my suit was working. It was two-piece and pretty skimpy, but of course at that age, there isn't much to show or hold back anyway. He and his pal Chipper pushed logs around in the water having fights and the girls got bored or worried about their tans, so we stretched out on towels and loosened our straps like the university kids did. I was careful to leave a space between my towel and Kate Coates' and to be the last girl to lie down. After a while the boys saw we weren't interested in watching them play warrior so they came up on the rocks, throwing a little water to make it seem like they did it only to annoy us. He stretched out between Kate and me. The next half hour was agony. I pretended to be asleep or very drowsy and managed to get my leg and arm partly onto his towel. He had lain down closer to me than his sister anyway, although he spent the time talking to her. They were twins and didn't treat each other meanly, like most of the brothers and sisters I knew. All that time I lay with half-closed lids praying, 'Please let him touch me, please let his arm come a little closer.' Then I knew it was getting nearly time for us to go back to the road where one of the mothers would pick us up and I said to myself, 'If he doesn't touch me by the time I count to ten I'm going to brush my hand over his when I sit up.' Nine, ten and I'd say, 'OK. This time I'm counting for real.' I could hear Cindy say, 'Hey, guys, we'd better get back up there or Mom's going to kill me.' He and Kate hadn't talked for a long time. I snuck a good look at him and he seemed fast asleep, his face toward me now. Then his arm moved, his eyes were still closed, but his hand brushed mine, suddenly closed over it, and our fingers spread around each other's. He opened his eyes, and I let mine open wide, and we didn't say a word. It was the first time any boy had held my hand like that. I mean not because he had to, in dancing class or a game.''

I paused, knowing I was wandering in slow circles toward the center, but I could not get there or anywhere in any other way.

"I don't think it amounted to much more than that. As I recall, we never even kissed. We spent a lot of time repeating that act in various places and occasions—at first always when we were with the others. We'd walk down the street in a bunch, and at some point his hand would find mine, the squeeze much more intentional than any casual brushing. Finally we were going places alone, taking walks along the tracks or onto the golf course and in the loneliest places we would stop and face each other and hold both hands and stare. Just stare.''

I could not help smiling when I remembered, not having thought of those ritual love gazes for a long time.

"They dropped me a block from home. Mr. Angier was mowing his lawn and idled the motor to stare and yell, 'Hi, cutie.' He lived with his mother, one of those genuine dirty old men who don't know they are, and during the past year I had crossed the borderline for him and now he treated me the way he did all the little girls on the block who had grown up, whistling jovially, calling out, copping a friendly feel whenever he got close enough in line at the local store while he complained about the price of the milk he held in the other hand. I tossed my head and kept going. I was Chris's woman. Get in line, Mr. Angier. I walked up the front steps to the house. The door was open, but the screen was locked. I called my brother's name but then remembered he had gone to Montreal for a few days. He was old enough so he really should have been living on his own, I guess, and he would for a month or so. But he couldn't keep a job. Mowing was his thing that summer. I called my mother. No answer. The cat came into view and saw me and did a little mewling circle in the sunshine near the door. I walked around the back.''

The house, patch-painted for years. Impossible color to match, Hob said, not caring anyway. A quilt of greenish yellows. No clear design. Peeling again. No car in the driveway. The sun in its late-afternoon dazzle, the little apple trees at the far end of the lawn thick with green nubbins in the darker leaves. The grass clipped and weeded and lush, Tim's pride and joy. The chair placed squarely in the patch of sun, its rectangle of shadow stretching toward the shed. ''Tim will be angry,'' I am thinking, ''because of the new patch of turf and then they'll argue and she will say, 'What is a lawn for if you can't sit on it? It's not just to look at.' ''

''She had on her favorite broad-brimmed hat. She was absolutely still in one of those long reclining chairs, the back lifted. I called to let her know I was home. She didn't answer. But she usually didn't if she was thinking or reading. I did not want to see anyone anyway. I wanted to be alone with my ecstasy, to stare at my hand. I went up to my room and sat on the edge of my bed and stared. I changed my clothes, then stared some more. I don't know how long. Once or twice I looked out and saw my mother still sitting there and I worried a little about her getting a sunburn if she was asleep, but she had the hat on and it shaded her. I imagined Chris sitting in his room in the Coates's summer house out in Shelburne and he was staring at his own hand and I started sending him messages. I told him to go to the phone and call me. So it started again. 'Please, let him telephone me.' Or, 'I'm going to count to ten and then he will get up and call me.' Nine, ten. Try again. The phone rang. I was suffocating when I picked it up. My father. I hated his voice then. But he sounded a little worried. He said he'd be home soon, but was Mother there? Yes. 'Everything OK, then?' Yes. Chris would be getting a busy signal. Hang up, Hob, hang up. But he chatted on a little. Finally he said, 'Maybe I'd better talk to Jane for a moment.' 'She's out back,' I said, seeing a long argument since I could tell by his tone of voice that they probably had parted company on bad terms, or worse than usual, and he would be checking out what variety of silence he would have to face when he returned. 'Well, just tell her I want to ask her something.' I went to the back door and yelled, 'Mom!' No reaction. 'Mother?' I was holding the receiver and he heard my yelling. I said to him, 'She's sleeping.' His voice was clear then and stiff as steel. 'Wake her.' I sighed. I was sure I was caught again in the middle of one of their real doozies. 'Julie. Wake her.' I put the phone down and slammed the screen door on the way out and walked onto the grass, digging my heels in, went up behind her, and said, 'Mom, wake up, Hob wants to talk to you,' and I noticed the odd posture of her head under the hat, her face staring down into her lap, and then I walked around and saw her wrists and the blood and the razor blade loose in one opened hand. And the flies.''

I stopped when my voice made me stop. When his hand touched my shoulder and then held it tightly, I did not shrug it off, but I did not look at him, either. His hand helped me find my voice.

"I dreamed all summer of waking my mother. A voice commanded me, and I obeyed. I was given the power to wake sleepers from stone, from wood, from spells, from sleep beyond sleep. My hand could do it. I could touch anyone and their lax or stiff bodies would stir, breathing would begin, they would turn and smile and open their eyes and I would weep for gratitude, thankful to them not only for waking but also for wanting to wake."

Only a small interval passed before he said simply, "Thank you for telling me that."

We sat for a while until he said even more quietly than before, "It isn't that the grief goes away. It's that you accept the grief as part of your life, forever."

We watched the light increase, and then I went to the door and pushed it open. The air had turned very mild again, a balmy, mid-summer wetness, and if the rain stopped, sunlight would shine through a thickly humid sky. In a few minutes he was beside me.

He breathed deeply. "Smells good this morning."

I held the screen door open. "Let's go."

We were in our bare feet.

"It's raining."

"Not hard."

"Where are we going?"

"It always rains in England." I took his hand. "Follow me."

We stepped out onto the patio. The first shock of water on my bare feet, on my hair and shoulders passed quickly. It was as warm as the breeze had suggested. We walked across the hard slate to the willow and stood under its canopy. I kissed him and we held on for a few seconds, and then we strolled across the unmown lawn, grass brushing wetly against ankles and shins, slowly up the rise to the fence hand in hand to where the world was stretching before us.

14

"That's odd." Michael peered through the windshield toward the single light in the upstairs window. "Dad must be home already, but I thought he said Tuesday."

He turned off the engine, and the bluster of a late September wind burst over us, whirling leaves against the car, then breaking over the dark field beyond us. I yawned and stretched. Sheldon had gone to visit friends in New Hampshire and we had indulged in a long weekend in Montreal, filling it with good food and late nights.

"The witches will be out practicing tonight." He jangled his key chain searching for the one to the front lock.

I breathed deeply as we stood in the cave of the porch. Time for the first frost, then Indian summer, those afternoons of raking the front yard and carrying leaves to the ledge at the end of the field where they would burn into the night, glaring red and sparking in a wind, acrid smoke sifting into our bedroom. The door swung open, we stepped in, lights flared on in the hallway, and the door was slammed behind us.

My chest constricted when the voice behind us said, "Just walk slow to where the chairs are."

Ed Bushy, his face scarlet, eyes wide and bulging at us, was strapped with rope to one of the chairs. His mouth was taped as if he had suffered some dreadful surgery. Behind him a face I had memorized from newspaper photographs was peering at us without expression, Leroy Haines holding to Ed's neck the point of our kitchen knife.

"You sit," Mindy said to Michael.

She had a gun. I did not know much about firearms, but it looked like the kind of carbine used by deer hunters.

"What is this?" Michael said stiffly, and I had the ridiculous notion that from here on we were to deliver lines learned from Grade B movies or television. But the small motion of Leroy's wrist, an inadvertent twitch as he shifted his feet, made it all very real.

"This is my brother Leroy."

"What do you want, Mindy?" I stared at her, trying to tell my gut to stay put, trying not to see Ed and the knife and Leroy. But I must have jerked my eyes like a frightened horse. I could not bear the blank, waxwork expression and pose of Leroy, that pricking I could feel in my own neck of tender skin under the point. Mindy held the gun as if she were used to it.

"First off, I want him to sit in that other chair." Her face was so tired and pale that the skin was tinged with gray. "Tell him to sit, Julie."

I did not need to say anything. Still staring at him, Mindy lifted the gun and pointed it directly at me, her finger on the trigger.

"Leroy's going to tie you down, Gardener."

I had never had a loaded gun pointed at me. Oh, all those tomboy rat-a-tats in backyards or chasing Tim in the woods, but the imagination working in the pattern of hide-and-seek, of make-believe heroics, cannot truly duplicate the moment when a long, hollow tube of indifferent metal holds its perfect circle toward you, receding to the chamber, the moment of explosion. I felt that giddy rush of standing too quickly, was afraid I could faint, and breathed deeply, concentrating on the deft motions of Leroy's hands as he bound Mike from behind. He drew the ropes tight on each circle of arm and legs but was not unnecessarily rough. Mindy let the barrel slope down when Michael was secure and finally she crooked it in her arm.

"He don't have to be taped anymore." She nodded to Bushey, and Leroy took one end of the tape, paused, began to pull. "Do it quick. Hurts less. I learned that in first aid."

Leroy jerked. One lip cracked and started bleeding.

"I would've warned you. That's how come they taped me." Ed licked his lip.

Leroy was standing beside him, staring down with his head to one side as if intensely curious about how Ed would react.

"I was driving home this evening. Saw a light on. Wasn't till I got home I thought that's odd, light hasn't been on while they've been away, and I tried to remember if both cars were in the drive, so I walked on over to check if you'd come home. Wish I'd just called the police."

"What do they want?"

Mike and Ed and I began talking to each other as if Mindy and Leroy were not there, or as if by talking to each other we could form a safe circle to exclude them.

"Don't know. I heard on the radio that he'd got loose from Waterbury. I didn't think at all of him being here. Just thought how upset you'd be to come home to that."

"Did they hurt you?"

"No. Couldn't do a thing when I saw her with that gun. Wish I'd known who she was when I give her that ride some time ago."

Michael broke our circle by turning to Mindy. "What do you want?"

In all the time I had seen Leroy Haines on television, held on each side by officers, led into hearings, shuffled into patrol cars, shown in some clips from an old high school basketball game, I had never heard him speak. His voice was throaty, half swallowed, and very monotonous, with a slight catch in some words that could have turned into a stutter but never did, and when he spoke he kept his eyes turned down as if he were counting the lacings in my shoes.

"They din't treat me right there. Mindy knows that. They pushed me around and kept asking me questions. I told them to leave me alone. I told them I was sorry if I done something bad, but I din't want to talk about it. I got enough trouble with all the other voices talking at me."

As if his averted gaze were a trap to make me open up my own face so he could see the full reaction to his words, he lifted his eyes and hammered them flat and unblinking onto my face, his long head thrust slightly forward, lips tautly shut. I did not want expression taken from me by force and struggled to keep my own face as immobile as his.

"I said, 'What do you want?' "

"We're not going to hurt anyone. I'm trying to help Leroy, that's all. He's my brother and I'm going to get him away from here. When I heard the news reports, like he says it was," and she flicked the barrel at Ed, "I knew where I'd probably find him. The police bugged me, staked out our house in case he tried to get home, but I lost them easy. He was there."

Mindy's gaze at me was almost affectionate, sharing something she and I knew, but I wanted no collusion with her.

"We walked along the lake, then the back roads. I figured if there was one place they wouldn't come, it would be here. Then, fuck it, I find no one home, so we had to bust in, camp out on your canned stuff. I couldn't figure what next. I looked all over for the keys to that car.''

"I bet I could start it. I know how. Mindy was going to let me tonight.''

I looked at Leroy again, this time in amazement. His expression had not changed, but the voice was proud, and I was witnessing what I had partly known all along—that he was still like a child, stunted or damaged beyond repair, but dangerous because he had the emotions of an adult with the ability of a child to cope with them. And he was staring at me, eyes yearning for something, maybe mere praise.

"Then he came. All I wanted was Julie in the first place. You and one of your cars and a place to hide for one day.''

I worried whether Ed might have a stroke. He was breathing heavily, anger pushing through his veins, a straining at the ropes to level one quick fist at each of them. And then I looked at Mike and he was staring at me, and that was the hardest part of all, his eyes caught in some limbo where anger, his own wound for Melissa torn open again, his need to see me safely out of all this, were whirling him. In that silence the wind broke over the roof, shaking the loose windows.

A car's lights passed slowly by, and Mindy went to the window. "We won't stay here longer. I'm taking her and one of the cars, and you're to remember I'll do anything to get my brother out of this. If you don't call the cops or anything you'll hear from her pretty soon.''

"Take me." Michael was staring at her.

Mindy shook her head. "Hell, no. I don't trust you. I want to talk to her, anyway. Where are the keys?''

Leroy stepped forward and put his hand in Michael's side pocket. Mike flinched violently to one side, almost tipping over, and Leroy pulled back, his eyes wide.

"Don't touch me.''

Leroy looked at him, blinking and confused.

"Go on," Mindy said.

Leroy stooped again, and this time Michael did not move, his jaw clenched. When he had the keys, Leroy came around to stand with his sister.

"Give them to Julie. She'll drive."

"I'll be all right," I said quietly to Michael. I was scared, perhaps more than I ever had been in my life, even if I knew Mindy had some code of honor defined strictly by her own needs. At that moment I was more frightened for Michael, his own sanity.

He looked at me and then to Mindy he said, "Don't harm her."

Mindy began to speak, but Leroy's voice came again with that taut hesitation of pushing words up the steep hill of his reluctance. "I never hurt nobody. On purpose, anyways. They told me what I done to your kid. But that wasn't me, if it's true. I wouldn't hurt nobody on purpose."

Mindy's lips were parted, eyes squinting at her brother's mouth like a ventriloquist, and that face for one of the few times I had known her was as expressive as the mourner grieving in the side panel of a Flemish triptych.

"Go on." She pulled the door open.

Leroy went out, Mindy waited for me, Michael and I looked at each other, and then I turned away.

I sat behind the wheel, Leroy beside me, Mindy behind us with her gun.

"Do your seat belt," she said to her brother.

In the glow from the dashboard I could see her oval, disembodied face in the mirror. Leroy did not have his knife. At first that gave me comfort. If he had carelessly left it near enough to the chairs, Mike and Ed could use it on their ropes, but when I thought of police stopping us, of being in this car if Leroy panicked or Mindy raged, I lost all hope. The lights flared into the stubble of the dark field. I backed around, and came to a stop at the road.

"Canada," Mindy said. "Drive fast when you can."

So I drove the same road I had just taken, on a journey that still is a mat of details as intense and jumbled as the dreams of a high fever. The order of things is unclear to me, but I was moving again through an interval of wrecked time. I had been to another country for a few days, driven back to my home, and now, in a body that only wanted to lie down in stillness and gather strength again in one place, I was driving with a madman and his sister over a road that looked familiar but that was altered forever. I had no idea where that road was taking us. Did Mindy at that moment? I wanted to ask. I could hear that impatient, yearning voice in me straining to ask, "When will we get there? How much longer do we have to go?'' For the moment, enough adrenaline had flooded into me to make me very alert. I kept silent, fearing that speaking might juggle Leroy or Mindy into violence. But I tried to concentrate, make plans. What was it that one did in situations like this? ''I have to go to the bathroom.'' ''We've run out of gas.'' ''I think we have a flat.'' Then running for it. Or a sudden swerve of the wheel. They both hit their heads on the doorframes. I drive the car into a tree.

My mind finally held perfectly still. We were somewhere north of St. Albans. I glanced at Leroy, strapped safely in his seat, hands on his knees, head thrust slightly forward as if he were being very polite and enjoying the scenery, glanced in the mirror at the dim form of Mindy sitting still in the center of the backseat, and decided all those solutions were the slick formulas of scripts I could never follow. What was left was the stern reality of three persons, none of whom really wanted to be where they were, hence each of them capable of any level of distortion. I was as dangerous as they were, even if less possessed of power for the moment. We stopped soon for gas, and I followed Mindy's instructions. She sat behind me, gun draped in Michael's raincoat. I paid, watched the attendant go back to the lit interior to punch the cash register.

''I have to go to the bathroom,'' I said.

She laughed. Leroy grinned quickly, then quit as if maybe he had overheard something he was not supposed to.

''This trip, sweetheart, you can do whatever you have to do in your pants.''

I think it was later, just south of the border, that Mindy said, ''Where were you guys? Traveling?'' And I told her, and we added to the surreal quality of the voyage by having a conversation about Montreal. She was genuinely curious, had never been there, wanted to, but she had enough trouble living with the Canucks in Burlington. As her interest began to wane, I tried to break the dream by saying, ''Mindy, can't we stop all this? It won't do any good.''

''They're not going to help him at that place.'' Did she not name it to keep Leroy quiet? His face was turned now toward his side window and we were talking about him as if he were not there. Maybe he wasn't. ''This is the only thing left that I can do. Hell,'' and she lapsed into the old bitterness, ''you're the last one I have to explain that to. You're the only one that's understood. And I told you you'd see him.''

"You'll be in as much trouble as he is if you go on."

"Trouble I can stand. But I also got to live with myself."

In Alburg she made me stop on the outskirts and she gave Leroy the tool kit and sent him out to steal some license plates from a parked car. He did that efficiently while she explained what I was to do at the border. I knew well enough how easy those crossings always were. The face peered at us through the half-open window, the light shone dimly onto Leroy's lap and mine. Yes, we were U.S. citizens. No, just going up to Montreal for a visit, pleasure. Yes, the car was mine. The guard's eyes swung lazily around the inside of the car, Mindy's voice said cheerily, "Say, what's the weather up there, d'you know?"

"Same as here." He stood back, his hand flicked to wave us on, an indifferent voice said, "Drive safely."

In those flat, dull plains near the Richelieu, Mindy told me to pull over into a field. She walked with me, standing back a little with the gun as I did what I needed in the stubble of a recently shorn corn-field. Back in the car, waiting for Leroy, she held a map of Canada out to me, I spread it under the light, and she said, "See the place called Sault Ste. Marie?"

My body sank into the wide expanse of miles.

"That's it. We're not going to send Leroy out into a foreign country. I want to take him back to the States. But out there where he's got a chance to get all the way West. I been over it with him. We get him into Michigan and he'll hitch his way or ride the boxcars to the Coast. They'll never find him in a place like California."

"I don't know if I can go that far. I'll sleep at the wheel."

"Move over."

Leroy's figure slipped into our headlights, pulling up the last inch of his fly.

"He can drive for a while. I don't want him to for long, because sometimes he gets confused when I tell directions. You sleep now."

I strapped myself in, watched Leroy readjust the seat, look around for the key, then shift. In the beginning he ground gears, but he knew how to drive. I lay back. At certain crossroads she told him what to do, leaned to motion and point right or left, talking in a slow, careful voice. I thought I would not sleep, certain my best hope was that Mindy would have to drop off eventually, and then an absolute darkness dragged me down and I knew nothing until she was shaking me, I was struggling against an enormous weight, and I woke to the same space I had left, but my head was heavy, ached, and I wondered if I would vomit.

"You got to drive again. Leroy's getting sleepy."

The trees were different—more pines. My gut rose, I held back against it, won, moved over to the vacated seat, and waited for Leroy to arrange himself.

"I like your car," he said flatly. "Drives real nice."

I rolled down my window, breathed in deeply. The air was colder and now I realized the heat was on in the car.

"Where are we?"

She leaned forward with the map. The distance we had traveled was not far enough to please me. After a while the sky began to pale, and she said abruptly, "Talk. Say things to me," and I knew she had to be tired. Leroy's leg jerked in his sleep.

We talked. Or I did most of it until she started accepting my silence again because the worst hours were over for her. Dawn. In the full light of day her face was deeply drawn but she said triumphantly, "I won't sleep now I can see. Turn off that heat."

Absolute monotony set in. Gas stops. Leroy was sent in for food at a McDonald's. I had long ago given up hope that we were being hunted for, that our plates would have been identified. Any police cars we saw were going about their usual business, and Mindy's vigilance was now on me or on the map, making sure we did not go off in wrong directions, more and more gaily telling us how far we had to go. And I will admit that I had moved into a whole new way of thinking about our trip because I could see no end to it until it was accomplished. I wanted now to reach the Soo as much as she did, and perhaps even some strange camaraderie became established. What we were doing together was so arduous. But then, suddenly, that illusion would be rent and I would be standing in the hallway to our house, looking straight ahead in the harsh light at the face and figure of the man who had killed Melissa, and I would feel heavy and sick again.

Rivers that she named for us, trees and outcroppings of rock, the expanse of a lake. I was doing the driving and would not give it up to

Leroy anymore. He seemed wearier than any of us, would nod, eyes rolling back, eyelids drooping, and then for miles he would slump against the door. I could not help looking at him when the road permitted, his jaw hanging slack, hands with palms up in his lap. They were delicate for someone who had lived so difficult a life—long fingers, slender thumbs, slightly calloused but not scarred and certainly not mutilated like Mindy's.

He groaned, rolled his head against the glass, muttered words in a whimper like a dog chasing rabbits in sleep. Mindy shook his shoulder and he bolted upright, straining forward against his seat belt and looking through the windshield as if he saw something he could not believe.

"You were dreaming," she said, and he slumped back into his seat.

"Fuck." He said it once like hitting the wall with his fist.

"Bad dreams?"

"They wouldn't leave me alone. I told them I don't know. Leave me alone. But they kept saying questions at me."

"You're not going back."

He nodded. "It's better now. The voices, they haven't come for days." He looked sideways past my face, as if the voices might come from there.

I tried to concentrate on anything. Hawks in flight. The signs of occasional motels. License numbers. At times I drove so automatically that I would jerk and grip the wheel after what seemed like long minutes of gliding that must have been dangerously close to sleep. Once I even saw Mindy nod, then lean back in her seat. Was this it? But we were in the middle of nowhere, a stretch of countryside where the main traffic was trucks piled high with chunks of pulpwood, and Leroy was in one of his alert moments, playing with the dial on the radio and finding nothing clear. I could certainly stop and leap out, but into where or what? How could I evade them, or who would help me there? I sped up, hoping she would keep sleeping, that we would enter a town, a settlement of some sort, but she jerked awake, saw my eyes in the mirror.

"Don't let me sleep, damn it," she said to Leroy, who looked back at her in surprise and in a heavily contrite voice said, "I'm sorry, Mindy."

In the Canadian Soo she made me drive around the town until we found a car with U.S. plates parked on a side street, and then she sent Leroy out to work again. But this time I thought I had more chance. If only the driver of that car would come, yell, confuse Leroy.

"Listen," she said tensely, her face close to my ear as we watched him stoop between the cars, those hands working quickly, "we're almost through it, you know? Don't blow it. I mean what I say about how I don't know what I'll do."

We drove to another back street, where he changed the plates on our car. We were from Wisconsin now, "and don't forget it," she said to me. "This town, Green Bay. That's where we'll say we're going."

No help from customs again. We were in a longer line this time, but if anything that only helped Mindy because the guards were trying to speed things up. Ever since then, on trips to Canada, with no gun held behind me, free to say or do whatever I want, I've been unable to suppress a misplaced anger at the casual indifference of customs, have felt myself on the verge of some insane scene in which I scream hysterically, "How do you know I'm not being made to do this? Why don't you make us all get out, frisk us, search the trunk, do something, save me?" No, Mindy told them, we had nothing to declare. We drove in a high arc over the locks, Leroy whistled and pointed excitedly, "Geesum, Mindy, look at the size of that boat with all the rocks in it."

Michigan. She was looking at the map again.

"We're going to let him off here, down by that road. Leroy, you can hitch, but don't get onto this road that goes over a big bridge. Just keep going straight for a while, toward a town called Marquette."

He listened and frowned. "Yes, Mindy."

We were by Lake Huron near a little town named Hessel when she told me to pull over. The roads were flat and straight. There had been only one long, slow rise as we sped south, and from its height we could see over the swampy land, the fields, the stunted pines.

"You get out, too," Mindy said to me.

Colder than I had expected. No wind, but air that must have crept down from northern Canada. We stood on the dirt beside the road. Leroy had his hands in his back pockets and he shivered slightly.

Mindy had not even bothered to bring out the rifle, but she did stay warily between the car and me.

"Here." she stripped off her sweater. "You take this."

"Naw." He shook his head, but she made him tie it around his waist.

"And this." She handed him all the bills in her wallet.

"What're you doing?" He looked at the wad in his fist. "This isn't mine."

"Goddamn it, Leroy, do what I say."

He looked crestfallen. "But that's your money."

"You got to have money. How do you think you're going to get to California?"

He nodded, stuffed the money into his side pocket. "Guess you're right."

"And this too." She took the folded map and tucked it into his jacket pocket.

We stood very still. The sun was cut in half by the horizon, and pines in the distance were magnified, motionless and twisted lines against the orange disk. We did not speak. No cars passed. It was as if we were waiting for some signal, or maybe to watch the sun go down, but we had formed a small circle in which no one was looking directly at another person but out through the spaces between us. We all started at a sudden whir when four birds rose nearby, cut an arc on rapid wings, headed straight toward the last rim of sun.

"Ducks," Leroy said heavily, his lean face following their flight.

She stepped forward, threw both arms around him, pinning his arms at his sides, her face flat into his chest. He looked surprised, started to bring up one hand to touch her head, but she stood back quickly.

"Go on." Her voice was flat. "You be careful and get there and stay out of trouble."

If I could not bear the look he gave her, how could she? Do people like Leroy suffer from a defect of imagination? He looked at her now as though he had never foreseen this moment, had not imagined that somewhere she would not be with him any longer or they would be saying good-bye, forever. His mouth opened, he started to speak, but instead his voice moaned, a long, unbroken exhaling of grief, and what was more eerie than the sound was that it did not break into

sobs or words but halted abruptly. The mouth closed, and his eyes
did not blink, staring hungrily as if already she were receding into the
distance. The silence following that howl hurt most of all.

She turned, barked, "Get in" at me, and I crossed quickly to my
seat behind the wheel. I started the car as she slid into the back.
Leroy still stood there, face toward us, arms slightly lifted, but now
the light, diffuse and fading, was behind him and I could not see his
expression.

"Go on! Go on!" she shrieked at me, her hand beating the top of
the seat.

I made a wide U-turn, paused, but she was still beating the seat,
her voice saying, "Go on! Go on!" I did. She dropped her forehead
onto the top of the seat. In the mirror I could see her humped form
and the receding mannequin with his hands held out stiffly into the
road waiting for some other figure to join him in a paralyzed dance.
Soon I could not distinguish him from the pines. She did not lift her
head from a silence worse than the sound of weeping.

"Now what?" I asked when we were approaching the border
again.

"He needs time. Go back the way we came."

She did not seem to care anymore about licenses or camouflage,
but we were soon through Sault Ste. Marie and onto the deserted section of road in darkness.

"I won't be able to go on and on like this, Mindy. I'll pass out
soon."

"We've got to go farther."

"We could pull over, let me sleep. There'll be a wreck if we
don't."

She was thinking, her face a pale mask with unmoving line for a
mouth until she whispered, "He'll make it, I know he will. He'll be
all right."

But I could not hold on anymore. The bitterness I had held back
so far because it seemed dangerous to show in Leroy's presence rose
in my mouth with an acrid taste. "Fine. But what about everyone
else? What about another woman or child sitting somewhere on a
bench when Leroy's voices come back or he blanks out on the world?
Maybe Melissa's blood is not on your hands, but from here on in,
you and your brother are acting together—you even more than he."

My shoulders tensed for a blow, but her head shook only once and she kept staring ahead, wide-eyed. Finally she said in that hoarse whisper, "I know."

I had more I could say, but a gray weariness descended. Since then I have imagined the brute satisfaction of beating down on Leroy's face with club or hammer or anything I can grasp in my dreams, but far worse is that residue of gray indifference that can sometimes take me when I think of him. Is that the true accomplishment of evil? Perhaps Leroy was too ill to be thought diabolical, but he becomes the instrument of the greatest evil, rousing in me that vast, weary inertia, the Devil's phrase, "What's the use?"

Mindy was still thinking, and once or twice her lips even moved slightly. She cleared her throat finally. "Listen, you heard him yourself say the voices weren't bothering him as much. Maybe he's getting better, maybe if he gets to a new place he'll find a job, be careful."

I shook my head. "But he doesn't even really think he killed her, Mindy. Be careful about what?"

"I have to take that chance."

Silence for a while, but I was gripping the ledge of a cliff with stiff fingers.

"Will you let me call Vermont? I want them to know I'm all right."

"Not yet. You'll tell them everything. I don't blame you. You will soon. But I want to give him a good lead."

"What are you going to do?"

"I don't care. They'll do something to me, I'm sure. I guess I'll find out."

"You're not going to run away too?"

"Where? If I was going to, I'd go with Leroy."

I drove and watched her and knew my chance would come soon. She had to be in worse shape than I was. She sat back, and soon I saw her head lowering, then snapping up, and finally she slumped sideways. I glanced over my shoulder. The gun was loose in her hands, her body leaned against one door. I drove for a while to let her sink far into sleep, biting my tongue, lips, pinching myself, finding pain wherever I could on my numb body.

The tall white pines were close to the road. We had not passed a house for miles, but ahead the road sign advertised a turnoff for a view of the river's bend. I slowed, braked easily, and came to a stop, leaving the lights and engine on. She had not moved. I turned and put my knees on the seat, reached back, thought of snatching the rifle, but when I touched it, her own hands slid away easily and the gun was mine. She moaned, her fingers curled and unclenched like a baby in restless sleep, then she was lax again. I put my finger on the trigger, made ready to wake her. But I was in an awkward position, so I opened my door quietly, stood out, and then opened hers. She was still sleeping, her body angling away toward the other door.

"Mindy."

A moan but no motion. With one hand I grasped her leg and shook it. Her head lifted, she jerked up on one elbow.

"Shit." She sat up all the way.

I backed away slightly.

"I went to sleep." Her tongue was heavy.

"You drive now. To the next gas station."

But she was shaking her head. "I won't if I don't want to."

"I can shoot this."

I thought she was laughing at the obvious false bravado of my statement.

"Damn thing never was loaded. Go on. Shoot it off."

She pushed her legs out, stood, put her hand toward me. I raised the gun. But she had me no matter what. Her hand was on the barrel, she reached along it, unclutched my fingers. She pointed it away and pulled the trigger a few times. Flat, metallic clicks.

"I had to use something, but I didn't want to risk an accident. Look. You know if we go at it hand to hand I'll beat the crap out of you, and you don't want to fight anyway. A deal. No point killing ourselves on the road. Let's sleep a while. I promise when it's light we'll drive to the next gas station and you can call and to hell with it."

Nothing for it. She would defend him those last hours, and I was not about to beat her brains in after she went to sleep. She lay down in the back and I took the front. I did not think I would sleep. My whole body ached now to hear Michael's voice, to have him know I was all right, and for a while I watched for the first tinge of light. But I woke to dawn, and both my arms were asleep so that at first I could not sit up. I did not bother to wake her. I started the car, spun out onto the road. It seemed as though that gas station would never arrive. As I pulled in, she sat up, rubbing her face with both hands. She climbed out too when she saw the place had a lunch counter.

"I need some coffee. You buying?"

I nodded. We went through the doorway together like two friends on a long trip, and a few truck drivers swiveled to take us in and then went back to their own conversation. She sat alone where the counter curved and I went to the phone. My first call was to Michael. I wanted to weep when I heard his voice, and I lost my own for a moment, and then he was saying, "Thank God, thank God," while I tried to tell him everything in a language I could not speak fast enough. I told him what I was going to do next and that I would call again afterward, and hung up. I called the police through the operator. Yes, they had been alerted. Was there still any danger? I looked at Mindy, holding her cup in both hands as if to warm them, the shortened fingers of her left hand showing starkly against the white porcelain.

"No."

I went back and sat beside her and ordered some coffee. "I called the police, too."

"I figured you would."

"Are you going to try to do anything? Get away?"

"Where to?"

"I'm going to tell them where Leroy's headed."

"He's on his own now."

"They'll find him, I hope."

"Don't rub it in."

We were silent for a while.

"You hungry?" I asked.

She was staring at her coffee, her pulpy face ashen. "You buying?"

So we had some eggs and bacon and toast, and we were almost finished by the time the police came, lights flashing. They pushed in fast, and everyone watched while they found out which one of us was the victim and handcuffed Mindy, and the proprietor kept saying to me, "Christ, lady, you didn't need to stay quiet, you know, we'd have helped. Kidnapped, can you imagine that?"

"No," I said to him, "I couldn't imagine that."

I followed the patrol car to their substation and I called Michael again to let him know exactly where we were.

"I'll drive back," I said when he asked if I wanted him to pick me up.

"Carefully, please."

"Ed's all right?"

"Relieved. I called him."

"I'll have to sleep a little first."

"Have they got Leroy?"

"No. But they will."

I paused, listening to that indifferent electronic space between us, the sound a wind might make on an empty planet.

"Michael, will you marry me?"

"I thought you'd never ask."

I still ached for him when we had hung up, my aversion to telephones not lessened. If I hated Mindy it was with anger for the stubborn geographical fact of having to drive so far before I could hold on to my Michael again. I had to sleep at a nearby motel in a strange bed because my body would not obey me any longer. But, thank God, I did not dream. And I was wrong about Leroy. I told them where he had planned to go, mentioned Marquette, but somewhere near Montreal I realized the fallacy of my statement to the police. Leroy would not have been capable of following directions. Surely he would have been lured onto that big bridge if only by his childlike curiosity trying to fill the pain of his new loneliness. And California? What was California to Leroy Haines? His simplemindedness would save him, if for him escape could be thought of as salvation.

I hated that car soon, could not help feeling the presence of the other people there, and I had no satisfaction from recalling my last view of Mindy slumped in her chair, her face rising to look at me, both hands having to come up to wave since they were shackled together.

15

Before I called Tim I went walking in the field, a stroll that had begun because the house was the wrong place to be on an unusually warm fall day, a warmth that was more and more precious as the season advanced into October. This fall had not yet produced a deep frost, and on such mornings I could imagine that the sun had reversed its slow and inevitable journey away from us. I kicked along the line of high grass where leaves from the row of maples had caught on windier days. Far to our left on the downward slope Ed Bushey rode his tractor. He waved and I flapped both of my arms. Since my return we were closer—not just to the Busheys but also to the people up and down the road who had heard of our recent difficulties. For all the space of its open fields and scattered houses, the landscape was smaller than I had known, or even thought I would welcome. But now, to kick the leaves, see Ed Bushey waving, a small figure in a sweep of land toward a bright horizon was touching a fine net of connections that spread invisibly out from all of us.

I stopped on the ledge of elephantine rock that sloped toward the east and the view of Camel's Hump. The wedding was to be in two days, and everything seemed ending and beginning again. Tentative moments, but I was very happy, or at least when I was happy, I was much more so than ever. I wanted to share that, or include Tim. Or was I ultimately attempting the impossible, to include Hob and to fill that emptiness I had sensed in his life? But fall in New England boasts of its own impossible vitality, a gesture of defiance before the bitter cold.

Gazing at the landscape, even dozing a few minutes after I lay back with the sun on my face, was not only a search for encouragement, it also was delay, so I turned back and went to the phone and called Tim. His wife answered. "You mean Randy? Who's calling? Oh, yes, just a moment, please." *Oh, yes?* Efficient as her tone was, I clung to that phrase in the silence while I waited. At least he had discussed his past with her, had not buried it so thoroughly that she did not know anything about me.

"Hello," the voice said through a very good connection.

"This is Julie."

"I know."

"Can we talk for a few minutes?"

"I think so."

"I have something to tell you, then a favor to ask. I should have called sooner, but . . ."

Where to begin, how to say enough magic words to charm him into coming? Suddenly more than anything else, I wanted him to come, to be there, but I was paralyzed. What was it? All that struggle of those past months? As the intervals of time connected like filings drawn into patterns by a magnet, the need spread back into years, into time even before memory.

"Julie? Are you still there?"

His voice saying my name. That was more magic than I possessed, as if he were giving me back a name I had not known was lost until he held it out to me.

"Tim." I declared it. A single syllable that was a sentence as long as my life.

"What is it, Julie? Something wrong?"

I found my voice again. "Everything is right. Or can be. Please come. To my wedding. Be Randy if you want. But I want to see you." I could hear him breathing in the silence. What if he hung up? What could I say? "I don't know how to say it. I thought I had a speech planned, a description, something to make you want to come. I don't. Can you come? It's day after tomorrow. His father and a few friends will be here. But I've just understood something." I swallowed. He was still there. "Something important will be missing without you. I can't pretend or make it easier for you not to come. I need you to be here." Then I simply gathered it all up into my hands and held it out to him. "I love you."

What could he do but be more than a little confused, even embarrassed? He could still say no. He had to be at least somewhat stunned. But instead of answering, he laughed. An easy, quiet laugh. "You haven't changed a bit."

I found myself grinning foolishly to the wall. "What do you mean?"

"Oh, seeming to be so clear and in control and then throwing it all away and asking for something in a way no one can refuse. You always got me, you know, even when I'd stood in my room and practiced saying no."

"You will, then, you will?"

"I think it can be managed."

I laughed now. "You haven't changed either."

A silence. "I suspect we both have, greatly. But we have a place to start, don't we?"

"Yes. Your wife too? She can come?"

"I'll call you back. My son is going to college next fall. We were thinking of coming East to look, and I think he can miss a week of school. I was going to write you anyway to let you know."

"You were?" I heard my voice rise with simple pleasure.

But he was still enough himself not to want the conversation to go much further. When we were younger, what brother Tim gave, he liked afterward to let you know he might not give again, or could even take back. Not that extreme now, because he let me babble on a little about Mike and myself and Sheldon, and then I told him briefly about Melissa so that he would not have to come into that unknowingly, and I could save all the part about Mindy and Leroy till later. But I could hear myself saying those clear and simple words about Melissa and knew that would have to be declared from time to time in all my life to come, a distillation into subjects and verbs.

We were about to hang up, his voice at first efficient in saying what he planned to do, then hesitating, saying, "Julie?"

"Yes."

"Thank you."

He was giving me something back, the tone of those words filling the hands I had held out to him.

When I went into the living room to join Sheldon and Michael I blurted, "My brother's coming."

"Brother?" Sheldon frowned. "What brother?"

"Hers. The only one."

"Mine."

"Why am I never told these things?"

"She's telling you now."

"He ran away from home. I haven't seen him since I was thirteen."

Sheldon thought for a moment. "You wouldn't make fun of me. But I can't help thinking you're telling me another story. By Cobb."

"No. About Cobb."

Michael made room for me to sit beside him. "Tell it. It's the good kind of story. With resurrections."

"Speak."

So I told Sheldon and he hardly interrupted me at all.

I looked for my brother in the man who came, at first staring at him so eagerly when he turned to talk to others that I suppose my gaze must have appeared half mad. But I was trying to chip away the years, return a shock of hair to that fast balding head, shape the features that were now comfortably ensconced in flesh and well-clipped moustache, make him lean and nervous and in quest of more than anything his mother, father, especially his sister could give. But he clung to his present self relentlessly until I surrendered to it. Occasionally he would start to say something, the words would be held back a moment as if he were making sure they were presentable, and his mouth would purse in a gesture I recognized as my mother's but totally altered to his own purpose. Hers would have led to a shrug, silence, the words told to go back to chambers and shamed into never reappearing, but his was only to be certain he wasted none, and what he saved then, he would use later. Time had been better to my brother than I had anticipated in my gloomier moments, especially in the person of his wife, Jenny, a very petite and energetic woman from Texas, so sprightly that even when she sat in one place by his side she scrolled arabesques around him with her eyes and hands and words. Why Hob had never mentioned Tim's marriage, which happened so soon after he left, baffled us both, since surely Hob had known of it.

If at times I saw Tim clearly as he had been, it was in the person of his son Reid, who was already taller than his father but as lean as Tim had been at that age. He dwarfed his mother, who said that first day, "My genes are retiring, even if I'm not," and Reid blushed, correcting her—"Recessive, Mom." "Well, I'm not that either." I blessed the presence of those two. Tim and I would have been too shy and slow to have come far in that first meeting without them, but

they gave him much to hold on to, and me a sense of welcome as if I
were the one who had come to visit. "I'm glad," she said to me that
first evening, those quick eyes holding on mine, "that you persisted.
He needs this. You will have to come visit us soon. That's only fair,"
and I promised.

On the morning of the wedding I risked telling Tim about Hob's
letter and asked him to read it.

He hesitated. "I did my time, Julie. I'm free of all this now. It's
addressed to you."

"And to you through me."

He held the pages folded, and he kept drawing one finger and
thumb along their edges as if pressing the crease so that it would not
open again. Then his hands stilled. "When you found Mother, Julie,
who did you blame?"

"Myself."

He looked up and nodded. "I blamed Hob."

"I know."

"No one blamed her."

"Should we have? I mean forever?"

"No. But it was the right place to start. I had to go all the way
back to the beginning to start there after it had gone far in wrong
directions. It took me a long time to learn how to grieve for her."

"Didn't Hob blame her?"

"If so, he didn't share that information. But that doesn't matter
too much to me anymore. I mean in that personal sense of what a
father and son might share. It might have a factual interest to me
now, I suppose I'd understand him better, but nothing can ever fill
in the blank of what he denied me, the right of a son to help console
his father. That's the problem of time. I've long ago forgiven him,
and after all I did not stay around long enough to give him much of a
chance, but understanding is no substitution for what we missed.
Anyway, I'll read it."

"Thank you." I stood. "Where's Reid?"

He smiled. "In the kitchen. Where he lives."

"I promised to go for a walk with him."

Reid was finishing a sandwich that seemed to have incorporated a
layer of at least one item from every shelf in the refrigerator.

"Can you walk?" I asked.

He nodded.

"But not talk?"

He pointed to his moving jaw, the bulge of cheeks. By the time we were on the patio he was capable of speech again, but Reid was at the age where some prompting was still necessary—a little shy, but very willing once he forgot to be. He had surprised us all the previous evening by arguing with Michael and Sheldon in a quiet, articulate firmness.

We were going to have to walk anyway before talking because Michael was mowing a large rectangle back from the patio. He pushed, the engine choked and complained at having to cut through the matted growth of our neglect. When he saw us, he waved, the motor almost stalled, and we walked on toward the fence, then over it. The weather was holding for us, bright and warm, but with storms and possible flurries expected that night.

If Reid was shy by nature and age, I was shy by role. Aunt Julie. That was something to grow accustomed to, and in the past twenty-four hours I had tried to walk around the term furtively, sizing it up. Now I decided on boldness, some attempt to seize and make it mine. I had encouragement from Reid. We found each other easy to talk to, a few times at dinner I had seen him staring at me with unguarded intensity, and twice that morning he had chosen to begin a conversation with me, albeit in a way that implied he was doing it because I was the only one nearby to talk to at that moment. So I confessed.

"I don't really know how to be an aunt, Reid. But I'm sorry I had to wait so long."

"Oh, that's all right. Actually Dad's told me about you sometimes. I used to ask him if he had brothers or sisters, and when Granddad and Nana came to visit, I'd ask him where his parents were."

"What did he say?"

Reid shrugged. "The truth. That they were dead."

I listened, not only to see if there would be more, but also to hear his words again in my own mind for any intonation. But they were facts as simple as the weather or time of day. "The truth . . . dead."

"Where do your grandparents live?"

"In Texas. Abilene. That's where Mom grew up. I like parts of Texas, but not that part much. Colorado is better anyway, and Vermont."

"Have you really seen Vermont before, or are you just trying to please your aunt?"

He blushed. "Neither. I mean I've seen pictures. Once after we spent Christmas in Texas I asked Dad what it was like where he grew up and he went out and bought a big picture book—mostly Vermont, but New England, too. I liked it. Anyway, what I've seen is fine."

We had turned the curve of the hill by the end of the maple grove, and the valley, the next ridge, then the distant shape of a hazy Camel's Hump were visible.

"Maybe you'll come here. To the university, I mean."

We stopped near the ledge and he stood with his arms crossed in front of him.

"I think I might. How come you're so much younger than Dad, do you know?"

I thought for a moment. "Actually, I don't. I guess they waited till later, or I could have been a mistake. Or Tim could have come sooner than they wanted." But even as I was finishing, the same feeling of puzzlement came over me that had been there when he mentioned Hob and Jane earlier, so I asked, "Does your father tell you much about our parents?"

"Oh, a little. I've seen his father's books in the library. I read one for school, but I don't think I understood it very well. It was about a boy and his parents and their farm. Seemed very sad to me. But English isn't my favorite subject. I know your mom died when Dad was young and how he ran away from home. She killed herself, which is too bad. And he had a rough time for years. Not just because of that. I mean the Army and being away from Mom and Korea and all."

Again, facts? Not quite. They were his facts by rights as strong as mine, the partnership of blood, but time had rendered them, and now they came back to me, different in substance.

"Someday I'll tell you about them, maybe. Or about Tim and me."

"I'd like that. Granddad tells me sometimes about when he was a child and all. It's pretty neat." He pointed to the bottom of the hill suddenly. "Do you own that stream?"

"Up to it."

"Can we walk down there?"

So we did, and as we made our way down the slope growing in with burdock and maple saplings, with alders near the water, I thought that at first the enormous effort of trying to tell one's life to a child or nephew, to transmit those tales that were the images governing my life, would be so impossible, so frustratingly inarticulate that some terrible isolation might result. But I had to stride to keep up with him, found myself again the little sister stretching to stay with a gangling, self-absorbed walker, and I wanted to catch hold of Reid's arm, sit down on the bank of that stream, tell him all I could remember, beginning with those walks by his father's side, in order to hear my own obsessions cool into history, making them as much his as mine. And then someday to hear him tell them back, or tell his own. But by the time we had come to a steep bank, the clear water clotted with the bright red and gold leaves, I felt no urgency. I could tell those tales not once, but again and again, and as differently as all their valences permitted, if he listened, or his children did. Or mine. Or I could even write it out for them and for myself.

"You know who I like?" he stared at the water. "I like Sheldon a lot, Mr. Gardener's father."

"So do I."

"When did Mr. Gardener's mother die?"

So I told him, and from there it was easy to go on. As we strolled slowly back up the hill, the sun so warm that we both took off our sweaters, I knew I had begun learning the art of telling stories, and Mike's family was a good place to begin. We watched two hawks rise in slow circles from a field beyond the house, maybe their last hunt before flying South. Michael was trundling a silent mower back to the shed.

"Almost time for a wedding," I said, and he laughed. As we crossed the fence I asked, "Am I doing all right?"

He looked puzzled.

"As an aunt."

He grinned. "You'll do. After all, you're the only aunt I've got."

"No competition. Then I stand a chance."

He was looking at his feet again when we turned to walk on. "I'll bet you'd beat them all anyway."

Tim stepped out onto the patio as we passed the willow.

"Your mother is looking for you. Something about a quick trip to town for a shirt and tie," and then Jenny was calling from one of the upstairs windows.

"My turn." Tim took me by the arm, but we went only as far as over the mowed lawn to the fence, where we stood leaning and looking back toward the house. "I've read the letter. Hard to read because even after all this time I can hear him, and I want to get up and stomp away. I never could win with words. Anyway, you did part of what he asked."

"What?"

"Brought us together again."

"I was working on that long before I read the letter. Even if I didn't know it." That seemed not to give Hob his due, though, so I added, "But it helped."

Too little time left for all the preparations I had neglected, and I was still dressing when Michael called impatiently, "They'll think you're reluctant."

On the patio the guests, some neighbors, friends were waiting. It was Reid's idea to arrange speakers outside, so we had music to help me over the flagstones to the lawn and the waiting Reverend Frasier and Michael. Sheldon gave me away, "Temporarily," he said. What did it matter that Purcell was cut off in midcadence, or that two local youths decided to drag-race up Mt. Philo Road as Frasier started to read? We had time enough to pause, and when he began again, it all went quickly enough. We said our vows, I watched the leaves at the far end of the field rise suddenly in a flourish of breeze that took its time to reach us, and then all our friends and music greeted us, Ed Bushey hugged me as if he thought I meant to run away, he passed what was left on to Tina, and Reid gave me a kiss on one cheek, which I insisted on parlaying into one for the other. We had champagne and an idle afternoon ahead, and now the music urged us to dance. I danced with Ed and Reid and Michael and Tim, who waltzed in amazingly graceful swoops and arcs, and finally with Sheldon in the center of a circle the others formed, moving in slow, precise steps, as if those hours and years we had sat and talked together were spent practicing for this. Sometime later we all went to a restaurant, and we increased with more wine and food and conversation the confusion of our joy. But good beginnings are always confusing.

16

We waited until the next spring to take our honeymoon, stopping in England on the way to Greece. What I recall best was York and the Mystery Plays, perhaps because London or Devon or even the city of York are places we have revisited and memory elides, but we have seen the plays only once. We were ushered to our seats high in the sunlight and we sat close together watching the stands fill slowly, the few props be moved into place in the wide stretch of platform and lawn under the high, ruined walls of the Abbey. Soon our knees were tight against the backs of the people below us, our backs pressed by those above, and to my side a family squeezed in, a young mother and father, a boy and girl, perhaps thirteen with long dark braids and a finely chiseled, serious face, sat between her mother and me. A slender body taut with expectation, she shook her head in annoyance when her brother leaned to offer her a piece of his chocolate. Her mother, with the same deep-sunken, watchful eyes but prominent bones that made her a much less delicate version of her daughter, smiled down at her child's intense frown toward the empty stage but did not let her see that expression when she turned to ask impatiently, "When will it start, Mummy?"

Did I smile too? I could not help remembering what it was like to sit in my purchased seat at theaters or movie houses when I was her age or younger, the curtain hanging still in front of me, everything I had waited for gathered ready to unfold behind that veil. As I looked at her I thought she would make this afternoon even more wonderful for me. I was there because I had heard this was a cultural event one must not miss, a rare opportunity to see the old plays performed authentically. She seemed there as an audience should be, perhaps would have been centuries before, her whole life concentrated.

The trumpets blew, God and his angels appeared high on broken parapets, Lucifer strutted with pride and writhed in envy against the making of a new world, and the long story of the world my world imitates each day, began. I leaned forward to hear the words, those simple, clear verses at first naîve in their rhymes and marked rhythms, then becoming the language of all speech and thought, simple only in the way the inner structure of all things are. I no longer saw the tiers of people, bare trees, and sky. I was lost in a story, and all my wishes and fears tangled themselves about the figures of Adam and Eve rising sleepily from clay, Noah marshaling his donkeys and dogs and cardboard cutouts of elephants into the ship he pounded together in spite of his neighbor's taunts. When Christ was born I knelt with those kingly figures whose tinfoiled crowns glinted as they journeyed in from the parking lot, I urged Mary and Joseph to flee on their donkey, perhaps the same one that balked that morning and would not let trucks pass by Bootham Bar, and I raged at the brutal soldiers who seized dolls wrapped in swaddling clothes from wailing mothers to dash them against stones of the wall or to rap the wooden stage with sounds as hollow as their cruel, efficient hearts. And all the time I knew I was watching more than what I was. I was also seeing whatever I had known or experienced—whether that wonder of a world rising into light or a summer morning when I stood on the peak of Camel's Hump after watching stars all night, or the terror those blank faces, gaunt hands showing through the slots of boxcars as their bored guards played a hand of cards and waited to load the next shipment, or a trench full of women and children from a small Asian village being pumped and sprayed by soldiers whose guns bucked and smoked and took all the men's concentration to fire correctly. Flee on your donkey, ride safely away—all my hope lay cradled in that actress's arms. I watched that baby grow into manhood, watched his short, intense lesson in what it is to be human.

He almost found that to be impossible and asked to be delivered, kneeling awake in a garden while his companions slept it off. But such deliverance was not why the long journey had begun even before He was born when angels flamed against a gateway in Eden. I went with Him to stand in the presence of Pilate and watched the mockery. On that cool day in York a man dressed only in a loincloth staggered over a stage under the weight of two beams on which I soon saw his hands and feet nailed by burly carpenters of that town and still He did not cry out until He spoke for all of us and asked his God, his Father, why he had been forsaken. In that moment my afternoon was torn by grief more terrible than any I had known because through that rent flooded all my griefs together. I turned to the child between us, and her face was wet with tears. She sat perfectly still, her weeping as old and quiet as the deepest sorrow. I looked up and saw the mother gazing at her child, her own eyes full, and neither of them seemed to breathe, they were so lost in what they saw.

I watched the figures below take Him down and wrap Him in a shroud, I watched the Marys mourn for Him, and He was claimed for burial. Satan and Death exulted, capering their little dance in short-lived victory before the stone was tossed aside and He rose to harrow the house that Lucifer built. Christ was resurrected and rose with the signs of His mortal wounds, and suddenly I could not sit there any longer. I turned to Michael, my mind utterly bewildered. He was in a haze I could not blink away. I stumbled down the row of stooped figures, bumping the backs of the people below me. The usher mistaking my need murmured, "All the way down, then left," but I descended nearly blind, sliding a taut hand along the rail, then turned onto the sloping lawn toward the trees and paths of the garden. "What is it, what are you doing?" my inner voice kept asking in dismay, "where are you going?" I came to a wide oak and sat against it, laid my head back, and closed my eyes. How can I say what I saw? The images elided, merged, whirled in their own new forms and were no clearer at times than Michael's face had been before I stumbled out.

I see hands, and like Art's they are rough from hewing and carrying, even flecked with blood from some violence, but they are lifted together, cupped toward light in a gesture so gentle that they belie their harsh scars. A woman sits in sunlight, her legs drawn primly under her skirt, and the dark shadow of a man rushes soundlessly up the lawn toward her, his arm raised to strike, but she lifts her own hands like knives against herself. I do not know if she is Melissa or my mother, but she becomes a weeping child, and she is walking slowly over a long bridge. I can see her because I am waiting huddled, my knees drawn up, staring at the child who comes and stops beside me and holds out a hand. I unfold slowly, take her hand in mine, and we walk together toward some unknown city on the other side. All I know is the touch of her hand curled entirely into mine, but that is all I need to know.

I heard the trumpets distantly, silence, then a long interval of applause as steady as the sound of falling rain. I stood near the exit and watched for Michael, looking at all the faces as they spilled out around me, men and women and children, nuns and clergymen and officers and women in dirndls, a group of kilted youths, and suddenly I was not certain I would know Michael because I was seeing all their faces, and how each was so different from the next that I might forget what his was like. But when he came, I saw no other face or body but his emerging from the crowd.

"Are you all right?"

"Wanted to be alone for a moment."

We could not stand still in the slow, forward pressure of the crowd so we joined it, strolling along the wide path toward the park gates.

"You missed the Day of Judgment."

"I heard it, though, and I didn't miss the Resurrection."

We held on to each other's hands after we were briefly separated.

"Ready to journey on?"

"To Greece."

Even for the dead, there is no finality. Haven't I seen my father's reputation rise, then settle into a plateau of solid appreciation? And more than even I know, Melissa is an inseparable part of our lives, of our identities. I can see how her presence in my life nudged it at an angle to its former path—small divergence at the time, but in decades the arc such an angle subtends is wide and I can look across that gap to the person I might have been. There is pleasure for me in being increasingly known in my own right—Julie Cobb, not just "daughter of J. Howard Cobb." I do not mind the latter when it comes, but I readily admit such equanimity is due to having my own reputation. The shapes I make of stone or wood seem to keep needing me to chisel them out of the unformed block, and if other people and some museums find them an enhancement of the air they displace, I am very glad. Mostly because I cannot stop, and after all, we cannot keep all of them.

We did not expect Sheldon to live through the previous winter, but he hung on. We are ready, he says he is too, but we never will be when it comes. He is pitiless in the way he mocks Mike's bald spot, placing a hand on his son's head in false blessing, saying, "Wait, you're not the hairy one," then boasting of his own full, white mane.

We have no children. Not for lack of trying at various times, and there were even moments when we lost ourselves in the hope, wondering if we could survive together without that other being. Not so now. The natural receding of that need was to be seen in our un-willingness to adopt a child or to consider various medical possibilities. Do we begin to suspect that we would have been un-happy later if we had not tried before? Our work and our lives together seem enough, but I willingly admit that not having children after trying is very different from choosing not to.

Sometimes Reid has occupied a territory between child and brother, but maybe that is true for all aunts. He came to the univer-sity, sputtered a little, and went through in five years, and like so many young people who cannot leave Vermont but who cannot find jobs, he has become a successful entrepreneur, running a small fresh fish store. He makes his own runs to Maine early in the morning, and I have gone a few times to be with him and talk and to have glimpses of the sun rising out of the ocean.

Mindy should have been prosecuted for kidnapping as well as aiding in her brother's escape, but the process of plea bargaining reduced her charge considerably. She was out on good behavior before long. She called to let me know she was headed for California, in spite of probation. "I can't stand this fucking cold asshole climate anymore," she said. I did not have much to say. Her voice could always tumble me back to places I did not want to be. "Don't worry about me," she said. "I can manage." I had not indicated such con-cern. She was still trying to make the world give back what she wanted. I gather the police came close to catching Leroy in those weeks after Mindy and I released him in Michigan. Somewhere in North Dakota a state trooper picked up a vagrant, and he was taken to the border. Evidently letting Montana worry about such people was their habit. Only the next day did the trooper match the bulletin with his hitchhiker, and by the time he had tried to excite an indif-ferent Montana State Patrol, the man was nowhere. Which is where he is for me forever, that intimate nowhere of dreams where sometimes a recognizable figure will stoop in a swamp near railroad tracks, maybe doing nothing but warming his hands, but I cannot see, and those are the dreams I struggle to wake from.

All that was easier for me to deal with then for Michael. At first, soon after we were married, his anger was mollified by the efforts we made, offering rewards through police departments and newspapers all over the West Coast. Then he focused his rage closer to home and tried to sue the authorities at the hospital for negligence, without success. Finally he did what I knew he would have to do if that terrible obsession with Leroy and his freedom were not to destroy him and us. He went on his own voyage that winter in search of Leroy Haines. He returned with himself to me, and for the first and only time in my life, I was gladly a Penelope.

Art died, a small notice in the paper. I tried to find out if there would be a service somewhere, or when he would be buried, but no one seemed to know. Some people are simply part of the landscape, and in those half-wild, unadorned places I still find his presence. I have never seen Bessy or Annette again. Perhaps they moved away.

We have lived through more brutal deaths than my society deserves, and that dead center of hidden imposthume, Richard Nixon, no less than Leroy Haines, inhabits my dreams, his handdog, paralytic face an image for me to inner death, betrayal, corruption, willed ignorance. We have watched astronauts fly high, but like the rest of us they came down to earth and have had to stay there, doing as well as they can. The moon was the focus of the world's attention as it probably will not be again for centuries to come, but I regard that satellite with a stubborn will to let it be itself—not the feat of our technology, not the goal of a rocketmaker's dreams, but what it always has been: a pale reflection of what our world might be if it had not hazarded life, inflexibly dark on one side, dependent for its light on the same sun that leaves us every night but will return. I love the moonlight, revealing in our clear nights that our most important star has left us only for a matter of hours.

Which leads me to this end, not really an end at all, but a stopping place. Of course, there is none. The story would not stand still, so I have told what rushed in, making history of my story. But this is an ending my father never could have written, since the voice that tells you this stops arbitrarily, not for the sake of form but because I can tell you no more than what I have lived. His characters ended at the final word, even if he could make you feel they did not. But my story does not end. It goes on, in ways you'll never know. Unless you can imagine.

But now I ask you to imagine another July. It is 1983. The lake we walk beside is cleaner than it was, the legacy of work by many people over these years. But it is far from what it should be, and I too spend time working for it when I can. That is part of my legacy from Melissa, who walked with me near Cedar Point and spoke passionately of matters that in my classrooms had been mere geography or natural process—Lake Erie, eutrophication. But this evening, it is our lake to walk beside and find a breeze to sit in while the sun goes down behind the Adirondacks. Again. And as it will again. It is repetition that I love now, the large patterns of days and seasons in which Michael and I can repeat the motions of our love.

We have found our breeze and I have guided us to our very private perch on a rock that slants to the water, the light-edged waves. Michael keeps his hand in mine, I sit, he lowers himself beside me. A single large gull wings by and does not swerve.

"First time I've felt cool all day." He smiles toward that sun. White and red sails dot the lake, each trying the wind in different directions.

"Mind if I swim?"

"As long as you don't go away like the little mermaid."

I take off my clothes and leave them beside him. The breeze now is even more soothing, and the water is almost cold. I look back to see him leaning on his elbows, legs stretched toward me. I slip into the water, paddle through the shallows, letting my breath come back, then swim. I cannot distinguish land from water now, the mountains are merely larger heaves of waves in the distance that the sun is sinking through. After a while I stop and turn and look back to the distant figure on the shore, motionless. I want him to move; I want him to see me.

I lift an arm and wave it slowly back and forth. For a moment he is absolutely still. The sky behind him is pale blue, darkening. I try to imagine the rim of the sun, the mountains, my arm smaller than the line of wave. He might not see me in such a wide landscape. I can hardly make him out now.

The thin line that is his figure rises, one arm waves to me or the sun or that flock of gulls I can hear mewing behind me. He is taking off the white speck of his shirt, bending out of sight for his shoes. He will wade into the water and swim out and we will go slowly back together. Already I can feel his wet, cool skin when we are standing on the rocks again. It will be dark but we will know each other as we always have, by touch.

I lie on my back and float in the water, watching the first stars appear, light that has been there but invisible, light sent to us millions of years ago, and I am waiting for him.